Mind Benders

There were two men and one woman left on Earth —and you'll never guess the outcome of their strange mating competition, in Ray Russell's bizarre "The Better Man."

The unmarked spaceship landing on the moon bore a cargo as unexpected as it was dangerous, in Walter M. Miller, Jr.'s great short novel "The Lineman."

The helpless inhabitants of the alien planet were doomed by Man, the destroyer, unless help came from an unimaginable source, in Chad Oliver's haunting "North Wind."

He thought he had at last outsmarted the diabolical creatures of his own creation, only to find they had one final terrible trick to play, in Ray Bradbury's unforgettably frightening "I, Mars."

These are just four of the ten superlative tales here presented for the first time in anthology form by one of the finest of science fictioneers, William F. Nolan.

A
Wilderness
of Stars
Stories of Man
in Conflict with Space

EDITED BY WILLIAM F. NOLAN

Introduction by Shelly Lowenkopf

A DELL BOOK

TO FORRY ACKERMAN,
who started me on the trail

ACKNOWLEDGMENTS

The Lineman by Walter M. Miller, Jr. was originally printed in the August 1957 issue of *The Magazine of Fantasy and Science Fiction*. Copyright © 1957 by Fantasy House, Inc. and reprinted by permission of the Harold Matson Company, Inc.

I, Mars by Ray Bradbury was originally printed in the April 1949 issue of *Super Science Stories*. Copyright © 1949 by

CONTENTS

INTRODUCTION

Shelly Lowenkopf

THESE STORIES revolve around the theme of Man in conflict with the outer reaches of Space. They also reflect vividly the less apparent theme of Man the Adapter, the truly great essayer of any environment he chooses.

Man has already taken a giant stride across the emptiness of Space. Because of this recent and significant advance, it is no longer satisfactory for writers merely to get us from Earth to the distant stars, nebulae, and asteroids. They must make us care about all the things we have yet to become. This is the theme that excites William F. Nolan, and he has chosen well; this collection of stories reflects the incisive nature of science fiction in dealing with new problems.

Nearly without exception, these problems are going to be holdovers, unresolved matters Man has brought with him into Space from Earth; loneliness, politics, prejudice, adaptiveness, and even more important, the question: How will we use what we find out There?

I mean this in the strictest sense. How will we treat and preserve what we encounter? How will we avoid cannibalizing the universe as we have the Earth? How will we make sure there is something left for the generations to come?

Not too many millennia past—a short span in science fiction terms—there was a great thrust of migration

across what we think of as the Bering Strait, and down
into what we call North America. The reason for this
push was one most familiar to us now—population explosion. Even back then, the world could be thought of
as overcrowded, especially when we recall that most of
the population were hunters, who needed great reaches
of land to support a small band of people.

In their enthusiasm for the newness and challenge of
their fresh surroundings, these not-too-distant predeces-
sors of ours systematically went about attacking the ecology of North America. Thus Man the Hunter, teaming up
with the last Ice Age, killed off all the large animals who
were potential beasts of burden. And by the time Man
the Inventor came up with the wheel, there were no animals left to haul wheeled vehicles. The net result: these
immigrants were able to develop only so far, and even
then, they were doomed. The next significant batch
of visitors to this continent who knew how to use the
wheel, and who brought in animals large enough to drive
wheeled vehicles, promptly took over, and haven't relin-
quished control yet.

It wasn't an immediate victory, but it was a pointed
one. As witness, this example is offered over several other
possibilities. The Plains Indians, using horses stolen from
the Spaniards, went on to a brief yet significant era of
greatness. On the other hand, the Paiute Indians were just
as successful as the Plains Indians in acquiring horses, yet
they compounded the mistake of their forebears and
bought an express ticket to extinction. Instead of using
the horse for work, hunting, and general mobility as the
Plains Indians did, the Paiutes, with the same options and
potentials open to them, chose to eat their horses.

Our journey into Space must be more careful, more
reasoned, and more concerned, lest we find ourselves out
There someday, with the wheel and nothing left to drive
it.

As you leaf through these pages now, and travel into
tomorrow, you'll see through different eyes that Man the
Adapter has his work cut out for him. This collection of

stories is particularly significant because it raises issues we cannot escape, exposes us to problems we have not yet solved, and brings us headlong into our own destiny while we still have something to do about it.

THE LINEMAN

Walter M. Miller, Jr.

For good and valid reasons of his own, Walter Miller, Jr. has retired as a storyteller. Over the last decade no new Miller science fiction has appeared— since the publication of his celebrated novel, A Canticle for Leibowitz, in 1959. This book has sold upwards of half a million copies, and is now scheduled for filming as a major Hollywood production.

Miller's last magazine story in the genre, "The Lineman," appeared in the August, 1957 issue of Fantasy and Science Fiction. A complete short novel of more than 20,000 words, it is here reprinted for the first time. It reflects the same mature top-of-the-field talent which produced Leibowitz. And, like that novel, it is of classic dimensions.

"The Lineman" is set on Earth's moon—man's first step out into a wilderness of stars. Miller's tough, rebellious construction workers, short of oxygen, hungry for sex, fearful of their killing environment, are delineated with force and depth.

Now, in book form, "The Lineman" takes its rightful place among the most memorable stories of the genre.

IT WAS August on Earth, and the newscast reported a heat wave in the Midwest: the worst since 2065. A letter from Mike Tremini's sister in Abilene said the chickens were dying and there wasn't enough water for the stock. It was the only letter that came for any of Novotny's men during that fifty-shift hitch on the Copernicus Trolley Project. Everybody read it and luxuriated in sympathy for Kansas and sick chickens.

- It was August on Luna too. The Perseids rained down with merciless impartiality; and, from his perch atop the hundred-foot steel skeleton, the lineman stopped cranking the jack and leaned out against his safety belt to watch two demolition men carrying a corpse out toward Fissure Seven. The corpse wore a deflated pressure suit. Torn fabric dragged the ground. The man in the rear carried the corpse's feet like a pair of wheelbarrow handles, and he continually tripped over the loose fabric; his head waggled inside his helmet as if he cursed softly and continuously to himself. The corpse's helmet was translucent with an interior coating of pink ice, making it look like a comic figure in a strawberry ice cream ad, a chocolate ragamuffin with a scoop for a head.

The lineman stared after the funeral party for a time until the team-pusher, who had been watching the slack span of 800 MCM aluminum conductors that snaked half a mile back toward the preceding tower, glanced up at the hesitant worker and began bellowing into his microphone. The lineman answered briefly, inspected the pressure gauge of his suit, and began cranking the jack again. With every dozen turns of the crank, the long snaking cable crept tighter across the lunar plain, straightening and lifting almost imperceptibly until at last the center-point cleared the ground and the cable swooped in a long graceful catenary between the towers. It trembled with fitful glistenings in the harsh sunglare. The lineman ignored the cable as he turned the crank. He squinted across the plains at the meteor display.

The display was not spectacular. It could be detected only as a slight turbulence in the layer of lunar dust that covered the ground, and an occasional dust geyser where a pea-sized bit of sky debris exploded into the crust at thirty miles per second. Sometimes the explosion was bright and lingering, but more often there was only a momentary incandescence quickly obscured by dust. The lineman watched it with nervous eyes. There was small chance of being hit by a stone of consequential size, but the eternal pelting by meteoric dust, though too fine to effect a puncture, could weaken the fabric of a suit and lead to leaks and blowouts.

The team-pusher keyed his mic switch again and called to the lineman on the tower. *"Keep your eyes on that damn jack, Relke! That clamp looks like she's slipping from here."*

The lineman paused to inspect the mechanism. *"Looks OK to me,"* he answered. *"How tight do I drag this one up?"*

The pusher glanced at the sagging span of steel-reinforced aluminum cable. *"It's a short stretch. Not too critical. What's the tension now?"*

The lineman consulted a dial on the jack. *"Going on forty-two hundred pounds, Joe."*

"Crank her up to five thousand and leave it," said the pusher. *"Let C-shift sag it in by the tables if they don't like it."*

"Yokay. Isn't it quitting time?"

"Damn near. My suit stinks like we're on overtime. Come on down when you reel that one in. I'm going back to the sleep wagon and get blown clear." The pusher shut off his oxygen while he transferred his hose connections from the main feeder supply to the walk-around bottles on his suit. He signaled "quitting time" at the men on the far tower, then started moon-loping his way across the shaggy terrain toward the train of rolling barracks and machinery that moved with the construction crew as the 200 kilovolt transmission line inched its way across the lunar landscape.

The lineman glanced up absently at the star-stung emptiness of space. Motion caught his eye. He watched with a puzzled frown, then hitched himself around to call after the departing team-pusher.

"Hey, Joe!"

The pusher stopped on a low rise to look back.

"*Relke?*" he asked, uncertain of the source of the voice.

"*Yeah. Is that a ship up there?*" The lineman pointed upward toward the east.

"*I don't see it. Where?*"

"*Between Arcturus and Serpens. I thought I saw it move.*"

The pusher stood on the low tongue of lava and watched the heavens for a time. "*Maybe—maybe not. So what if it is, Relke?*"

"*Well . . .*" The lineman paused, keying his mic nervously. "*Looks to me like it's headed the wrong direction for Crater City. I mean—*"

The pusher barked a short curse. "*I'm just about fed up with that superstitious drivel!*" he snapped. "*There* aren't *any non-human ships, Relke. And there aren't any non-humans.*"

"*I didn't say—*"

"*No, but you had it in mind.*" The pusher gave him a scornful look and hiked on toward the caterpillar train.

"Yah. If you say so, Joe," Relke muttered to himself. He glanced again at the creeping point of light in the blackness; he shrugged; he began cranking up the slack span again. But the creeping point kept drawing his gaze while he cranked. When he looked at the tension indicator, it read 5,600 pounds. He grunted his annoyance, reversed the jack ratchet, and began letting out the extra 600 pounds.

The shift-change signal was already beeping in his headsets by the time he had eased it back down to 5,000, and the C-shift crewmen were standing around the foot of the tower jeering at him from below.

"*Get off it, boy. Give the men a chance.*"

"*Come on down, Relke. You can let go. It ain't gonna drop.*"

He ignored the razzing and climbed down the trainward side of the tower: Larkin and Kunz walked briskly around to meet him. He jumped the last twenty-five feet, hoping to evade them, but they were waiting for him when his boots hit the ground.

"We want a little talk with you, Relke, my lad," came Larkin's rich, deceptively affable baritone.

"Sorry, Lark, it's late and I—" He tried to sidestep them, but they danced in and locked arms with him, one on each side.

"Like Lark told you, we want a little talk," grunted Kunz.

"Sure, Harv—but not right now. Drop by my bunk tank when you're off shift. I been in this straight jacket for seven hours. It doesn't smell exactly fresh in here."

"Then, Sonny, you should learn to control yourself in your suit," said Larkin, his voice all mellifluent with smiles and avuncular pedagoguery. *"Let's take him, Harv."*

They caught him in a double armlock, hoisted him off the ground, and started carrying him toward a low lava ridge that lay a hundred yards to the south of the tower. He could not kick effectively because of the stiffness of the suit. He wrenched one hand free and fumbled at the channel selector of his suit radio. Larkin jerked his stub antenna free from its mounting before Relke could put in a call for help.

"Tch tch tch," said Larkin, waggling his head.

They carried him across the ridge and set him on his feet again, out of sight of the camp. *"Sit down, Sonny. We have seeeerious matters to discuss with you."*

Relke heard him faintly, even without the antenna, but he saw no reason to acknowledge. When he failed to answer, Kunz produced a set of jumper wires from his knee pocket and clipped their suit audio circuits into a three-way intercom, disconnecting the plate lead from an r.f. stage to insure privacy.

"You guys give me a pain in the hump," growled the lineman. "What do you want this time? You know damn well a dead radio is against safety rules."

"It *is?* You ever hear of such a rule, Kunz?"

"Naah. Or maybe I did, at that. It's to make things easy for work spies, psych checkers, and time-and-motion men, ain't that it?"

"Yeah. You a psych checker or a time-and-motion man, Relke?"

"Hell, you guys known damn well I'm not—"

"Then what are you stalling about?" Larkin's baritone lost its mellowness and became an ominous growl. "You came nosing around, asking questions about the Party. So we let you in on it. We took you to a cell meeting. You said you wanted to join. So we let you in on two more meetings. Then you chickened out. We don't like that, Relke. It smells. It smells like a dirty informing rat!"

"I'm no damn informer!"

"Then why did you welsh?"

"I didn't welsh. I never said I'd join. You asked me if I was in favor of getting the Schneider-Volkov Act repealed. I said 'yes.' I still say 'yes.' That doesn't mean I want to join the Party."

"Why not, Relke?"

"Well, there's the fifty bucks, for one thing."

"Wh-a-a-at! One shift's wages? Hell, if that's all that's stopping you—Kunz, let's pay his fifty bucks for him, okay?"

"Sure. We'll pay your way in, Relke. I don't hold it against a man if he's a natural born tightwad."

"Yeah," said Larkin. "All you gotta do is sign up, Sonny. Fifty bucks, hell—that's less than union dues. If you can call that yellow-bellied obscenity a union. Now how about it, Relke?"

Behind the dark lenses of his glare goggles, Relke's eyes scanned the ground for a weapon. He spotted a jagged shard of volcanic glass and edged toward it.

"Well, Relke?"

"No deal."

"Why not?"

"That's easy. I plan on getting back to Earth someday. Conspiracy to commit mutiny rates the death penalty."

"Hear what he said, Lark? He calls it mutiny."

"Yeah. Teacher's little monitor."

"C'mere, informer."

They approached him slowly, wearing tight smiles. Relke dived for the shard of glass. The jumper wires

jerked tight and broke loose, throwing them off balance
for a moment. He came up with the glass shard in one
fist and backed away. They stopped. The weapon was as
good as a gun. A slit suit was the ultimate threat. Relke
tore the dangling wires loose from his radio and backed
toward the top of the ridge. They watched him somberly,
not speaking. Larkin waved the lineman's stub antenna
and looked at him questioningly. Relke held out a glove
and waited for him to toss it. Larkin threw it over his
shoulder in the opposite direction. They turned their
backs on him. He loped on back toward the gravy train,
knowing that the showdown had been no more than post-
poned. Next time would be worse. They meant to in-
criminate him, as a kind of insurance against his informing. He had no desire to be incriminated, nor to inform—
but try to make them believe that.

Before entering the clean-up tank, he stopped to glance
up at the heavens between Arcturus and Serpens. The
creeping spot of light had vanished—or moved far from
where he had seen it. He did not pause to search. He
checked his urine bottle in the airlock, connected his
hoses to the wall valves, and blew the barn-smell out of
his suit. The blast of fresh air was like icy wine in his
throat. He enjoyed it for a moment, then went inside the
tank for a bath.

Novotny was waiting for him in the B-shift line crew's
bunkroom. The small pusher looked sore. He stopped pac-
ing when Relke entered.

"Hi, Joe."

Novotny didn't answer. He watched while Relke stowed
his gear, got out an electric razor, and went to the wall
mirror to grind off the blond bristles.

"Where you been?" Novotny grunted.

"On the line where you saw me. I jacked that last span
up tighter than you told me. I had to let her back down
a little. Made me late getting in."

The pusher's big hand hit him like a club between the
shoulder blades, grabbed a handful of coverall, and
jerked him roughly around. The razor fell to the end of
the cord. Novotny let go in back and grabbed a handful

in front. He shoved the lineman back against the wall.

Relke gaped at him blankly.

"Don't give *me* that wide blue-eyed dumb stare, you sonofabitch!" the pusher snapped. "I saw you go over the hill with Kunz and Larkin."

Relke's Adam's apple did a quick genuflection. "If you saw me go, you musta seen *how* I went."

Novotny shook him. "What'd they want with you?" he barked.

"Nothing."

Joe's eyes turned to dark slits. "Relke, I told you, I told the rest of my men. I told you what I'd do to any sonofabitch on my team that got mixed up with the Party. Pappy don't allow that crap. Now shall I do it to you here, or do you want to go down to the dayroom?"

"Honest, Joe, I'm not mixed up in it. I got interested in what Larkin had to say—back maybe six months ago. But I never signed up. I never even meant to."

"Six months? Was that about the time you got your Dear John letter from Fran?"

"Right after that, Joe."

"Well, that figures. So what's Larkin after you about now?"

"I guess he wonders why I asked questions but never joined."

"I don't want your guesses. What did he say out there, and what did you say to him?"

"He wanted to know why I didn't sign up, that's all."

"And you told him what?"

"No deal."

"So?"

"So, I came on back and took a shower."

Novotny stared at him for a few seconds. "You're lying," he grunted, but released him anyway. "OK, Relke, but you better listen to this. You're a good lineman. You've stayed out of trouble. You get along with the rest of the team. If you got out of line in some *other* way, I'd figure it was about time you let off some steam. I'd stick up for you. But get mixed up with the Party—and I'll stomp you. When I'm through stomping you, I'll report you off my team. Understand?"

"Sure, Joe."

Novotny grunted and stepped away from him. "No hard feelings, Relke."

"Naah." The lineman went back to the mirror and started shaving again. That his hand remained steady was a surprise to him. Novotny had never before laid a hand on him, and Relke hoped the first time would be the last. He had watched Joe mop up the dayroom with Benet for playing fast and loose with safety rules while working a hotstick job, and it put Benet in sick bay for three days. Novotny was small, but he was built like a bunker. He was a fair overseer, but he handled his men in the only way he knew how to handle them on such a job. He expected self-discipline and self-imposed obedience, and when he didn't get it, he took it as a personal insult and a challenge to a duel. Out on the lava, men were pressure-packed, hermetically sealed charges of high explosive blood and bone; one man's folly could mean the death of several others, and there was no recourse to higher authority or admonitions from the dean, with a team on the lava.

"What's your grudge against the Party, Joe?" Relke asked while he scraped under his neck.

"No grudge. Not as long as Benet, Braxton, Relke, Henderson, Beasley, Tremini, and Novotny stay out of it. No grudge at all. I'm for free love and nickel beer as much as the next guy. But I'm not for getting my ass shot off. I'm not for fouling up the whole Lunar project just to get the Schneider-Volkov Act repealed, when you can't get it repealed that way anyhow. I'm not for facing a General Space Court and getting sentenced to blowout. That's all. No grudge."

"What makes you think a general strike couldn't force repeal, Joe?"

The pusher spat contemptuously at the disposal chute and missed. "A general strike on the Lunar Project? Hell, Relke, use your head. It'd never work. A strike against the government is rough to pull off, even on Earth. Up

here, it'd be suicide. The Party's so busy yelling about
who's right and who's wrong and who's getting a raw
deal—and what they ought to do about it—that they forget the important point: who's in the driver's seat. So
what if we shut down Copernicus and all the projects like
this one? Copernicus has a closed ecology, its own plant
animal cycle, sure. We don't need much from Earth to
keep it running—but there's the hitch: don't need *much*.
The ecology slips out of balance now and then. Every
month or two it has to get a transfusion from Earth.
Compost bacteria, or a new strain of algae because our
strain starts mutating—it's always something like that. If
a general strike cut us off from Earth, the World Parliament could just sit passing solemn gas through their waffle-
bottom chairs and wait. They could debate us to death in
two months."

"But world opinion—"

"Hell, *they* make world opinion, not *us*."

Relke stopped shaving and looked around. "Joe?"

"Yah."

"Kunz and Larkin'd kill me for telling you. Promise
not to say anything?"

The pusher glowered at him for a moment. "Look,
Relke, nobody brutalizes Joe Novotny's men. I'll handle
Kunz and Larkin. You'd better spill. You think it's in-
forming if you tell *me?*"

Relke shook his head. "Guess not. OK, Joe. It's this:
I've been to three cell meetings. I heard some stuff. I
think the strike's supposed to start come sundown."

"I heard that too. If it does, we'll all be—" He broke
off. The cabin's intercom was suddenly blaring.

*Attention, all personnel, attention. Unidentified bird at
thirty degrees over horizon, south-southwest, braking fire
for landing in our vicinity. All men on the line take cover.
Safety team to the ready room on the double. Rescue
team scramble, rescue team scramble.*

Relke rolled the cord neatly around the razor and
stared at it. "I'll be damned," he muttered. "It *was* a ship
I saw. What ship would be landing way the hell out
here?" He glanced around at Novotny.

The pusher was already at the periscope viewer, his face buried in the sponge rubber eyepieces. He cranked it around in a search pattern toward the south-southwest.

"See anything?"

"Not yet . . . *yeah,* there she is. Braking in fast—now what the hell!"

"Give me a look."

They traded turns at the viewer.

"She's a fusion furnace job. Cold fusion. Look at that blue tail."

"Why land way out here?"

The hatch burst open and the rest of the men spilled in from the dayroom. A confused babble filled the cabin. "I tole ya and I tole ya!" said Bama Braxton. "That theah mine shaff at Tycho is the play-yun evvy-dance. Gennlemen, weah about to have stranjuhs in ouah midst."

"Cut that superstitious bullspit, Brax," Novotny grunted. "There *aren't* any aliens. We got enough bogeys around here without you scaring the whoop out of yourself with that line of crap."

"Theah ahn't no aliens!" Braxton howled. "Theah ahn't no *aliens?* Joe, you blind?"

"He right, Joe," said Lije Henderson, Bama's chief crony. "That mine shaff speak fo' itself."

"That mine's a million years old," Joe snorted, "and they're not even sure it's a mine. I said drop it."

"That *ship* speak fo' itself!"

"Drop it! This isn't the first time a ship overshot Crater City and had to set down someplace else. Ten to one it's full of Parliament waffle-bottoms, all complaining their heads off. Maybe they've got a meteor puncture and need help quick."

The closed-circuit intercom suddenly buzzed, and Novotny turned to see the project engineer's face on the small viewer.

"Are all your men up and dressed, Joe?" he asked when Novotny had answered the call.

"EVERYBODY PIPE DOWN! Sorry, Suds. No—well, except for Beasley, they're up. Beasley's logging sack time."

"The hell Beasley is!" complained Beasley from his bunk. "With you verbing nouns of a noun all yapping like—"

"Shut up, Beez. Go on, Suds."

"We got contact with that ship. They've got reactor troubles. I tried to get Crater City on the line, but there's an outage on the circuit somewhere. I need some men to take a tractor and backtrack toward Copernicus. Look for a break in the circuit."

"Why call me?"

"The communication team is tied up, Joe."

"Yeah, but I'm not a communic—"

"Hell!" Brodanovitch exploded. "It doesn't take an electronics engineer to splice a broken wire, does it?"

"OK, Suds, we'll go. Take it easy. What about that ship?"

The engineer paused to mop his face. He looked rather bleak suddenly. "I don't know if it's safe to tell you. But you'll find out anyhow. Watch out for a riot."

"Not a runaway reactor—"

"Worse, Joe. Women."

"WOMEN!" It was a high piping scream from Beasley. "Did he say *women?*" Beasley was out of bed and into his boots.

"WOMEN!" They came crowding around the intercom screen.

"Back off!" Novotny barked. "Go on, Suds."

"It's a troupe of entertainers, Joe. Clearance out of Algiers. They say they're scheduled for a performance in Crater City, come nightfall. That's all I know, except they're mostly women."

"Algiers! Jeez! Belly dancers . . . !"

The room was a confused babble.

"Wait a minute," said Suds. His face slid off the screen as he talked to somebody in the boss tank. Moments later he was back. "Their ship just put down, Joe. Looks like a safe landing. The rescue team is out there. You'll pass the ship on the way up the line. Get moving."

"Sure, Suds." Novotny switched off and looked around at the sudden scramble. "I'll be damned if you do!" he yelled. "You can't all go. Beasley, Henderson—"

"No, bigod you don't, Joe!" somebody howled. "Draw straws!"

"OK. I can take three of you, no more."

They drew. Chance favored Relke, Braxton, and Henderson. Minutes later they crowded into the electric runabout and headed southeast along the line of stately steel towers that filed back toward Copernicus. The ship was in sight. Taller than the towers, the nacelles of the downed bird rose into view beyond the broken crest of a distant lava butte. She was a freight shuttle, space-constructed and not built for landing on Earth. Relke eyed the emblem on the hull of her crew nacelle while the runabout nosed onto the strip of graded roadbed that paralleled the transmission line back to Crater City. The emblem was unfamiliar.

"That looks like the old *RS Voltaire*," said the lineman. "Somebody must have bought her, Joe. Converted her to passenger service."

"Maybe. Now keep an eye on the telephone line."

The pusher edged the runabout toward the trolley rods. The overhead power transmission line had been energized by sections during the construction of it, and the line was hot as far as the road had been extended. Transformer stations fed energy from the 200 kilovolt circuit into the 1,500 volt trolley bars that ran down the center of the roadbed. Novotny stopped the vehicle at the end of the finished construction and sidled it over until the feeler arms crackled against the electrified bus rods and locked in place. He switched the batteries to "charge" and drove on again.

"Relke, you're supposed to be watching that talk circuit, not the ship."

"OK, Joe, in a minute."

"You horny bastard, you can't see their bloomers through that titanium hull. Put the glasses down and watch the line."

"OK, just a minute. I'm trying to find out who owns her. The emblem's—"

"Now, dammit!"

"No marking on her except her serial number and a picture of a rooster—and something else that's been painted over."

"RELKE!"

"Sure, Joe, OK."

"Girls!" marveled Lije Henderson. "Whenna lass time you touch a real girl, Brax?"

"Don' ass me, Lije! I sweah, if I evum touch a lady's li'l pink fingah right now, I could—"

"Hell, I could jus' sittin' heah lookin' at that ship. Girls. God! Lemme have those glasses, Relke."

Novotny braked the runabout to a halt. "All right, get your helmets on," he snapped. "Pressure your suits. I'm going to pump air out."

"Whatthehell! *Why*, Joe?"

"So you can get out of this heap. You're walking back. I'll go on and find the break myself."

Braxton squealed like a stuck pig; a moment later all three of them were on him. "Please, Joe. . . . Fuh the love a heaven, Joe, have a haht. . . . Gawd, *women!*"

"Get off my lap, you sonofabitch!" he barked at Braxton, who sat on top of him, grabbing at the controls. "Wait—I'll tell you what. Put the damn binoculars down and watch the line. Don't say another damn word about dames until we find the break and splice it. Swear to that, you bastards, and you can stay. I'll stop at their ship on our way back, and then you can stare all you want to. OK?"

"Joe, I sweah on a stack of—"

"All right, then watch the line."

They drove on in silence. The ship had fired down on a flat stretch of ground about four miles from the construction train, a few hundred yards from the trolley road. They stared at it as the runabout crawled past, and Novotny let the vehicle glide to a halt.

"The ramp's out and the ladder's down," said Relke. "Somebody must have come out."

"Unglue your eyes from that bird and look around," Novotny grunted. "You'll see why the ladder's down." He jerked his thumb toward a row of vehicles parked near the massive ship.

"The rescue team's wagons. But wheah's the rescue team?"

No crewmen were visible in the vicinity of the ship or the parked runabouts. Novotny switched on the radio, punched the channel selector, and tried a call, reading the call code off the side of the safety runabout.

"*Double Able Niner, this is One Four William. Talk back, please.*"

They sat in silence. There was nothing but the hiss of solar interference from the radio and the sound of heavy breathing from the men.

"Those lucky ole bastahds!" Braxton moaned. "You know wheah they gone, gennlemen? I know wheah they gone. They clambered right up the ladies' ladduh. I taya, alright—"

"Knock it off. Let's get moving. Tell us on the way back."

"Those lucky ole—"

The runabout moved ahead across the glaring land.

Relke: "Joe?"

"Yeah?"

"Joe, on our way back, can we go over and see if they'll let us climb aboard?"

Novotny chuckled. "I thought you were off dames, Relke. I thought when Fran sent you the Dear John, you said dames were all a bunch of—"

"Damn, Joe! You could have talked all day without saying 'Fran.' " The lineman's throat worked a brief spasm, and he stared out across the broken moonscape with dismal eyes.

"Sorry I mentioned it," Novotny grunted. "But sure, I guess one of us could walk over and ask if they mind a little more company on board."

Lije: "*One* of us! Who frinstance—*you?*"

Joe: "No, you can draw for it—not now, you creep! Watch the line."

They watched in silence. The communication circuit

was loosely strung on temporary supports beside the road-bed. The circuit was the camp's only link with Crater City, for the horizon interposed a barrier to radio reception, such reception being possible only during the occasional overhead transits of the lunar satellite station which carried message-relaying equipment. The satellite's orbit had been shifted to cover a Russian survey crew near Clavius, however, and its passages over the Trolley Project were rare.

"I jus' *thought*," Lije muttered suddenly, smacking his fist in his palm.

Relke: "Isn't that getting a little drastic, Lije?"

"I jus' thought. If we fine that outage, less don' fix it!"

Joe: "What kind of crazy talk is that?"

"Lissen, you know what ole Suds want to call Crater City *fo'*? He want to call 'em so's they'll senn a bunch of tank wagons down heah and tote those gals back to town. Thass what he want to call 'em fo'!"

Braxton slapped his forehead. "Luvva God! He's right. Y'all heah that? Is he right, Joe, or is he right?"

"I guess that's about the size of it."

"We mi'not evum get a look at 'em!" Braxton wailed.

"Less don' fix it, Joe!"

"I sweah, if I evum touch one of theah precious li'l fingahs, I'd—"

"Shut up and watch the line."

Relke: "Why didn't he use a bridge on the circuit and find out where the break was, Joe?"

"A bridge won't work too well on that line."

"How fah we gonna keep on drivin', Joe?"

"Until we find the break. Relke, turn up that blower a little. It's beginning to stink in here."

"Fresh ayah!" sighed Braxton as the breeze hit them from the fan.

Relke: "I wonder if it's fresh. I keep wondering if it doesn't come out foul from the purifier, but we've been living in it too long to be able to tell. I even dream about it. I dream about going back to Earth and everybody runs away from me. Coughing and holding their noses. I can't get close to a girl even in a dream anymore."

"Ah reckon a head-shrinker could kill hisself a-laughin' over that one."

"Don't talk to me about head-shrinkers."

"Watch the damn line."

Braxton: "Talk about *dreams!* Listen, I had one lass sleep shift that I oughta tell y'all about. Gennlemen, if she wasn't the ohnriest li'l—"

Novotny cursed softly under his breath and tried to keep his eyes on both the road and the communications circuit.

Relke: "Let 'em jabber, Joe. I'll watch it."

Joe: "It's bad enough listening to a bunch of jerks in a locker room bragging about the dames they've made. But Braxton! Braxton's got to brag about his dreams. Christ! Send me back to Earth. I'm fed up."

"Aww, Joe, we got nothin' else to talk about up heah."

They drove for nearly an hour and a half without locating the outage. Novotny pulled the runabout off the hot trolleys and coasted to a stop. "I'm deflating the cab," he told them. "Helmets on, pressure up your suits."

"Joe, weah not walkin' back from heah!" Bama said flatly.

"Oh, blow yourself out, Brax!" the pusher said irritably. "I'm getting out for a minute. C'mon, get ready for vacuum."

"Why?"

"Don't say *why* to me outside the sleep-tank, corn pone! Just do it."

"Damn! Novotny's in a humah! Les say 'yessah' to him, Bama."

"You too, Lije!"

"Yessah."

"Can it." Novotny got the pressure pumped down to two pounds, and then let the rest of the air spew out slowly into vacuum. He climbed out of the runabout and loped over to the low-hanging spans of the communication circuit. He tapped into it with the suit audio and listened for a moment. Relke saw his lips moving as he tried a call, but nothing came through the lineman's suit radio.

After about five minutes, he quit talking and beckoned the rest of them back to the runabout.

"That was Brodanovitch," he said after they were inside and the pressure came up again. "So the circuit break must be on up ahead."

"Oh, hell, we'll *nevah* get a look at those ladies!"

"Calm down. We're going back——" He paused a moment until the elated whooping died down. "Suds says let them send a crew out of Copernicus to fix it. I guess there's no hurry about moving those people out of there."

"The less hurry, the bettuh . . . *hot dawg!* C'mon, Joe, roll it!" Bama and Lije sat rubbing their hands. Only Relke seemed detached, his enthusiasm apparently cooled. He sat staring out at the meteor display on the dust-flats. He kept rubbing absently at the ring finger of his left hand. There was no ring there, nor even a mark on the skin. The pusher's eye fell on the slow nervous movement.

"Fran again?" Joe grunted.

The lineman nodded.

"I got my Dear John note three years ago, Relke."

Relke looked around at him in surprise. "I didn't know you were married, Joe."

"I guess I wasn't as married as I thought I was."

Relke stared outside again for awhile. "How do you get over it?"

"You don't. Not up here on Luna. The necessary and sometimes sufficient condition for getting over a dame is the availability of other dames. So, you don't."

"Hell, Joe!"

"Yeah."

"The movement's not such a bad idea."

"Can it!" the pusher snapped.

"It's true. Let women come to Crater City, or send us home. It makes sense."

"You're only looking at the free love and nickel beer end of it, Relke. You can't raise kids in low gravity. There are five graves back in Crater City to prove it. Kids' graves. Six feet long. They grow themselves to death."

"I know but . . ." He shrugged uncomfortably and watched the meteor display again.

"When do we draw?" said Lije. "Come on Joe, less draw for who goes to talk ouah way onto the ship."

Relke: "Say, Joe, how come they let dames in an entertainment troupe come to the moon, but they won't let our wives come? I thought the Schneider-Volkov Act was supposed to keep all women out of space, period."

"No, they couldn't get away with putting it like that. Against the WP constitution. The law just says that all personnel on any member country's lunar project must be of a single sex. Theoretically some country—Russia, maybe—could start an all-girl lunar mine project, say. Theoretically. But how many lady muckers do you know? Even in Russia."

Lije: "When do we draw? Come on, Joe, less draw."

"Go ahead and draw. Deal me out."

Chance favored Henderson. "Fastuh, Joe. Hell, less go fastuh, befo' the whole camp move over theah."

Novotny upped the current to the redline and left it there. The long spans of transmission line, some of them a mile or more from tower to tower, swooped past in stately cadence.

"There she is! Man!"

"You guys are building up for a big kick in the rump. They'll never let us aboard."

"Theah's two more cahs pahked over theah."

"Yeah, and still nobody in sight on the ground."

Novotny pulled the feelers off the trolleys again. "OK, Lije, go play John Alden. Tell 'em we just want to look, not touch."

Henderson was bounding off across the flats moments after the cabin had been depressurized to let him climb out. They watched him enviously while the pressure came up again. His face flashed with sweat in the sunlight as he looked back to wave at them from the foot of the ladder.

Relke glanced down the road toward the rolling construction camp. "You going to call in, Joe? Ought to be able to reach their antenna from here."

"If I do, Brodanovitch is sure to say 'haul ass on back to camp.'"

"Never mind, then! Forget I said it!"

The pusher chuckled. "Getting interested, Relke?"

"I don't know. I guess I am." He looked quickly toward the towering rocket.

"Mostly you want to know how close you are to being rid of her, maybe?"

"I guess—Hey, they're letting him in."

"That lucky ole bastuhd!" Bama moaned.

The airlock opened as Lije scaled the ladder. A helmet containing a head of unidentifiable gender looked out and down, watching the man climb. Lije paused to wave. After a moment's hesitancy, the space-suited figure waved back.

"*Hey, up theah, y'all mind a little company?*"

The party who watched him made no answer. Lije shook his head and climbed on. When he reached the lock, he held out a glove for an assist, but the figure stepped back quickly. Lije stared inside. The figure was holding a gun. Lije stepped down a rung. The gun beckoned impatiently for him to get inside. Reluctantly Lije obeyed.

The hatch closed. A valve spat a jet of frost, and they watched the pressure dial slowly creep to ten psi. Lije watched the stranger unfasten his helmet, then undid his own. The stranger was male, and the white goggle marks about his eyes betrayed him as a spacer. His thin dark features suggested Semitic or Arabic origins.

"*Parlez-vous français?*"

"Naw," said Lije. "Sho' don't. Sorry."

The man tossed his head and gave a knowing snort. "It is necessaire that we find out who you are," he explained, and brandished the weapon under Lije's nose. He grinned a flash of white teeth. "Who send you here?"

"Nobody send me. I come unduh my own steam. Some fellas in my moonjeep pulled cahds, and I—"

"Whup! You are—ah *ein Unteroffizier? Mais non,* wrong sprach—you *l'officiale?* Officer? Company man?"

"Who, me? Lahd, no. I'm juss a hot-stick man on B-shif'. You muss be lookin' fo' Suds Brodanovitch."

"Why you come to this ship?"

"Well, the fellas and I heard tell theah was some gals, and we—"

The man waved the gun impatiently and pressed a button near the inner hatch. A red indicator light went on.

"Yes?" A woman's voice, rather hoarse. Lije's chest heaved with sudden emotion, and his sigh came out a bleat.

The man spoke in a flood of French. The woman did not reply at once. Lije noticed the movement of a viewing lens beside the hatch; it was scanning him from head to toe.

The woman's voice shifted to an intimate contralto. "OK, dearie, you come right in here where it's nice and warm."

The inner hatch slid open. It took Lije a few seconds to realize that she had been talking to him. She stood there smiling at him like a middle-aged schoolmarm.

"Why don't you come on in and meet the girls?"

Eyes popping, Lije Henderson stumbled inside.

He was gone a long time.

When he finally came out, the men in Novotny's runabout took turns cursing at him over the suit frequency. *"Fa chrissake, Henderson, we've been sitting here using up oxy for over an hour while you been horsing around . . ."* They waited for him with the runabout, cabin depressurized.

Lije was panting wildly as he ran toward them. *"Lissen to the bahstud giggle,"* Bama said disgustedly.

"Y'all juss don' know, y'all juss don' KNOW!" Lije was chanting between pants.

"Get in here, you damn traitor!"

"Hones', I couldn' help myself. I juss couldn'."

"Well, do the rest of us get aboard her, or not?" Joe snapped.

"Hell, go ahead, man! It's wide open. Evahthing's wide open."

"Girls?" Relke grunted.

"Girls, God yes! Girls."

"You coming with us?" Joe asked.

Lije shook his head and fell back on the seat, still panting. *"Lahd, no! I couldn't stand it. I juss want to lie heah and look up at ole Mamma Earth and feel like a human again."* He grinned beatifically. *"Y'all go on."*

Braxton was staring at his crony with curious suspicion. *"Man, those must be some entuhtainuhs! Whass the mattah with you, Lije?"*

Henderson whooped and pounded his leg. *"Hoo hoo! Hooeee! You mean y'all still don' know what that ship is?"*

They had already climbed out of the tractor. Novotny glared back in at Lije. *"We've been waiting to hear it from you, Henderson,"* he snapped.

Lije sat up grinning. *"That's no stage show troupe! That ship, so help me Hannah, is a—hoo hoo hooee—is a goddam flyin' HO-house."* He rolled over on the seat and surrendered to laughter.

Novotny looked around for his men and found himself standing alone. Braxton was already on the ladder, and Relke was just starting up behind.

"Hey, you guys come back here!"

"Drop dead, Joe."

Novotny stared after them until they disappeared through the lock. He glanced back at Lije. Henderson was in a grinning beatific trance. The pusher shrugged and left him lying there, still wearing his pressure suit in the open cabin. The pusher trotted after his men toward the ship.

Before he was halfway there, a voice broke into his headsets. *"Where the devil are you going, Novotny? I want a talk with you!"*

He stopped to glance back. The voice belonged to Brodanovitch, and it sounded sore. The engineer's runabout had nosed in beside Novotny's; Suds sat in the cab and beckoned at him angrily. Joe trudged on back and climbed in through the vehicle's coffin-sized airlock. Brodanovitch glared at him while the pusher removed his helmet.

"What the devil's going on over there?"

"At the ship?" Joe paused. Suds was livid. "I don't know exactly."

"I've been calling Safety and Rescue for an hour and a half. Where are they?"

"In the ship, I guess."

"You *guess!*"

"Hell, chief, take it easy. We just got here. I don't know what's going on."

"Where are your men?"

Novotny jerked his thumb at the other runabout. "Henderson's in there. Relke and Brax went to the ship."

"And that's where you were going just now, I take it," Suds snarled.

"Take that tone of voice and shove it, Suds! You know where you told me to go. I went. Now I'm off. We're on our own time unless you tell us different."

The engineer spent a few seconds swallowing his fury. "All right," he grunted. "But every man on that rescue squad is going to face a Space Court, and if I have any say about it, they'll get decomped."

Novotny's jaw dropped. "Slow down, Suds. Explosive decompression is for mutiny or murder. What're you talking about?"

"Murder."

"Wha-a-at?"

"That's what I call it. A demolition man—Hardin, it was—had a blowout. With only one man standing by on the rescue gear."

"Meteor dust?"

"Yeah."

"Would it have made any difference if Safety and Rescue had been on the job?"

Suds glowered. "Maybe, maybe not. An inspector might have spotted the bulge in his suit before it blew." He shook an angry finger toward the abandoned Safety & Rescue vehicles. "Those men are going to stand trial for negligent homicide. It's the principle, damn it!"

"Sure, Suds. I guess you're right. I'll be right back."

Henderson was sleeping in his pressure suit when Novotny climbed back into his own runabout. The cab was still a vacuum. He got the hatch closed, turned on the air pumps, then woke Henderson.

"Lije, you been with a woman?"

"Nnnnnngg-*nnnng!* I hope to tell!" He shot a quick glance toward the rocket as if to reassure himself as to its reality. "And man, was she a little—"

Joe shook him again. "Listen. Brodanovitch is in the next car. Bull mad. I'll ask you again. You been with a woman?"

"Woman? You muss of lost yoah mine, Joe. Lass time I saw a woman was up at Atlanta." He rolled his eyes up toward the Earth crescent in the heavens. "Sure been a long ole time. Atlanta . . . *man!*"

"That's better."

Lije jerked his head toward Brodanovitch's jeep. "What's ole wet blanket gonna do? Chase those gals out of here, I 'spect?"

"I don't know. That's not what he's frothing about, Lije. Hardin got killed while the S&R boys were shacking up over there. Suds doesn't even *know* what's in that ship. He acts like he's got about a dozen troubles running loose at once, and he doesn't know which way to grab."

"He don't even *know?* How we evah gonna keep him from findin' out?" Lije shot another glance at the ship and jumped. "Uh-oh! Looka theah! Yonder they come. Clamberin' down the ladies' ladduh. Theah's Joyce and Lander and Petzel—other one looks like Crump. Half the Safety team, Joe. Hoo-eee! They got that freshly bred look. You can evum tell it from heah. Uh-oh!"

Brodanovitch had climbed out of his runabout. Bellowing at his mic, he charged toward the ship. The S&R men took a few lopes toward their vehicles, saw Brodanovitch, and stopped. One man turned tail and bolted for the ladder again. Gesturing furiously, the engineer bore down on them.

"Leave the radio off, Joe. Sure glad we don' have to listen to that bull bellow."

They sat watching the safety men, who managed somehow to look stark naked despite their bulgey pressure suits. Suds stalked toward them like an amok runner, beating a gloved fist into his palm and working his jaw at them.

"Suds don' know how to get along with men when he *want* to get along with 'em, and he don' know how to fuss at 'em when he don't want to get along. Man, look how he rave!"

"Yeah. Suds is a smart engineer, but he's a rotten overseer."

The ship's airlock opened again and another man started out. He stopped with one foot on the top rung of the ladder. He looked down at Brodanovitch and the S&R men. He pulled his leg back inside and closed the hatch. Novotny chuckled.

"That was Relke, the damn fool."

Lije smote his forehead. "Look at Suds! They tole him! They went an *tole* him, Joe. We'll nevah get back in that ship now."

The pusher watched the four figures on the plain. They were just standing there. Brodanovitch had stopped gesticulating. For a few seconds he seemed frozen. His head turned slowly as he looked up at the rocket. He took three steps toward it, then stopped.

"He gonna have apoplexy, thass what he gonna have."

Brodanovitch turned slowly. He gave the S&R men a blank look, then broke into a run toward his tractor.

"I'd better climb out," Joe said.

He met the engineer beside the command runabout. Suds's face was a livid mask behind the faceplate. *"Get in,"* he snapped at the pusher.

As soon as they were inside, he barked, "Drive us to Crater City."

"Slow down, Suds."

"Joe. That ship. Damn brothel. Out to fleece the camp."

"So what're you going to do in Crater City?"

"Tell Parkeson, what else?"

"And what's the camp going to be doing while you're gone?"

That one made him pause. Finally he shook his head. "Drive, Joe."

Novotny flipped the switch and glanced at the gauges. "You haven't got enough oxygen in this bug to last out the trip."

"Then we'll get another one."

"Better take a minute to think it over, Suds. You're all revved up. What the hell can Parkeson do?"

"What can he *do?* What can—migawd, Joe!" Suds choked.

"Well?"

"He can get that ship out of here, he can have those women interned."

"How? Suppose they refuse to budge. Who appointed Parkeson king of creation? Hell, he's only *our* boss, Suds. The moon's open to any nation that wants to send a ship, or to any corporation that can get a clearance. The W.P. decided that a long time ago."

"But it's illegal—those women, I mean!"

"How do you know? Maybe their racket's legal in Algiers. That's where you told me they had clearance from, didn't you? And if you're thinking about the Schneider-Volkov Act, it just applies to the Integrated Projects, not wildcat teams."

Brodanovitch sat silent for a few moments, his throat working. He passed a shaky hand over his eyes. "Joe, we've got to keep discipline. Why can't I ever make the men understand that? On a moon project, it's discipline or die. You know that, Joe."

"Sure I know it. You know it. Parkeson knows it. The First Minister of the Space Ministry knows it. But the men don't know it, and they never will. They don't know what the word 'discipline' means, and it's no good trying to tell them. It's an overseer's word. It means your outfit's working for you like your own arms and legs. One brain and one body. When it cracks, you've just got a loose handful of stray men. No coordination. You can see it, but they can't see it. 'Discipline' is just a dirty word in the ranks, Suds."

"Joe, what'll I do?"

"It's your baby, not mine. Give it first aid. Then talk to Parkeson later, if you want to."

Suds sat silent for half a minute, then: "Drive back to the main wagon."

Novotny started the motors. "What are you going to do?"

"Announce Code Red, place the ship off limits, put an armed guard on it, and hope the Crater City crew gets that telephone circuit patched up quick. That's all I can do."

"Then let me get a safe distance away from you before you do it."

"You think it'll cause trouble?"

"Good Lord, Suds, use your head. You've got a campful of men who haven't been close to a dame in months and years, even to talk to. They're sick, they're scared, they're fed-up, they want to go home. The Party's got them bitter, agitated. I'd hate to be the guy who puts those women off limits."

"What would you do?"

"I'd put the screws on the shift that's on duty. I'd work hell out of the crews that are supposed to be on the job. I'd make a horrible example out of the first man to goof off. But first I'd tell the off-duty team-pushers they can take their crews over to that ship, one crew at a time, and in an orderly manner."

"*What?* And be an accomplice? Hell, no!"

"Then do it your own way. Don't ask me."

Novotny parked the runabout next to the boss-wagon. "Mind if I use your buggy for awhile, Suds?" he asked. "I left mine back there, and I've got to pick up my men."

"Go ahead, but get them back here—fast."

"Sure, Suds."

He backed the runabout out again and drove down to B-shift's sleep-wagon. He parked again and used the airlock phone. "Beasley, Benet, the rest of you—come on outside."

Five minutes later they trooped out through the lock. "What's the score, Joe?"

"The red belts are ahead, that's all I know."

"Come on, you'll find out."

"Sleep! I haven't had no sleep since—*Say!* You takin' us over to that ship, Joe?"

"That's the idea."

"YAYHOO!" Beasley danced up and down. "Joe, we love ya!"

"Cut it. This is once-and-once-only. You're going once, and you're not going again."

"Who says?"

"Novotny says."

"But *why?*" Benet wailed.

"What did you say?"

"I said 'why!' "

"OK. I'll tell you why. Brodanovitch is going to put the ship off limits. If I get you guys in under the wire, you've got no gripe later on—when Suds hangs out the big No."

"Joe, that's chicken."

Novotny put on the brakes. "Get out and walk back, Benet."

"Joe—!"

"Benet."

"Look, I didn't mean anything."

Novotny paused. If Brodanovitch was going to try to do things the hard way, he'd lose control of his own men unless he gave them loose rein for a while first—keeping them reminded that he still *had* the reins. But Benet was getting out of hand lately. He had to decide. Now.

"Look at me, Benet."

Benet looked up. Joe smacked him. Benet sat back, looking surprised. He wiped his nose on the back of a glove and looked at the red smear. He wiped it again. The smear was bigger.

"You can stay, Benet, but if you do, I'll bust your hump after we get back. You want it that way?"

Benet looked at the rocket; he looked at Joe; he looked at the rocket. "Yeah. We'll see who does the busting. Let's go."

"All right, but do you see any other guys taking their teams over?"

"No."

"But you think you're getting a chicken deal."

"Yeah."

The pusher drove on, humming to himself. As long as he could keep them alternately loving him and hating him, everything was secure. Then he was Mother. Then they didn't stop to think or rationalize. They just reacted to Mother. It was easy to handle men reacting, but it wasn't so easy to handle men thinking. Novotny liked it the easy way, especially during a heavy meteor fall.

"It is of no importance to me," said Madame d'Annecy, "if you are the commandant of the whole of space, M'sieur. You wish entrance, I must ask you to contribute thees small fee. It is not in my nature to become unpleasant like thees, but you have bawl in my face, M'sieur."

"Look," said Brodanovitch, "I didn't come over here for . . . for what you think I came over here for." His ears reddened. "I don't want a girl, that is."

The madame's prim mouth made a small pink O of sudden understanding. "Ah, M'sieur, I begin to see. You are one of those. But in that I cannot help you. I have only girls."

The engineer choked. He started toward the hatch. A man with a gun slid into his path.

"Permit yourself to be restrained, M'sieur."

"There are four men in there that are supposed to be on the job, and I intend to get them. And the others too, while I'm at it."

"Is it that you have lost your boy friend, perhaps?"

Brodanovitch croaked incomprehensibly for a moment, then collapsed onto a seat beside the radar table that Madame d'Annecy was using for an accounting desk. "I'm no fairy," he said.

"I am pleased to hear it, M'sieur. I was beginning to pity you. Now if you will please sign the sight draft, so that we may telecast it—"

"I am *not* paying twelve hundred dollars just to get my men out of there!"

"I do not haggle, M'sieur. The price is fixed."

"Call them down here!"

"It cannot be done. They pay for two hours, for two hours they stay. Undisturbed."

"All right, let's see the draft."

Madame d'Annecy produced a set of forms from the map case and a small gold fountain pen from her ample bosom. "Your next of kin, M'sieur?" She handed him a blank draft.

"Wait a minute! How did you know where my account—"

"Is it not the correct firm?"

"Yes, but how did you know?" He looked at the serial number on the form, then looked up accusingly. "This is a telecopy form. You have a teletransmitter on board?"

"But of course! We could not risk having payment stopped after services rendered. The funds will be transferred to our account before you leave this ship. I assure you, we are well protected."

"I assure you, you are all going to jail."

Madame d'Annecy threw back her head and laughed heartily. She said something in French to the man at the door, then smiled at the unhappy engineer. "What law prevails here, M'sieur?"

"UCOJE does. Uniform Code of Justice, Extraterrestrial. It's a semi-military—"

"U.N.-based, I believe?"

"Certainly."

"Now I know little of thees matters, but my attorneys would be delighted, I am certain, if you can tell me: which articles of thees UCOJE is to be used for inducing us to be incarcerated?"

"Why . . . Uh . . ." Suds scratched nervously at one corner of his moustache. He glanced at the man with the gun. He gazed forlornly at the sight draft.

"Exactly!" Mme. d'Annecy said brightly. "There have been no women to speak of on the moon since the unfortunate predicament of *les enfants perdus*. The moonborn grotesque ones. How could they think to pass laws against thees—thees *ancien* establishment, thees *maison intime*—when there are no women, eh M'sieur?"

"But you falsified your papers to get clearance. You must have."

"But no. Our clearance is 'free nation,' not 'world federal.' We are an entertainment troupe, and my government's officials are most lenient in defining 'entertainment.' *Chacun à son gout*, eh?"

Suds sat breathing heavily. "I can place this ship off limits."

"If you can do that, if the men do not come"—she shrugged eloquently and spread her hands—"then we will simply move on to another project. There are plenty of others. But do you think thees putting us off limits will make you very popular with your men?"

"I'm not trying to win a popularity contest," Suds wheezed. "I'm trying to finish the last twelve miles of this line before sundown. You've got to get out of here before there's a complete work stoppage."

"Thees project. It is important? Of an urgent nature?"

"There's a new uranium mine in the crater we're building toward. There's a colony there without an independent ecology. It has to be supplied from Copernicus. Right now, they're shooting supplies to them by rocket missile. It's too far to run surface freight without trolley service— or reactor-powered vehicles the size of battleships and expensive. We don't have the facilities to run a fleet of self-powered wagons that far."

"Can they not run on diesel, perhaps?"

"If they carry the oxygen to burn the diesel with, and if everybody in Copernicus agrees to stop breathing the stuff."

"*Embarras de choix.* I see."

"It's essential that the line be finished before nightfall. If it isn't, that mine colony will have to be shipped back to Copernicus. They can't keep on supplying it by bird. And they can't move out any ore until the trolley is ready to run."

Mme. d'Annecy nodded thoughtfully. "We wish to make the cordial entente with the lunar workers," she murmured. "We do not wish to cause the *bouleversement*—

the disruption. Let us then negotiate, M'sieur."

"I'm not making any deals with you, lady."

"Ah, but such a hard position you take! I was but in-
tending to suggest that you furnish us a copy of your
camp's duty roster. If you will do that, Henri will not
permit anyone to visit us if he is—how you say?—goofing
off. Is it not that simple?"

"I will not be a party to robbery!"

"How is it robbery?"

"Twelve hundred dollars! Pay for two day-hitches. Lunar days. Nearly two months. And you're probably planning to fleece them more than once."

"*A bon marché!* Our expenses are terrific. Believe me,
we expect no profit from this first trip."

"First trip and last trip," Suds grumbled.

"And who has complained about the price? No one so
far excepting M'sieur. Look at it *thus;* it is an investment." She slid one of the forms across the table. "Please
to read it, M'sieur."

Suds studied the paper for a moment and began to
frown. "*Les Folies Lunaires,* Incorporated . . . a North
African corporation . . . in consideration of the sum of
one hundred dollars in hand paid by—who?—Howard
Beasley!—aforesaid corporation sells and grants to Howard Beasley . . . *one share of common stock!*"

"M'sieur! Compose yourself! It is no fraud. Everybody
gets a share of stock. It comes out of the twelve hundred.
Who knows? Perhaps after a few trips, there will even be
dividends. M'sieur? But you look positively ill! Henri,
bring brandy for the gentleman."

"So!" he grated. "That's the way it goes, is it? Implicate
everybody—nobody squawks."

"But certainly. It is for our own protection, to be sure,
but it is really stock."

"Blackmail."

"But no, M'sieur. All is legal."

Henri brought a plastic cup and handed it to him; Suds
shook his head.

"Take it. M'sieur. It is real brandy. We could bring

only a few bottles, but there is sufficient pure alcohol for the mixing of cocktails."

The small compartment was filled with the delicate perfume of the liquor; Brodanovitch glanced longingly at the plastic cup.

"It is seventy-year-old Courvoisier, M'sieur. Very pleasant."

Suds took it reluctantly, dipped it toward Mme. d'Annecy in self-conscious toast, and drained it. He acquired a startled expression; he clucked his tongue experimentally and breathed slowly through his nose.

"Good Lord!" he murmured absently.

Mme. d'Annecy chuckled. "M'sieur has forgotten the little pleasures. It was a shame to gulp it so. *Encore, Henri.* And one for myself, I think. Take time to enjoy this one, M'sieur." She studied him for a time while Henri was absent. She shook her head and began putting the forms away, leaving out the sight draft and stock agreement which she pushed toward him, raising one inquisitive brow. He gazed expressionlessly at them. Henri returned with the brandy; Madame questioned him in French. He seemed insistently negative for a time, but then seemed to give grudging assent. *"Bien!"* she said, and turned to Brodanovitch: "M'sieur, it will be necessary only for you to purchase the share of stock. Forget the fee."

"What?" Suds blinked in confusion.

"I said—" The opening of the hatch interrupted her thought. A dazzling brunette in a filmy yellow dress bounced into the compartment, bringing with her a breath of perfume. Suds looked at her and emitted a loud guttural cluck. A kind of glazed incredulity kneaded his face into a mask of shocked granite wearing a supercilious moustache. The girl ignored his presence and bent over the table to chat excitedly in French with Mme. d'Annecy. Suds's eyes seemed to find a mind and will of their own; involuntarily they contemplated the details of her architecture, and found manifest fascination in the way she relieved an itch at the back of one trim calf by rubbing it vigorously with the instep of her other foot while she leaned over the desk and bounced lightly on tiptoe as she spoke.

"M'sieur Brodanovitch, the young lady wishes to know —M'sieur Brodanovitch?—*M'sieur!*"

"What—? Oh." Suds straightened and rubbed his eyes. "Yes?"

"One of your young men has asked Giselle out for a walk. We have pressure suits, of course. But is it safe to promenade about this area?" She paused. "M'sieur, *please!*"

"What?" Suds shook his head. He tore his eyes away from the yellow dress and glanced at a head suddenly thrust in through the hatch. The head belonged to Relke. It saw Brodanovitch and withdrew in haste, but Suds made no sign of recognition. He blinked at Madame again.

"M'sieur, is it safe?"

"What? Oh. I suppose it is." He gulped his brandy and poured another.

Mme. d'Annecy spoke briefly to the girl, who, after a hasty *merci* and a nod at Suds went off to join Relke outside. When they were gone, Madame smilingly offered her pen to the engineer. Suds stared at it briefly, shook his head, and helped himself to another brandy. He gulped it and reached for his helmet. La d'Annecy snapped her fingers suddenly and went to a locker near the bulkhead. She came back with a quart bottle.

"M'sieur will surely accept a small token?" She offered the bottle for his inspection. "It is Mumms 2064, a fine year. Take it, M'sieur. Or do you not care for champagne? It is our only bottle, and what is one bottle of wine for such a crowd? Take it—or would you prefer the brandy?"

Suds blinked at the gift while he fastened his helmet and clamped it. He seemed dazed. She held the bottle out to him and smiled hopefully. Suds accepted it absent-mindedly, nodded at her, and stepped into the airlock. The hatch slid closed.

Mme. d'Annecy started back toward her counting table. The alarm bell burst into a sudden brazen clamor. She looked back. A red warning signal flashed balefully. Henri burst in from the corridor, eyed the bell and the light, then charged toward the airlock. The gauge by the hatch showed zero pressure. He pressed a starter button, and a meter hummed to life. The pressure needle crept upward. The bell and the light continued a frenetic complaint. The motor stopped. Henri glanced at the gauge, then swung open the hatch. *"Allons! Ma foi, quelle merde!"*

Mme. d'Annecy came to peer around him into the small cubicle. Her subsequent shriek penetrated to the farthest corridors. Suds Brodanovitch had missed his last chance to become a stockholder.

"It wasn't yo' fault, Ma'am," said Lije Henderson a few minutes later as they half-led, half-carried her to her compartment. "He know bettuh than to step outside with that bottle of booze. You didn't know. You couldn' be 'spected to know. But he been heah long enough to know—a man make one mistake, thass all. BLOOIE."

Blooie was too graphic to suit Madame; she sagged and began retching.

"C'mon, Ma'am, less get you in yo hammock." They carried her into her quarters, eased her into bed, and stepped back out on the catwalk.

Lije mopped his face, leaned against a tension member, and glanced at Joe. "Now how come you s'pose he had that bottle of fizzling giggle water up close to his helmet that way, Joe?"

"I don't know. Reading the label, maybe."

"He sho' muss have had something on his mine."

"Well, it's gone now."

"Yeah. BLOOIE. Man!"

Relke had led the girl out through the lock in the reactor nacelle in order to evade Brodanovitch and a possible command to return to camp. They sat in Novotny's runabout and giggled cozily together at the fuzzy map of Earth that floated in the darkness above them. On the ship's fuselage, the warning light over the airlock hatch began winking, indicating that the lock was in use. The girl noticed it and nudged him. She pointed at the light.

"Somebody coming out," Relke muttered. "Maybe Suds.

We'd better get out of here." He flipped the main switch and started the motor. He was backing onto the road when Giselle caught his arm.

"Beel! Look at the light!"

He glanced around. It was flashing red.

"Malfunction signal. Compressor trouble, probably. It's nothing. Let's take a ride. Joe won't care." He started backing again.

"*Poof!*" she said suddenly.

"What?"

"Poof. It opened, and *poof*—" She puckered her lips and blew a little puff of steam in the cold air to show him. "So. Like smoke."

He turned the car around in the road and looked back again. The hatch had closed. There was no one on the ladder. "Nobody came out."

"*Non.* Just poof."

He edged the car against the trolley rails, switched to autosteering, and let it gather speed.

"Beel?"

"Yeah, kid?"

"Where you taking me?"

He caught the note of alarm in her voice and slowed down again. She had come on a dare after several drinks, and the drinks were wearing off. The landscape was frighteningly alien, and the sense of falling into bottomlessness was ever-present.

"You want to go back?" he asked gloomily.

"I don't know. I don't like it out here."

"You said you wanted some ground under your feet."

"But it doesn't feel like ground when you walk on it."

"Rather be inside a building?"

She nodded eagerly.

"That's where we're going."

"To your camp?"

"God, no! I'm planning to keep you to myself."

She laughed and snuggled closer to him. "You can't. Madame d'Annecy will not permit—"

"Let's talk about something else," he grunted quickly.

"OK. Let's talk about Monday."

"Which Monday?"

"Next Monday. It's my birthday. When is it going to be Monday, Bill?"

"You said *Bill*."

"Beel? That's your name, isn't eet? Weeliam Q. Relke, who weel not tell me what ees the Q?"

"But you said *Bill*."

She was silent for a moment. "OK, I'm a phony," she muttered. "Does the inquisition start now?"

He could feel her tighten up, and he said nothing. She waited stiffly for a time. Gradually she relaxed against him again. "When's it going to be Monday?" she murmured.

"When's it going to be Monday where?"

"Here, anywhere, silly!"

He laughed. "When will it be Monday all over the universe?"

She thought for a moment. "Oh. Like time zones. OK, when will it be Monday here?"

"It won't. We just have periods, hitches, and shifts. Fifty shifts make a hitch, two hitches make a period. A period's from sunrise to sunrise. Twenty-nine and a half days. But we don't count days. So I don't know when it'll be Monday."

It seemed to alarm her. She sat up. "Don't you even have *hours?*" She looked at her watch and jiggled it, listened to it.

"Sure. Seven hours in a shift. *We* call them hours, anyhow. Forty-five seconds longer than an Earth hour."

She looked up through the canopy at the orb of Earth. "When it's Monday on Earth, it'll be Monday here too," she announced flatly.

Relke laughed. "OK, we'll call it that."

"So when will it start being Monday on Earth?"

"Well, it'll start at twenty-four different times, depending on where you are. Maybe more than twenty-four. It's August. Some places, they set the clocks ahead an hour in Summer."

She looked really worried.

"You take birthdays pretty seriously?" he asked.

"Only this one. I'll be—" She broke off and closed her mouth.

"Pick a time zone," Relke offered, "and I'll try to figure out how long until Monday starts. Which zone? Where you'd be now, maybe?"

She shook her head.

"Where you were born?"

"That would be—" She stopped again. "Never mind. Forget it." She sat brooding and watching the moonscape.

Relke turned off the road at the transformer station. He pulled up beside a flat-roofed cubicle the size of a sentrybox. Giselle looked at it in astonishment.

"*That's* a building?" she asked.

"That's an entrance. The 'building's' underground. Come on, let's seal up."

"What's down there?"

"Just a transformer vault and living quarters for a substation man."

"Somebody *lives* down there?"

"Not yet. The line's still being built. They'll move somebody in when the trolley traffic starts moving."

"What do we want to go down there for?"

He looked at her forlornly. "You'd rather go back to the ship?"

She seemed to pull herself together professionally. She laughed and put her arms around him and whispered something in French against his ear. She kissed him hard, pressed her forehead against his, and grinned. "C'mon, babee! Let's go downstairs."

Relke felt suddenly cold inside. He had wanted to see what it felt like to be alone with a woman again in a quiet place, away from the shouting, howling revelry that had been going on aboard the ship. Now he knew what it was going to feel like. It was going to feel counterfeit. "Christ!" he grunted angrily. "Let's go back!" He reached roughly around her and cut on the switch again. She recoiled suddenly and gaped at him as he started the motor and turned the bug around.

"Hey!" She was staring at him oddly, as if seeing him for the first time.

Relke kept his face averted and his knuckles were white on the steering bar. She got up on her knees on the seat and put her hands on his shoulders. "Bill. Good Lord, you're *crying!*"

He choked out a curse as the bug hit the side of the cut and careened around on the approach to the road. He lost control, and the runabout went off the approach and slid slowly sideways down a gentle slope of crushed-lava fill. A sharp clanking sound came from the floor plates.

"Get your suit sealed!" he yelled. "Get it sealed!"

The runabout lurched to a sudden stop. The cabin pressure stayed up. He sat panting for a moment, then started the motor. He let it inch ahead and tugged at the steering bar. It was locked. The bug crept in an arc, and the clanking resumed. He cut off the motor and sat cursing softly.

"What's wrong?"

"Broke a link and the tread's fouled. We'll have to get out."

She glanced at him out of the corner of her eye. He was glowering. She looked back toward the sentrybox entrance to the substation and smiled thoughtfully.

It was chilly in the vault, and the only light came from the indicator lamps on the control board. The pressure gauge inside the airlock indicated only eight pounds of air. The construction crew had pumped it up to keep some convection currents going around the big transformers, but they hadn't planned on anyone breathing it soon. He changed the mixture controls, turned the barostat up to twelve pounds, and listened to the compressors start up. When he turned around, Giselle was taking off her suit and beginning to pant.

"*Hey,* stay in that thing!" he shouted.

His helmet muffled his voice, and she looked at him blankly. "*What?*" she called. She was gasping and looking around in alarm.

Relke sprinted a few steps to the emergency rack and grabbed a low pressure walk-around bottle. When he got back, she was getting blue and shaking her head drunkenly. He cracked the valve on the bottle and got the hose connection against her mouth. She nodded quickly and sucked on it. He went back to watch the gauges. He found the overhead lighting controls and turned them on. Giselle held her nose and anxiously sipped air from the bottle. He nodded reassuringly at her. The construction crews had left the substation filled with nitrogen-helium mixture, seeing no reason to add rust-producing moisture and oxygen until someone moved into the place; she had been breathing inert gases, nothing more.

When the partial oxygen pressure was up to normal, he left the control panel and went to look for the communicator. He found the equipment, but it was not yet tied into the line. He went back to tell the girl. Still sipping at the bottle, she watched him with attentive brown eyes. It was the gaze of a child, and he wondered about her age. Aboard ship, she and the others had seemed impersonal automata of Eros; painted ornaments and sleekly functional decoys designed to perform stereotyped rituals of enticement and excarnation of desire, swiftly, lest a customer be kept waiting. But here in stronger light, against a neutral background, he noticed suddenly that she was a distinct individual. Her lipstick had smeared. Her dark hair kept spilling out in tangled wisps from beneath a leather cap with fleece ear flaps. She wore a pair of coveralls, several sizes too large and rolled up about the ankles. With too much rouge on her solemnly mischievous face, she looked ready for a role in a girls' school version of *Chanticler*.

"You can stop breathing out of the can," he told her. "The oxygen pressure's okay now."

She took the hose from her mouth and sniffed warily. "What was the matter? I was seeing spots."

"It's all right now."

"It's cold in this place. Are we stuck here?"

"I tried to call Joe, but the set's not hooked up. He'll come looking for us."

"Isn't there any heat in here? Can't you start a fire?"

He glanced down at the big 5,000 kva transformers in the pit beyond the safety rail. The noise of corona discharge was very faint, and the purr of thirty-two cycle hum was scarcely audible. With no trucks drawing power from the trolley, the big pots were cold. Normally, eddy current and hysteresis losses in the transformers would keep the station toast-warm. He glanced at a thermometer. It read slightly under freezing: the ambient temperature of the subsurface rock in that region.

"Let's try the stationman's living quarters," he grunted. "They usually furnish them fancy, as bunk tanks go. Man has to stay by himself out here, they want to keep him sane."

A door marked PRIVATE flipped open as they approached it. A cheery voice called out: *"Hi, Bo. Rugged deal, ain't it?"*

Giselle started back in alarm. "Who's there?"

Relke chuckled. "Just a recorded voice. Back up, I'll show you."

They moved a few paces away. The door fell closed. They approached it again. This time a raucous female squawked at them: *"Whaddaya mean coming home at this hour? Lemme smell your breath."*

Giselle caught on and grinned. "So he won't get lonesome?"

"Partly, and partly to keep him a little sore. The stationmen hate it, but that's part of the idea. It gives them something to talk back to and throw things at."

They entered the apartment. The door closed itself, the lights went on. Someone belched, then announced: *"I get just as sick of looking at you as you do looking at me, button head. Go take a bath."*

Relke flushed. "It can get pretty rough sometimes. The tapes weren't edited for mixed company. Better plug your ears if you go in the bathroom."

Giselle giggled. "I think it's cute."

He went into the kitchenette and turned on all the burners of the electric range to help warm the place. "Come stand next to the oven," he called, "until I see if

the heat pumps are working." He opened the oven door.
A libidinous purr came from within.

"*Dah-ling, now why bother with breakfast when you
can have meee?*"

He glanced up at Giselle.

"*I* didn't say it," she giggled, but posed invitingly.

Relke grinned and accepted the invitation.

"You're not crying now," she purred as he released her.

He felt a surge of unaccountable fury, grunted, "Excuse me," and stalked out to the transformer vault. He
looked around for the heat pumps, failed to find them,
and went to lean on the handrail overlooking the pit. He
stood there with his fists in his pockets, vaguely anguished
and enraged, for no reason he understood. For a moment
he had been too close to feeling at home, and that
brought up the wrath somehow. After a couple of minutes he shook it off and went back inside.

"Hey, I wasn't teasing you," Giselle told him.

"What?"

"About crying."

"Listen," he said irritably, "did you ever see a looney
or a spacer without leaky eyes? It's the glare, that's all."

"Is that it? Huh—want to know something? I can't cry.
That's funny. You're a man and you can cry, but I can't."

Relke watched her grumpily while she warmed her behind at the oven. *She's not more than fifteen*, he decided
suddenly. It made him a little queasy. *Come on, Joe,
hurry.*

"You know," she went on absently, "when I was a little girl, I got mad at . . . at somebody, and I decided I
was never going to cry anymore. I never did, either. And
you know what?—now I can't. Sometimes I try and I try,
but I just *can't*." She spread her hands to the oven, tilted
them back and forth, and watched the way the tendons
worked as she stiffened her fingers. She seemed to be
talking to her hands. "Once I used an onion. To cry, I
mean. I cut an onion and rubbed some of it on a handkerchief and laid the handkerchief over my eyes. I cried
that time, all right. That time I couldn't stop crying, and
nobody could make me stop. They were petting me and

scolding me and shaking me and trying to give me smelling salts, but I just couldn't quit. I blubbered for two days. Finally Mother Bernarde had to call the doctor to give me a sedative. Some of the sisters were taking cold towels and—"

"Sisters?" Relke grunted.

Giselle clapped a hand to her mouth and shook her head five or six times, very rapidly. She looked around at him. He shrugged.

"So you were in a convent."

She shook her head again.

"So what if you were?" He sat down with his back to her and pretended to ignore her. She was dangerously close to that state of mind which precedes the telling of a life history. He didn't want to hear it; he already knew it. So she was in a nunnery; Relke was not surprised. Some people had to polarize themselves. If they broke free from one pole, they had to seek its opposite. People with no middle ground. Black, or if not black, then white, never gray. Law, or criminality. God, or Satan. The cloister, or a whorehouse. Eternally a choice of all or nothing-at-all, and they couldn't see that they made things that way for themselves. They set fire to every bridge they ever crossed—so that even a cow creek became a Rubicon, and every crossing was on a tightrope.

You understand that too well, don't you, Relke? he asked himself bitterly. There was Fran and the baby, and there wasn't enough money, and so you had to go and burn a bridge—a 240,000-mile bridge, with Fran on the other side. And so, after six years on Luna, there would be enough money; but there wouldn't be Fran and the baby. And so, he had signed another extended contract, and the moon was going to be home for a long long time. *Yeh, you know about burned bridges, all right, Relke.*

He glanced at Giselle. She was glaring at him.

"If you're waiting for me to say something," she snapped, "you can stop waiting. I don't have to tell you anything."

"I didn't ask you anything."

"I was just a novice. I didn't take permanent vows."

"All *right*."

"They wouldn't let me. They said I was—unstable. They didn't think I had a calling."

"Well, you've got one now. Stop crawling all over me like I said anything. I didn't ask you any questions."

"You gave me that pious look."

"Oh, garbage!" He rolled out of the chair and loped off to the room. The stationman's quarters boasted its own music system and television (permanently tuned to the single channel that broadcast a fairly narrow beam aimed at the lunar stations). He tried the television first, but solar interference was heavy.

"Maybe it'll tell us when it's going to be Monday," she said, coming to watch him from the doorway.

He gave her a sharp look, then softened it. The stove had warmed the kitchen, and she had stepped out of the baggy coveralls. She was still wearing the yellow dress, and she had taken a moment to comb her hair. She leaned against the side of the doorway, looking very young but excessively female. She had that lost pixie look and a tropical climate tan too.

"Why are you looking at me that way?" she asked. "Is this all we're going to do? I mean, just wait around until somebody comes? Can't we dance or something?" She did a couple of skippity steps away from the door jamb and rolled her hips experimentally. One hip was made of India rubber. "Say! Dancing ought to be fun in this crazy gravity." She smirked at him and posed alluringly.

Relke swallowed, reddened, and turned to open the selector cabinet. *She's only a kid, Relke.* He paused, then dialed three selections suitable for dancing. *She's only a kid, damn it!* He paused again, then dialed a violin concerto. *A kid—back home they'd call her "jail bait."* He dialed ten minutes' worth of torrid Spanish guitar. *You'll hate yourself for it, Relke.* He shuddered involuntarily, dialed one called *The Satyricon of Lily Brown, an orgy in New African Jazz (for adults only).*

He glanced up guiltily. She was already whirling around the room with an imaginary partner, dancing to the first selection.

Relke dialed a tape of Palestrina and some plainchant, but left it for last. Maybe it would neutralize the rest.

She snuggled close and they tried to keep time to the music—not an easy task, with the slow motion imposed by low gravity mismatched to the livelier rhythms of dancing on Earth. Two attempts were enough. Giselle flopped down on the bunk.

"What's that playing now, Bill?"

"Sibelius. Concerto for Something and Violin. I dunno."

"Bill?"

"Yeah."

"Did I make you mad or something?"

"No, but I don't think—" He turned to look at her and stopped talking. She was lying on her back with her hands behind her head and her legs cocked up, balancing her calf on her other knee and watching her foot wiggle. She was lithe and brown and . . . ripe.

"Damn," he muttered.

"Bill?"

"Uh?"

She wrinkled her nose at him and smiled. "Don't you even know what you wanted to come over here for?"

Relke got up slowly and walked to the light switch. He snapped it.

"*Oh, dahling!*" said a new voice in the darkness. "*What if my husband comes home!*"

After Sibelius came the Spanish guitar. The African jazz was wasted.

Relke sat erect with a start. Giselle still slept, but noises came from the other room. There were voices, and a door slammed closed. Shuffling footsteps, a muffled curse. "Who's there?" he yelled. "Joe?"

The noises stopped, but he heard the hiss of someone whispering. He nudged the girl awake with one elbow. The record changer clicked, and the soft chant of an *Agnus Dei* came from the music system.

"Oh, God! It's Monday!" Giselle muttered sleepily.

"A dame," grunted a voice in the next room.

"Who's there?" Relke called again.

"We brought you some company." The voice sounded familiar. A light went on in the other room. "Set him down over here, Harv."

Relke heard rattling sounds and a chair scraped back. They dumped something into the chair. Then the bulky silhouette of a man filled the doorway. "Who's in here, anyhow?" He switched on the lights. The man was Larkin. Giselle pulled a blanket around herself and blinked sleepily.

"Is it Monday?" she asked.

A slow grin spread across Larkin's face. "Hey Harv!" he called over his shoulder. "Look what we pulled out of the grab bag! Come look at lover boy. . . . Now, Harv—is that sweet? Is that romantic?"

Kunz looked over Larkin's shoulder. "Yuh. Real homey, ain't it. Hiyah, Rat. Lookit that cheese he's got with him. Some cheese. Round like a provolone, huh? Hiyah, cheesecake, know you're in bed with a rat?"

Giselle glanced questioningly at Relke. Relke was surveying the tactical situation. It looked unpromising. Larkin laughed.

"Look at him, Harv—wondering where he left his shiv. What's the matter, Relke? We make you nervous?" He stepped inside, Kunz followed.

Relke stood up in bed and backed against the wall. "Get out of the way," he grunted at Giselle.

"Look at him!" Larkin gloated. "Getting ready to kick. You planning to kick somebody, sonny?"

"Stay back!" he snapped. "Get out of here, Giselle!"

"*A l'abri? Oui—*" She slid off the bed and darted for the door. Kunz grabbed at her, but she slipped past. She stopped in the doorway and backed up a step. She stared into the next room. She put her hand to her mouth. "Oh! *Oh!*" she yelped. Larkin and Kunz glanced back at her. Relke lunged off the bed. He smashed against Larkin, sent him sprawling into Kunz. He dodged Giselle and sprinted for the kitchen and the cutlery rack. He made it a few steps past the door before he saw what Giselle had seen. Something was sitting at the table, facing the door. Relke stopped in his tracks and began backing away. The something at the table was a blistered carica-ture of a man, an icy frost-figure in a deflated pressure suit. Its mouth was open, and the stomach had been forced up through . . . He closed his eyes. Relke had seen men blown out, but it hadn't gotten any pleasanter to look at since the last time.

"Get him, Harv!"

They pinned his arms from behind. "Heading for a butcher knife, Relke?" He heard a dull crack and felt his head explode. The room went pink and hazy.

"That's for grabbing glass on us the other day, Sonny."

"Don't mess him up too much, Lark. The dame's here."

"I won't mess him up. I'll be real clean about it."

The crack came again, and the pink haze quivered with black flashes.

"That's for ratting on the Party, Relke."

Dimly he heard Giselle screaming at them to stop it.

"Take that little bitch in the other room and play house with her, Harv. I'll work on Sonny awhile, and then we'll trade around. Don't wear her out."

"Let go," she yelled. "Take your hands off—listen, I'll go in there with you if you'll quit beating him. Now stop—"

Another crack. The pink haze flew apart, and black-ness engulfed him. Time moved ahead in jerks for awhile. First he was sitting at the table across from the corpse. Larkin was there too, dealing himself a hand of solitaire. Loud popular music blared from the music system, but he could hear Kunz laughing in the next room. Once Giselle's voice cried out in protest. Relke moved and groaned. Larkin looked his way.

"Hey, Harv—he's awake. It's your turn."

"I'm busy," Kunz yelled.

"Well, hurry up. Brodanovitch is beginning to thaw."

Relke blinked at the dead man. "Who? Him? Brodan—" His lips were swollen, and it was painful to talk.

"Yeah, that's Suds. Pretty, isn't he? You're going to look like that one of these days, kid."

"You—killed—Suds?"

Larkin threw back his head and laughed. "Hey, Harv, hear that? He thinks we killed Suds."

"What happened to him, then?"

Larkin shrugged. "He walked into an airlock with a bottle of champagne. The pressure went down quick, the booze blew up in his face, and there sits Suds. A victim of imprudence, like you. Sad looking schlemazel, isn't he?"

"Wha'd you bring him here for?"

"You know the rules, Sonny. A man gets blown out, they got to look him over inch by inch, make sure it wasn't murder."

Giselle cried out again in protest. Relke started to his feet, staggering dizzily. Larkin grabbed him and pushed him down.

"Hey, Harv! He's getting frisky. Come take over. The gang'll be rolling in pretty quick."

Kunz came out of the bunkroom. Larkin sprinted for the door as Giselle tried to make a run for it. He caught her and dragged her back. He pushed her into the bunkroom, went in after her, and closed the door. Relke lunged at Kunz, but a judo cut knocked numbness into the side of his neck and sent him crashing against the wall.

"Relke, get wise," Harv growled. "This'll happen every now and then if you don't join up."

The lineman started to his feet. Kunz kicked him disinterestedly. Relke groaned and grabbed his side.

"We got no hard feelings, Relke. . . ." He chopped his boot down against the back of Relke's neck. "You can join the Party any time."

Time moved ahead in jerks again.

Once he woke up. Brodanovitch was beginning to melt, and the smell of brandy filled the room. There were voices and chair scrapings and after a while somebody carried Brodanovitch out. Relke lay with his head against the wall and kept his eyes closed. He assumed that if the apartment contained a friend, he would not still be lying here on the floor; so he remained motionless and waited to gather strength.

"So that's about the size of it," Larkin was telling someone. "Those dames are apt to be dynamite if they let them into Crater City. We've got enough steam whipped up to pull off the strike, but what if that canful of cat meat walks in on Copernicus about sundown? Who's going to have their mind on politics?"

"Hell, Lark," grunted a strange voice. "Parkeson'll never let them get in town."

"No? Don't be too damn sure. Parkeson's no idiot. He knows trouble's coming. Hell, he could *invite* them to Crater City, pretend he's innocent as a lamb, just didn't know what they are, but take credit for them being there."

"Well, what can we do about it?"

"Cripple that ship."

"Wha-a-at?"

"Cripple the ship. Look, there's nothing else we can do on our own. We've got no orders from the Party. Right before we break camp, at sundown, we cripple the ship. Something they can't fix without help from the base."

"Leave them *stuck* out here?"

"Only for a day or two. Till the Party takes over the base. Then *we* send a few wagons out here after dark and pick up the wenches. Who gets credit for dames showing up? The Party. Besides, it's the only thing we dare do without orders. We can't be sure what'd happen if Parkeson walked in with a bunch of Algerian whores about the time the show's supposed to start. And says, 'Here, boys, look what Daddy brought.' "

"Parkeson hasn't got the guts."

"The hell he hasn't. He'd say *that* out of one side of his mouth. Out of the other side, he'd be dictating a vigorous protest to the WP for allowing such things to get clearance for blasting off, making it sound like they're at fault. That's just a guess. We've got to keep those women out of Crater City until we're sure, though. And there's only one way: cripple the ship."

There were five or six voices in the discussion, and Relke recognized enough of them to understand dimly that a cell meeting was in progress. His mind refused to function clearly, and at times the voices seemed to be speaking in senseless jargon, although the words were plain enough. His head throbbed and he had bitten a piece out of the end of his tongue. He felt as if he were lying stretched out on a bed of jagged rocks, although there was only the smooth floor under his battered person.

Giselle cried out from the next room and beat angrily on the door.

Quite mindlessly, and as if his body were being directed by some whimsical puppet master, Relke's corpse suddenly clambered to its feet and addressed itself to the startled conspirators.

"Goddam it, gentlemen, can't you let the lady out to use the crapper?"

They hit him over the head with a jack handle.

He woke up again. This time he was in the bunkroom. A faint choking sound made him look up. Giselle sat on the foot of the bed, legs tightly crossed, face screwed up. She was trying to cry.

"Use an onion," he told her thickly, and sat up. "What's the matter?"

"It's Monday now."

"Where are they?"

"They left. We're locked in."

He fell back with a groan. A stitch in his side felt like a broken rib. He turned his face to the wall. "What's so great about Monday?" he muttered.

"Today the others are taking their vows."

When he woke up again, Novotny was watching him from the foot of the bed. The girl was gone. He sat up and fell back with a groan.

"Fran," he said.

"It wasn't Fran, it was a hustler," said Joe. "I had Beasley take her back. Who busted you?"

"Larkin and Kunz."

"It's a good thing."

"What?"

"They saved me the trouble. You ran off with the jeep."

"Sorry."

"You don't have to be sorry. Just watch yourself, that's all."

"I wanted to see what it was like, Joe."

"What? Playing house with a wench?"

He nodded.

"What was it like?"

"I don't know."

"You woke up calling her Fran."

"I did?"

"Yah. Before you start feeling that way, you better ask Beasley what they did together on the rug while you were asleep, Romeo."

"What?"

"She really knows some tricks. Mme. d'Annecy really educates her girls. You been kissing and cooing with her, Relke?"

"I'm sick, Joe. Don't."

"By the way, you better not go back. The Madame's pretty sore at you."

"Why?"

"For keeping the wench gone so long. There was going to be a show. You know, a circus. Giselle was supposed to be in it. You might say she had the lead role."

"Who?"

"Giselle. Still feel like calling her Fran?—Hey! if you're going to vomit, get out of bed."

Relke staggered into the latrine. He was gone a long time.

"Better hurry up," Novotny called. "Our shift goes on in half an hour."

"I can't go on, Joe."

"The hell you can't. Unless you want to be sent up N.L.D. You know what they do to N.L.D. cases."

"You wouldn't report me N.L.D."

"The hell I wouldn't, but I don't have to."

"What do you mean?"

"Parkeson's coming, with a team of inspectors. They're probably already here, and plenty sore."

"About the ship? The women?"

"I don't know. If the Commission hear about those bats, there'll be hell to pay. But who'll pay it is something else."

Relke buried his face in his hands and tried to think. "Joe, listen. I only half remember, but . . . there was a cell meeting here."

"When?"

"After Larkin and Kunz worked me over. Some guys came in, and . . ."

"Well?"

"It's foggy. Something about Parkeson taking the women back to Crater City."

"Hell, that's a screwy idea. Who thinks that?"

Relke shook his head and tried to think. He came out of the latrine mopping his face on a towel. "I'm trying to remember."

Joe got up. "All right. Better get your suit. Let's go pull cable."

The lineman breathed deeply a few times and winced at the effect. He went to get his suit out of the hangar, started the routine safety check, and stopped halfway through. "Joe, my suit's been cut."

Novotny came to look. He pinched the thick corded plastic until the incision opened like a mouth. "Knife," he grunted.

"Those sons of—"

"Yah." He fingered the cut. "They meant for you to find it, though. It's too conspicuous. It's a threat."

"Well, I'm fed up with their threats. I'm going to—"

"You're not going to do anything, Relke. *I'm* going to do it. Larkin and Kunz have messed around with my men one time too often."

"What have you got in mind, Joe?"

"Henderson and I will handle it. We'll go over and have a little conference with them, that's all."

"Why Henderson? Look, Joe, if you're going to stomp them, it's *my* grudge, not Lije's."

"That's just it. If I take you, it's a grudge. If Lije and I do it, it's just politics. I've told you guys before—leave the politics to me. Come on, we'll get you a suit from the emergency locker."

They went out into the transformer vault. Two men wearing blue armbands were bending over Brodanovitch's corpse. One of them was fluently cursing unknown parties who had brought the body to a warm place and allowed it to thaw.

"Investigating team," Novotny muttered. "Means Parkeson is already here." He hiked off toward the emergency lockers.

"Hey, are you the guy that left this stiff near a stove?" one of the investigators called out to Relke.

"No, but I'll be glad to rat on the guys that did, if it'll get them in trouble," the lineman told him.

"Never mind. You can't hang them for being stupid."

"What are you going to do with *him?*" Relke asked, nodding at the corpse.

"Promote him to supervisory engineer and give him a raise."

"Christ but they hire smart boys for the snooper team, don't they? What's your I.Q., friend? I bet they had to breed you to get smart."

The checker grinned. "You looking for an argument, Slim?"

Relke shook his head. "No, I just asked a question."

"We're going to take him back to Copernicus and bury him, friend. It takes a lot of imagination to figure that out, doesn't it?"

"If he was a class three laborer, you wouldn't take him back to Copernicus. You wouldn't even bury him. You'd just chuck him in a fissure and dynamite the lip."

The man smiled. Patient cynicism was in his tone. "But he's *not* a class three laborer, Slim. He's Mister S.K. Brodanovitch. Does that make everything nice and clear?"

"Sure. Is Parkeson around?"

The checker glanced up and snickered. "You're a chum of his, I guess? Hear that, Clyde? We're talking to a wheel."

Relke reddened. "Shove it, chum. I just wondered if he's here."

"Sure, he's out here. He went over to see that flying bordello you guys have been hiding out here."

"What's he going to do about it?"

"Couldn't say, friend."

Novotny came back with an extra suit.

"Joe, I just remembered something."

"Tell me about it on the way back."

They suited up and went out to the runabout. Relke told what he could remember about the cell meeting.

"It sounds crazy in a way," Novotny said thoughtfully. "Or maybe it doesn't. It *could* mess up the Party's strike plans if Parkeson brought those women back before sundown. The men want women back on the moon project. If they can get women bootlegged in, they won't be quite so ready to start a riot on the No Work Without a Wife theme."

"But Parkeson'd get fired in a flash if—"

"If Parliament got wind of it, sure. Unless he raised the squawk later himself. UCOJE doesn't mention prostitution. Parkeson could point out that some national codes on Earth tolerate it. Nations with delegates in the Parliament, and with work teams on the moon. Take the African team at Tycho. And the Japanese team. Parkeson himself is an Aussie. Whose law is he supposed to enforce?"

"You mean maybe they can't keep ships like that from visiting us?"

"Don't kid yourself. It won't last long. But maybe long enough. If it goes on long enough, and builds up, the general public will find out. You think that wouldn't cause some screaming back home?"

"Yeah. That'll be the end."

"I'm wondering. If there turns out to be a profit in it for whoever's backing d'Annecy, well—anything that brings a profit is pretty hard to put a stop to. There's only one sure way to stop it. Kill the demand."

"For women? Are you crazy, Joe?"

"They could bring in decent women. Women to marry. That'll stop it."

"But the kids. They can't have kids."

"Yeah, I know. That's the problem, and they've got to start solving it sometime. Hell, up to now, they haven't been trying to solve it. When the problem came up, and the kids were dying, everybody got hysterical and jerked the women back to Earth. That wasn't a solution, it was an evasion. The problem is growth-control—in low gravity. It ought to have a medical answer. If this d'Annecy dame gets a chance to keep peddling her wares under the counter, well—she'll force them to start looking for a solution."

"I don't know, Joe. Everybody said homosexuality would force them to start looking for it—after Doc Reiber made his survey. The statistics looked pretty black, but they didn't do anything about it except send us a shipful of ministers. The fairies just tried to make the ministers."

"Yeah, but this is different."

"I don't see how."

"Half the voters are women."

"So? They didn't do anything about homosex—"

"Relke, wise up. Listen, did you ever see a couple of Lesbians necking in a bar?"

Relke snickered. "Sure, once or twice."

"How did you feel about it?"

"Well, this once was kind of funny. You see, this one babe had on—"

"Never mind. You thought it was funny. Do you think it's funny the way MacMillian and Wickers bill and coo?"

"That gets pretty damn nauseating, Joe."

"Uh-huh, but the Lesbians just gave you a giggle. Why?"

"Well, I don't know, Joe, it's—"

"I'll tell you why. You like dames. You can understand other guys liking dames. You like dames so much that you can even understand two dames liking each other. You can see what they see in each other. But it's incongruous, so it's funny. But you *can't* see what two fairies see in each other, so that just gives you a bellyache. Isn't that it?"

"Maybe, but what's that got to do with the voters?"

"Ever think that maybe a woman would feel the same way in reverse? A dame could see what MacMillian and Wickers see in each other. The dame might morally disapprove, but at the same time she could sympathize. What's more, she'd be plenty sure that she could handle that kind of competition if she ever needed to. She's a woman, and wotthehell, Wickers is only a substitute woman. It wouldn't worry her too much. Worry her morally, but not as a personal threat. Relke, Mme. d'Annecy's racket is a personal threat to the home girl and the womenfolk."

"I see what you mean."

"Half the voters are women."

Relke chuckled. "Migod, Joe, if Ellen heard about that ship . . ."

"Ellen?"

"My older sister. Old maid. Grim."

"You've got the idea. If Parkeson thinks of all this . . ." His voice trailed off. "When is Larkin talking about crippling that ship?"

"About sundown, why?"

"Somebody better warn the d'Annecy dame."

The cosmic gunfire had diminished. The Perseid shrapnel still pelted the dusty face of the plain, but the gram-impact-per-acre-second had dropped by a significant fraction, and with it fell the statistician's estimate of dead men per square mile. There was an ion storm during the first half of B-shift, and the energized spans of high voltage cable danced with fluttering demon light as the trace-pressure of the lunar "atmosphere" increased enough to start a glow discharge between conductors. High current surges sucked at the line, causing the breakers to hiccup. The breakers tried the line three times, then left the circuit dead and waited for the storm to pass. The storm meant nothing to the construction crews except an increase in headset noise.

Parkeson's voice came drawling on the general call frequency, wading waist-deep through the interference caused by the storm. Relke leaned back against his safety strap atop the trusswork of the last tower and tried to listen. Parkeson was reading the Articles of Discipline, and listening was compulsory. All teams on the job had stopped work to hear him. Relke gazed across the plain toward the slender nacelles of the bird from Algiers in the distance. He had gotten used to the ache in his side where Kunz had kicked him, but it was good to rest for a time and watch the rocket and remember brown legs and a yellow dress. Properties of Earth. Properties belonging to the communion of humanity, from which fellowship a Looney was somehow cut off by 238,000 miles of physical separation.

"We've got a job to finish here," Parkeson was telling the men.

Why? What was in space that was worth the wanting? What followed from its conquest? What came of finishing the job?

Nothing.

Nothing.

Nothing. Nothing anybody ever dreamed of or hoped for.

Parkeson scolded on. *"I know the question that's foremost in your minds,"* his voice continued, *"but you'd better forget it. Let me tell you what happens if this line isn't finished by sundown.* (But by God, it *will* be finished!) *Listen, you wanted women. All right, now you've all been over to visit the uh—'affectionate institution'— and you got what you wanted; and now the work is behind schedule. Who gives a damn about the project, eh? I know what you're thinking. 'That's Parkeson's worry.' OK, so let's talk about what you're going to breathe for the next couple of periods. Let's talk about how many men will wind up in the psycho-respiratory ward, about the overload on the algae tanks. That's not your responsibility either, is it? You don't have to breathe and eat. Hell, let Nature take care of air and water, eh? Sure. Now look around. Take a good look. All that's between you and that hungry vacuum out there is ten pounds of man-made air and a little reinforced plastic. All that keeps you eating and drinking and breathing is that precarious life-cycle of ours at Copernicus. That plant-animal feedback loop is so delicately balanced that the biology team gets the cold shakes every time somebody sneezes or passes gas. It has to be constantly nursed. It has to be planned and kept on schedule. On Earth,*

Nature's a plenum. You can chop down her forests, kill off her deer and buffalo, and fill her air with smog and hot isotopes; the worst you can do is cause a few new deserts and dust bowls, and make things a little unpleasant for a while.

"Up here, we've got a little bit of Nature cooped up in a bottle, and we're in the bottle too. We're cultured like mold on agar. The biology team has to chart the ecology for months in advance. It has to know the construction and survey teams are going to deliver exactly what they promise to deliver, and do it on schedule. If you don't deliver, the ecology gets sick. If the ecology gets sick, you get sick.

"Do you want another epidemic of the chokers like we had three years back? That's what'll happen if there's a work slowdown while everybody goes off on a sex binge at that ship. If the line isn't finished before sundown, the ecology gets bled for another two weeks to keep that mine colony going, and the colony can't return wastes to our cycle. Think it over, but think fast. There's not much time. 'We all breathe the same air'—on Earth, that's just a political slogan. Here, we all breathe it or we all choke in it. How do you want it, men?"

Relke shifted restlessly on the tower. He glanced down at Novotny and the others who lounged around the foot of the steel skeleton listening to Parkeson. Lije caught his eye. He waved at Relke to haul up the hoist-bucket. Relke shook his head and gave him a thumbs-down. Henderson gestured insistently for him to haul it up. Relke reeled the bucket in. It was empty, but chalked on the sides and bottom was a note from Lije: "They toll me what L and K did to you and yr girl. I and Joe will take care of it, right after this sermon. You can spit on my fist first if you want. Lije."

Relke gave him a half-hearted screw-twist signal and let the bucket go. Revenge was no good, and vicarious revenge was worse than no good; it was hollow. He thought of asking Joe to forget it, but he knew Joe wouldn't listen. The pusher felt his own integrity was involved, and a matter of jurisdictional ethics: nobody can push my men around but me. It was gang ethics, but it seemed inevitable somehow. Where there was fear, men huddled in small groups and counted their friends on their fingers, and all else was Foe. In the absence of the family, there had to be the gang, and fear made it quarrelsome, jealous, and proud.

Relke leaned back against his strap and glanced up toward Earth. The planet was between quarter and half phase, for the sun was lower in the west. He watched it and tried to feel something more than a vague envy. Sometimes the heartsick nostalgia reached the proportions of idolatrous adoration of Gaea's orb overhead, only to subside into a grudging resentment of the gulf between worlds. Earth—it was a place where you could stop being afraid, a place where fear of suffocation was not, where fear of blowout was not, where nobody went berserk with the chokers or dreamed of poisoned air or worried about short-horn cancer or burn blindness or meteoric dust or low-gravity muscular atrophy. A place where there was wind to blow your sweat away.

Watching her crescent, he felt again that vague anger of separation, that resentment against those who stayed at home, who had no cause for constant fear, who could live without the tense expectancy of sudden death haunting every moment. One of them was Fran, and another was the one who had taken her from him. He looked away quickly and tried to listen to the coordinator.

"This is no threat," Parkeson was saying. *"If the line isn't finished on time, then the consequences will just happen, that's all. Nobody's going to punish you, but there are a few thousand men back at the Crater who have to breathe air with you. If they have to breathe stink next period—because you guys were out having one helluva party with Madame d'Annecy's girls—you can figure how popular you'll be. That's all I've got to say. There's still time to get the work back on schedule. Let's use it."*

Parkeson signed off. The new engineer who was replacing Brodanovitch gave them a brief pep-talk, implying that Parkeson was a skunk and would be forced to eat his own words before sundown. It was the old hard-guy-soft-guy routine: first a bawling-out and then a buttering-up. The new boss offered half of his salary to the first team to forge ahead of its own work schedule. It was not stated nor even implied that Parkeson was paying him back.

The work was resumed. After half an hour, the safety beeper sounded on all frequencies, and men switched back to general call. Parkeson and his party were already heading back toward Copernicus.

"Blasting operation at the next tower site will occur in ten minutes," came the announcement. *"Demol team requests safety clearance over all of zones two and three, from four forty to five hundred hours. There will be scatter-glass in both zones. Zone two is to be evacuated immediately, and all personnel in zone three take line-of-sight cover from the red marker. I repeat: there will be scatter-glass . . ."*

"That's us," said Novotny when it was over. "Everybody come on. Brax, Relke, climb down."

Braxton swore softly in a honeysuckle drawl. It never sounded like cursing, which it wasn't, but like a man marveling at the variety of vicissitudes invented by an ingenious universe for the bedevilment of men. "I sweah, when the angels ahn't shootin' at us from up in Perseus, it's the demol boys. Demol says froggie, and eve'body jumps. It gives 'em that suhtain feelin' of impohtance. Y'all know what I think? I got a thee-orry. I think weah all really dead, and they don' tell us it's hell weah in, because not tellin' us is paht of the tohture."

"Get off the damn frequency, Brax, and stay off!" Novotny snapped when the Alabaman released his mic button. "I've told you and Henderson before—either learn to talk fast, or don't talk on the job. If somebody had a slow leak, he'd be boiling blood before he could scream —with you using the frequency for five minutes to say 'yeah.' "

"Mistuh Novotny! My mothuh always taught me to speak slowly and de-stinct-ly. If you think that yo' Yankee upbringin' . . ."

Joe rapped on his helmet until he shut up, then beckoned to Henderson. "Lije, we got twenty minutes."

"Yeah, Joe, want to go see a couple of guys now?" He flashed white teeth and stared back toward the barrack train.

"Think we can handle it in twenty minutes?"

"I don' know. It seem like a short time to do a real good job of it, but maybe if we don't waste any on preliminary fisticuffin' . . ."

"Hell, they didn't waste any ceremony on Relke."

"Less go, then!" He grinned at Relke and held out his fist. "Spit on it?"

Relke shook his head. Henderson laughed. "Wanted to see if you'd go ptooey in your helmet."

"Come on, Lije. The rest of you guys find cover."

Relke watched the two of them lope off toward the rolling barracks. "Hey, Joe," he called after a few seconds.

The lopers stopped to look back. "Relke?"

"Yeah. Don't lose."

"What?"

"They'll say I sicced you. Don't lose."

"Don't worry." They loped again. The longer Relke watched them, the less he liked the idea. If they didn't do a pretty thorough job on Kunz and Larkin, things would be worse for Relke than if they did nothing at all. Then there was the movement to think about; he didn't know to what extent *they* looked out for their own.

Relke walked out of the danger zone and hiked across the hill where he could get a clear view of the rocket. He stopped for a while on the slope and watched four distant figures moving around on the ground beneath the towering ship. For a moment, he thought they were women, but then he saw that one of them was coiling mooring cable, and he knew they were ship's crew. What sort of men had the d'Annecy women been able to hire for such a job? he wondered.

He saw that they were getting ready to lift ship. *Lift ship!*

Relke was suddenly running toward them without knowing why. Whenever he topped a rise of ground and could see them, he tried calling them, but they were not using the project's suit frequency. Finally he found their voices on the seldom used private charter band, but they were speaking French.

One of the men looped a coil of cable over his shoulder and started up the ladder toward the lock. Relke stopped atop an outcropping. He was still two or three miles from the ship. The "isobar" valve system for the left knee of his suit had jammed, and it refused to take up the increased pressure caused by flexure. It was like trying to bend a fully inflated rubber tire, and he hobbled about for a moment with one leg stiff as a crutch.

"Listen!" he called on the p.c. frequency. "You guys at the ship. Can you hear me?" He was panting, and he felt a little panicky. The man on the ladder stopped climbing and looked around.

There was a staccato exchange in French.

"No, no! Over here. On the rock." He waved at them and jumped a few times. "Look toward the camp. On the rock."

They conversed heatedly among themselves for a time.

"Don't any of you speak English?" he begged.

They were silent for a moment. "Whoevair ees?" one of them ventured. "You conversation with wrong radio, M'sieur. Switch a button."

"No, no. I'm trying to call you . . ."

A carrier drowned him out.

"We close for business," the man said. "We go now." He started climbing again.

"Listen!" Relke yelled. "Ten thousand dollars. Everything."

"You crazy man."

"Look, it won't get you in any trouble. I've got plenty in the bank. I'll pay—"

The carrier cut him off again.

"You crazy. Get off the air. We do not go to Earth now."

"Wait! Listen! Tell Giselle . . . No, let me talk to her. Get her to use the radio. It's important."

"I tell you, we close for business now." The man

climbed in the airlock. The others climbed up behind. They were jeering at him. This time it sounded like Arabic. He watched until they were all inside.

White fury lanced the ground and spread in a white sheet beneath the ship and roiled up in a tumult of dust and expanding gasses. It climbed on a white fan, gathering velocity. Relke could still make it out as a ship when its course began arcing away from the vertical. It was beginning a trajectory in the direction of Copernicus. When it was out of sight, he began trudging back toward the work site. He was nearly an hour overdue.

"Where you been?" Novotny asked him quietly after watching him hobble the last quarter of a mile in stony silence. He was squinting at the lineman with that faintly puzzled look that Relke recognized as a most ominous omen. The squint was lopsided because of a cut under one eye, and it looked like a chip was missing from a tooth.

Relke showed his stiff leg and bounced the heel against the ground a couple of times. "I walked too far, and the c.p. valves got jammed. Sorry, Joe."

"You don't have to be sorry. Let's see."

The pusher satisfied himself that the suit was malfunctioning. He waved the lineman toward the barrack train. "Go to supply and get it fixed. Get back on the double. You've slowed us down."

Relke paused. "You sore, Joe?"

"We're on duty. I don't get sore on duty. I save it up. Now—haul ass!"

Relke hobbled off. "What about . . . what you went for, Joe?" he called back. "What happened?"

"I told you to keep your nose out of politics!" the pusher snapped. "Never mind what happened."

Joe, Relke decided, was plenty sore. About something. Maybe about a beating that backfired. Maybe about Relke taking an hour awol. Either way, he was in trouble. He thought it over and decided that paying a bootleg ship ten thousand to take him back to Earth with them hadn't been such a hysterical whim after all.

But then he met Larkin in the supply wagon. Larkin

was stretched out flat on his back, and a medic kept saying, "Who did it to you? Who did it to you?" and Larkin kept telling him to go to hell out of a mouth that looked like a piece of singed stew meat. Kunz was curled up on a blanket and looked even worse. He spat in his sleep and a bit of tooth rattled across the deck.

"Meanest bunch of bastards I ever saw," the clerk told Relke while he checked in the suit. "They don't even give you a chance. Here were these two guys sleeping in their bunks and not bothering anybody, and what do you think?"

"I quit thinking. What?"

"Somebody starts working them over. Wham. Don't even wake them up first. Just wham. You ever see anything like it? Mean, John, just mean. You can't even get a shift's sleep anymore. You better go to bed with a knife in your boot, John."

"It's Bill."

"Oh. What do you suppose makes a guy that mean anyway?"

"I don't know. Everybody's jumpy, I guess."

The clerk looked at him wisely. "There you have put your finger on it, John. Looney nerves. The jitters. Everybody's suit-happy." He leaned closer and lowered his voice. "You know how I tell when the camp's getting jittery?"

"Listen, check me out a suit. I've got to get back to the line."

"Now wait, this'll surprise you. I can tell better than the psych checkers when everybody's going on a slow panic. It's the sleeping bag liners."

"What?"

"The bed wetters, John. You'd be surprised how many grown men turn bed wetters about the middle of a hitch. At first, nobody. Then somebody gets killed on the line. The bag liners start coming in for cleaning. By the end of the hitch, the wash tank smells like a public lavatory, John. Not just the men, either. Some of the engineers. You know what I'm doing?"

"Look, Mack, the suit . . ."

"Not Mack. Frank. Look, I'll show you the chart." He got out a sheet of paper with a crudely drawn graph on it. "See how it goes? The peak? I've done ten of them."

"Why?"

The clerk looked at him blankly. "For the idea box, John. Didn't you know about the prizes? Doctor Esterhall ought to be glad to get information like this."

"Christ, they'll give you a medal, Charley. Now give me my damn suit before I get it myself. I'm due on the line."

"OK, OK. You got the jitters yourself, haven't you?" He went to get the suit. "I just happened to think," he called back. "If you've been turning in liners yourself, don't worry about me. I don't keep names, and I don't remember faces."

"You blab plenty, though," Relke grumbled to himself.

The clerk heard him. "No call to get sore, John."

"I'm not sore, I'm just in a hurry. If you want to beg for a stomping, it's nothing to me."

The clerk came back bristling. "Who's going to stomp?"

"The bed wetters, I guess." He started getting into the suit.

"Why? It's for science, isn't it?"

"Nobody likes to be watched."

"There you put your finger on it, John. It's the watching part that's worst. If they'd only quit watching us, or come out where we could see them! You know what I think? I think there's some of them among us. In disguise." The clerk smirked mysteriously at what-he-knew-but-wouldn't-tell.

Relke paused with a zipper halfway up. "Who do you mean—watching? Checkers?"

The clerk snorted and resumed what he had been doing when Relke entered: he was carefully taping his share of stock in Mme. d'Annecy's venture up on the wall among a display of pin-ups. "You know who I mean," he muttered.

"No, I don't."

"The ones that dug that mine, that's who."

"Aliens? Oh, bullspit."

"Yeah? You'll see. They're keeping an eye on us, all right. There's a guy on the African team that even talked to some of them."

"Nuts. He's not the first guy that ever talked to spooks. Or demons. Or saucer pilots. You don't have to be a Looney to be a lunatic."

That made the clerk sore, and he stomped off to his sanctum to brood. Relke finished getting into the suit and stepped into the airlock. Some guys had to personify their fear. If there was danger, somebody must be responsible. They had to have an Enemy. Maybe it helped, believing in gremlins from beyond Pluto. It gave you something to hate when your luck was bad.

He met Joe just outside the lock. The pusher was waiting to get in.

"Hey, Pappy, I own up. I was goofing off awhile ago. If you want to be sore——" Relke stopped. Something was wrong. Joe was breathing hard, and he looked sick.

"Christ, I'm not sore! *Not now!*"

"What's wrong, Joe?"

The pusher paused in the hatchway. "Run on back to the line. Keep an eye on Braxton. I'm getting a jeep. Back in a minute." He went on inside and closed the hatch.

Relke trotted toward the last tower. After a while he could hear Braxton talking in spasms on the frequency. It sounded like sobbing. He decided it *was* sobbing.

"Theah just isn't any God," Bama was moaning. "Theah just couldn't be a God and be so mean. He was the bes' frien' a man evah had, and he nevah did nothin' to deserve it. Oh, God, oh, God, why did it have to be *him?* Theah jus' can't be any God in Heaven, to treat a man that way, when he been so . . ." Braxton's voice broke down into incoherent sobbing.

There was a man lying on the ground beside the tower. Relke could see Benet bending over him. Benet was clutching a fistful of the man's suit. He crossed himself slowly and stood up. A safety team runabout skidded to

a halt beside the tower, and three men piled out. Benet
spread his hands at them in a wide shrug and turned his
back.

"What happened?" Relke asked as he loped up to
Beasley.

"Bama was welding. Lije walked over to ask him for a
wrench or something. Bama turned around to get it, and
Lije sat down on the strut with the hot weld."

"Blow out?"

"He wasn't that lucky. Call it a fast slowout."

Novotny drove up, saw the safety jeep, and started bellowing furiously at them.

"Take it easy, chum. We got here as quick as we
could."

"Theah jus' can't be any God in Heaven . . ."

They got Henderson in the safety runabout. Novotny
manufactured a hasty excuse to send Braxton off with
them, for grief had obviously finished his usefulness for
awhile. Everybody stood around in sickly silence and
stared after the jeep.

"Benet, you know how to pray," Novotny muttered.
"Say something, altar boy."

"Aw, Joe, that was fifteen years ago. I haven't lived
right."

"Hell, who has? Go ahead."

Benet muttered for a moment and turned his back. *"In
nomine Patris et Filii et Spiritus Sancti . . ."* He paused.

"Can't you pray in English?" Joe asked.

"We always said it in Latin. I only served at a few
masses."

"Go ahead."

Benet prayed solemnly while they stood around with
bowed heads and shuffled their boots in the dust. Nobody
understood the words, not even Benet, but somehow it
seemed important to listen.

*"Requiem aeternam dona ei, Domine. Et lux perpetua
luceat . . ."*

Relke looked up slowly and let his eyes wander slowly
across the horizon. There were still some meteorites com-

ing in, making bright little winks of fire where they bit
into the plain. Deadly stingers out of nowhere, heading
nowhere, impartially orbiting, random as rain, random as
death. The debris of creation. Relke decided Braxton was
wrong. There was a God, all right, maybe personal, maybe not, but there was a God, and He wasn't mean. His
universe was a deadly contraption, but maybe there wasn't
any way to build a universe that wasn't a deadly contraption—like a square circle.

He made the contrapation, and He put Man in it, and
Man was a fairly deadly contraption himself. But the
funny part of it was, there wasn't a damn thing the universe
could do to a man that a man wasn't built to endure. He
could even endure it when it killed him. And gradually he
could get the better of it. It was the consistency of matched
qualities—random mercilessness and human endurance—
and it wasn't mean, it was a fair match.

"Poor Lije. God help him."

"All right," Novotny called. "Let's pull cable, men."

"Yeah, you know what?" said Beasley. "Those dames
went to Crater City. The quicker we get the line finished,
the quicker we get back. Damn Parkeson anyhow!"

"Hell, why do you think he let them go there, Beeze?"
Tremini jeered. "So we'd work our butts off to finish
quick, that's why. Parkeson's no idiot. If he'd sent them
packing for somewhere else, maybe we'd finish, maybe
we wouldn't."

"Cut the jawing. Somebody run down and get the twist
out of that span before she kinks. Relke, start taking up
slack."

Atop the steel truss that supported the pendulous in-
sulators, the lineman began jacking up the slack line. He
glanced toward the landing site where the ship had been,
and it was hard to believe it had ever been there at all.
A sudden improbable dream that had come and gone and
left nothing behind. Nothing? Well, there was a share of
stock . . .

"Hey, we're all capitalists!" Relke called.

Benet hooted. "Take your dividends out in trade."

"Listen, someday they'll let dames come here again

and get married. That's one piece of community property you better burn first."

"That d'Annecy dame thought of everything."

"Listen, that d'Annecy dame is going to force an issue. She'll clean up, and a lot of guys will throw away small fortunes, but before it's over, they'll let women in space again. Now quit jawing, and let's get to work."

Relke glanced at the transformer station where he had taken the girl. He tried to remember what she looked like, but he got Fran's face instead. He tried to transmute the image into Giselle's, but it stayed Fran. Maybe he hadn't really seen Giselle at all. Maybe he had looked at her and seen Fran all along, but it had been a poor substitution. It had accomplished one thing, though. He felt sorry for Fran now. He no longer hated her. She had stuck it out a long time before there had been another guy. And it was harder for a wife on Earth than it was for a husband on Luna. She had to starve in the midst of plenty. He had only to deny himself what he couldn't get anyhow, or even see. She was the little girl with her nose against the bakery window. He was only fasting in the desert. It was easy; it put one beyond temptation. To fast in a banquet hall, one had to be holy. Fran wasn't holy. Relke doubted he'd want a wife who was holy. It could get damnably dull.

A quick glance at Earth told him it was still in the skyless vault. Maybe she'll come, if they ever let them come, he thought wistfully. Maybe the guy'll be a poor substitute, and she'll figure out who she's really married to, legal instruments notwithstanding. Maybe . . . O God, let her come! . . . women had no business on Luna, but if they didn't then neither did men, nor Man, who had to be a twosome in order to be recognizably human.

"Damn it, Relke, work that jack!" Joe yelled. "We got to build that line!"

Relke started cranking again, rocking his body to the rhythm of the jack, to the rhythm of echoes of thought. Got to build the line. Damn it, build the line. Got to build the line. Build the damn line. The line was part of a living thing that had to grow. The line was yet another creeping of life across a barrier, a lungfish flopping from pool to pool, an ape trying to walk erect across still another treeless space. Got to build the line. Even when it kills you, got to build the line, the bloody endless line. The lineman labored on in silence. The men were rather quiet that shift.

I, MARS

Ray Bradbury

As I pointed out in my anthology, Three to the Highest Power, *the dividing line between a Bradbury fantasy and a Bradbury science fiction story is often very thin. The present selection proves my point. As in Bradbury's "The Veldt," the machine-made world of "I, Mars," takes on a life of its own to threaten the human protagonist. Bradbury does not ask us to believe in the scientific aspects of his fable; he simply expects us to enjoy the fantasy.*

"I, Mars" has been lost in the pages of Super Science Stories *for twenty years, having appeared a full season before* The Martian Chronicles *was first published by Doubleday. This story, a direct companion piece to the book, examines with humor and zest the bizarre methods one man might employ to ward off loneliness and insanity amid the dead cities and sand-dusted seas of Mars.*

THE PHONE rang.

A gray hand lifted the receiver.

"Hello."

"Hello, Barton?"

"Yes."

"This is Barton."

"What?"

"This is Barton!"

"It can't be. This phone hasn't rung in twenty years."

The old man hung up.

Brrrrinnnng!

His gray hand seized the phone.

"Hello, Barton," laughed the voice. "You have forgotten, haven't you?"

The old man felt his heart grow small and like a cool stone. He felt the wind blowing in off the dry seas and the blue hills of Mars. After twenty years of silence and cobwebs and now, tonight, on his eightieth birthday, with a ghastly scream, this phone had wailed to life.

"Who did you think it was?" said the voice. "A rocket captain? Did you think someone had come to rescue you?"

"No."

"What's the date?"

Numbly, "July 20th, 2097."

"Good Lord. Sixty years! Have you been sitting there that long? Waiting for a rocket to come from Earth to rescue you?"

The old man nodded.

"Now, old man, do you know who I am?"

"Yes." The dry pale lips trembling. "I understand. I remember. I am Emil Barton and you are Emil Barton."

"With one difference. You are eighty. I am only twenty. All of life before me!"

The old man began to laugh and then to cry. He sat holding the phone like a lost child. The conversation was impossible, and should not be continued, and yet he went on with it. When he got hold of himself he held the phone close to his withered lips and said, in deepest anguish, "Listen! You there! Listen, oh God, if I could warn you! How can I? You're only a voice. If I could show you how lonely the years are. End it, kill yourself! Don't wait! If you knew what it is to change from the thing you are to the thing that is me, today, here, now, at this end."

"Impossible." The voice of the young Barton laughed,

far away. "I've no way to tell if you ever get this call. You're talking to a transcription. This is 2037. Sixty years in your past. Today, the atom war started on Earth. All colonials were called home from Mars, by rocket. I got left behind!"

"I remember," whispered the old man.

"Alone on Mars," laughed the young voice. "A month, a year, who cares? There are foods and books. In my spare time I've made transcription libraries of ten thousand words, responses, my voice, connected to phone relays. In later months I'll call, have someone to talk with."

"Yes," murmured the old man, remembering.

"Forty-sixty years from now my own transcripto-tapes will ring me up. I don't really think I'll be here on Mars that long; it's just a beautifully ironic idea of mine, something to pass the time. Is that really you, Barton? Is that really me?"

Tears fell from the old man's eyes. "Yes!"

"I've made a thousand Bartons, tapes, sensitive to all questions, my voice, in one thousand Martian towns. An army of Bartons over Mars, while I wait for the rockets to return."

"You fool," the old man shook his head, wearily. "You waited sixty years. You grew old waiting, always alone. And now you've become me and you're still alone in the empty cities."

"Don't expect my sympathy. You're like a stranger, off in another country. I can't be sad. I'm alive when I make these tapes. And you're alive when you hear them. Both of us, to the other, incomprehensible. Neither can warn the other, even though both respond, one to the other, one automatically, the other warmly and humanly. I'm human now. You're human later. I can't cry, because not knowing the future I can only be optimistic. These hidden tapes can only react to a certain number of stimuli from you. Can you ask a dead man to weep?"

"Stop it!" cried the old man. He felt the familiar great seizures of pain. Nausea moved through him, and blackness. "Stop it! Oh God, but you were heartless. Go away!"

"Were, old man? I *am*. As long as the tapes glide on,

as long as secret spindles and hidden electronic eyes read
and select and convert words to send to you, I'll be
young, cruel, blunt. I'll go on being young and cruel long
after you're dead. Goodby."

Click.

Barton sat holding the silent phone a long while. His
heart gave him intense pain.

What insanity it had been, in those first secluded years,
fixing the telephonic brains, the tapes, the circuits, sched-
uling calls on time relays:

Brrrrinnnng!

"Morning, Barton. This is Barton. Seven o'clock. Rise
and shine!"

Brrrrinnnng!

"Barton calling. You're to go to Mars Town at noon.
Install a telephonic brain. Thought I'd remind you."

"Thanks."

Brrrrinnnng!

"Barton? Barton. Have lunch with me? The Rocket
Inn?"

"Right."

Brrrrinnnng!

"That you, B.? Thought I'd cheer you. Firm chin, and
all that. The rescue rocket might come tomorrow, to
save you."

"Yes, tomorrow, tomorrow, tomorrow, tomorrow."

Click.

But forty years had burned into smoke. Barton had
muted the insidious phones and their clever, clever repar-
tee. He had sealed them into silences. They were to call
him only after he was eighty, if he still lived. And now
today, the phones ringing, and the past breathing in his
ear, sighing, whispering, murmuring, and remembering.

Brrrrinnnng!

He let it ring.

"I don't have to answer it," he thought.

Brrrrinnnng!

"There's no one there at all," he thought.

Brrrrinnnng!

"It's like talking to yourself," he thought. "But different. Oh God, how different."

He felt his hands crawl unconsciously toward the phone.

Click.

"Hello, old Barton, this is young Barton. One year older, though. I'm twenty-one today. In the last year I've put voice brains in two hundred towns on Mars. I've populated it with arrogant Bartons!"

"Yes." The old man remembered those days six decades ago, those nights of rushing over blue hills and into iron valleys of Mars, with a truckful of machinery, whistling, happy. Another telephone, another relay. Something to do. Something clever and wonderful and sad. Hidden voices. Hidden, hidden. In those young days when death was not death, time was not time, old age a faint echo from the long blue cavern of years ahead. That young idiot, that sadistic fool, never thinking to reap the harvest so sown.

"Last night," said Barton, aged twenty-one, "I sat alone in a movie theater in an empty town. I played an old Laurel and Hardy. God, how I laughed."

"Yes."

"I got an idea today. I recorded my voice one thousand times on one tape. Broadcast from the town, it sounds like a thousand people living there. A comforting noise, the noise of a crowd. I fixed it so doors slam in town, children sing, music boxes play, all by clockworks. If I don't look out the window, if I just listen, it's all right. But if I look, it spoils the illusion. I guess I'm getting lonely."

The old man said, "Yes. That was your first sign."

"What?"

"The first time you admitted you were lonely."

"I've experimented with smells. As I walk down the deserted streets, the smells of bacon and eggs, ham steak, filets, soups, come from the houses. All done with hidden machines. Clever?"

"Fantasy. Madness."

"Self-protection, old man."

"I'm tired." Abruptly, the old man hung up. It was too much. The past pouring over him, drowning him. . . .

Swaying, he moved down the tower stairs to the streets of the town.

The town was dark. No longer did red neons burn, music play, or cooking smells linger. Long ago he had abandoned the grim fantasy of the mechanical lie. Listen! Are those footsteps? Smell! Isn't that strawberry pie! No, he had stopped it all. What had he done with the robots? His mind puzzled. Oh, yes . . .

He moved to the dark canal where the stars shone in the quivering waters.

Underwater, in row after fish-like row, rusting, were the robot populations of Mars he had constructed over the years, and, in a wild realization of his own insane inadequacy, had commanded to march, one two three four! into the canal deeps, plunging, bubbling like sunken bottles. He had killed them and shown no remorse.

Brrrrinnnng.

Faintly a phone rang in a lightless cottage.

He walked on. The phone ceased.

Brrrrinnnng. Another cottage ahead, as if it knew of his passing. He began to run. The ringing stayed behind. Only to be taken up by a ringing from now this house— Brrrrinnnng! now that, now here, there! He turned the corner. A phone! He darted on. Another corner. Another phone!

"All right, all right!" he shrieked, exhausted. "I'm coming!"

"Hello, Barton."

"What do you want!"

"I'm lonely. I only live when I speak. So I must speak. You can't shut me up forever."

"Leave me alone!" said the old man, in horror.

"This is Barton, age twenty-four. Another couple of years gone. Waiting. A little lonelier. I've read *War and Peace*, drunk sherry, run restaurants with myself as waiter, cook, entertainer. And tonight, I star in a film at the

Tivoli. Emil Barton in *Love's Labor Lost,* playing all the parts, some with wigs, myself!"

"Stop calling me," the old man's eyes were fiery and insane. "Or I'll kill you!"

"You can't kill me. You'll have to find me, first!"

"I'll find you!" A choking.

"You've forgotten where you hid me. I'm everywhere in Mars, in boxes, in houses, in cables, towers, underground! Go ahead, try! What'll you call it? Telecide? Suicide? Jealous, are you? Jealous of me here, only twenty-four, bright-eyed, strong, young, young, young? All right, old man, it's war! Between us. Between me! A whole regiment of us, all ages from twenty to sixty, against you, the real one. Go ahead, declare war!"

"I'll kill you!" screamed Barton.

Click. Silence.

"Kill you!" He threw the phone out the window, shrieking.

In the midnight cold, the ancient automobile moved in deep valleys. Under Barton's feet on the floorboard were revolvers, rifles, dynamite. The roar of the car was in his thin, tired bones.

I'll find them, he thought. Find and destroy, all of them. Oh, God, God, how can he do this to me?

He stopped the car. A strange town lay under the late twin moons. There was no wind.

He held the rifle in his cold hands. He peered at the poles, the towers, the boxes. Where? Where was this town's voice hidden? That tower? Or that one there! Where! So many years ago. So long gone. So forgotten. He turned his head now this way, now that, wildly. It must be that tower! Was he certain? Or this box here, or the transformer half up that tower?

He raised the rifle.

The tower fell with the first bullet.

All of them, he thought. All of the towers in this town will have to be cut apart. I've forgotten. Too long.

The car moved along the silent street.

Brrrrinnnng!

He looked at the deserted drugstore.

Brrrrinnnng!

Pistol in hand, he entered.

Click.

"Hello, Barton? Just a warning. Don't try to rip down all the towers, blow things up. Cut your own throat that way. Think it over . . ."

Click.

He stepped out of the phone booth slowly and moved into the street and listened to the telephone towers humming high in the air, still alive, still untouched. He looked at them and then he understood.

He could not destroy the towers. Suppose a rocket came from Earth, impossible idea, but suppose it came tonight, tomorrow, next week? and landed on the other side of the planet, and used the phones to try to call Barton, only to find the circuits dead?

Barton dropped his gun.

"A rocket won't come," he argued, softly, logically with himself. "I'm old. It won't come now. It's too late."

But suppose it came, and you never knew, he thought. No, you've got to keep the lines open.

Brrrrinnnng.

He turned dully. His eyes were blinking and not seeing. He shuffled back into the drugstore and fumbled with the receiver.

"Hello?" A strange voice.

"Please," pleaded the old man, brokenly. "Don't bother me."

"Who's this, who's there? Who is it? Where are you?" cried the voice, surprised.

"Wait a minute." The old man staggered. "This is Emil Barton, who's that?"

"This is Captain Leonard Rockwell, Earth Rocket 48. Just arrived from New York."

"No, no, no."

"Are you there, Mr. Barton?"

"No, no, it can't be, it just can't."

"Where are you?"

"You're lying, it's false!" The old man had to lean against the booth wall. His blue eyes were cold blind. "It's you, Barton, making fun of me, lying to me again!"

"This is Captain Rockwell. We just landed in New Schenectady. Where are you?

"In Green Town," he gasped. "That's a thousand miles from you."

"Look, Barton, can you come here?"

"What?"

"We've repairs on our rocket. Exhausted from the flight. Can you come help?"

"Yes, yes."

"We're at the tarmac outside town. Can you rush by tomorrow?"

"Yes, but—"

"Well?"

The old man petted the phone, pitifully. "How's Earth? How's New York? Is the war over? Who's President now? What happened?"

"Plenty of time for gossip when you arrive."

"Is everything fine?"

"Fine."

"Thank God." The old man listened to the far voice. "Are you sure you're Captain Rockwell?"

"Damn it, man!"

"I'm sorry!"

He hung up and ran.

They were here, after many years, unbelievable, his own, who would take him back to Earth seas and skies and mountains.

He started the car. He would drive all night. Could he do it? What of his heart—It would be worth a risk, to see people, to shake hands, to hear them near you.

The car thundered in the hills.

That voice. Captain Rockwell. It couldn't be himself, forty years ago. He had never made a recording like that. Or had he? In one of his depressive fits, in a spell of drunken cynicism, hadn't he once made a false tape of a false landing on Mars with a synthetic captain, an imaginary crew? He jerked his gray head, savagely. No. He was a suspicious fool. Now was no time to doubt. He must run under the moons of Mars, hour on hour. What a party they would have!

The sun rose. He was immensely tired, full of thorns and brambles of weakness, his heart plunging and aching, his fingers fumbling the wheel, but the thing that pleased him most was the thought of one last phone call: Hello, young Barton, this is old Barton. I'm leaving for Earth today! Rescued! He chuckled weakly.

He drove into the shadowy limits of New Schenectady at sundown. Stepping from his car he stood staring at the rocket tarmac, rubbing his reddened eyes.

The rocket field was empty. No one ran to meet him. No one shook his hand, shouted, or laughed.

He felt his heart roar into pain. He knew blackness and a sensation of falling through the open sky. He stumbled toward an office.

Inside, six phones sat in a neat row.

He waited, gasping.

Finally:

Brrrrinnnng.

He lifted the heavy receiver.

A voice said, "I was wondering if you'd get there alive."

The old man did not speak, but stood with the phone in his hands.

The voice continued, "An elaborate joke. Captain Rockwell reporting for duty, sir. Your orders, sir?"

"You," groaned the old man.

"How's your heart, old man?"

"No!"

"Hoped the trip would kill you. Had to eliminate you some way, so I could live, if you call a transcription living."

"I'm going out now," replied the old man, "and blow it all up. I don't care. I'll blow up everything until you're all dead!"

"You haven't the strength. Why do you think I had you travel so far, so fast? This is your last trip!"

The old man felt his heart falter. He would never make

the other towns. The war was lost. He slid into a chair and made low sobbing, mournful noises from his loose mouth. He glared at the five other, silent phones. As if at a signal, they burst into silver chorus! A nest of ugly birds screaming!

Automatic receivers popped up.

The office whirled. "Barton, Barton, Barton!!"

He throttled the phone in his hands, the voice, the youth, the time of long ago. He mashed, choked it and still it laughed at him. He throttled it. He beat it. He kicked at it. He hated it with hands and mouth and blind raging eye. He furled the hot wire like serpentine in his fingers, ripped it into red bits which fell about his stumbling feet.

He destroyed three other phones. There was a sudden silence.

And as if his body now discovered a thing which it had long kept secret, it seemed to decay upon his tired bones. The flesh of his eyelids fell away like flower petals. His mouth became a withered rose. The lobes of his ears melting wax. He pushed his chest with his hands and fell face down. He lay still. His breathing stopped. His heart stopped.

After a long spell, the remaining two phones rang.

Twice. Three times.

A relay snapped somewhere. The two phone voices were connected, one to the other.

"Hello, Barton?"

"Yes, Barton?"

"What's happened?"

"I don't know. Listen."

The silent room. The old man did not stir on the floor. The wind blew in the broken window. The air was cool.

"Congratulate me, Barton, this is my twenty-sixth birthday!"

"And I'm twenty-four!"

"Congratulations!"

Laughter drifted out the window into the dead city.

SUNJAMMER

Arthur C. Clarke

In collaboration with director Stanley Kubrick, Arthur C. Clarke created the most successful and controversial science fiction property ever made: 2001: A Space Odyssey. No one who sees this extraordinary film (or reads the book by Clarke) remains unmoved. The concept has engendered delight, awe, anger, and fierce debate within science fiction ranks. In 2001 Clarke explores the vast wonder and terror of space in cinematic terms, as he has been doing for many years within a book-and-magazine framework. We are not sitting in a theater, watching a movie; we are there, in space, knowing that this is how it will be, must be, when man enters the star wilderness.

Now, in "Sunjammer," the miracle is repeated. We are part of a great fleet of sunships, dangerously racing one another to the death, far out beyond Earth. "Sunjammer" is an exciting example of the creative imagination and technical brilliance which has always marked the work of Arthur C. Clarke.

THE ENORMOUS disc of sail strained at its rigging, already filled with the wind that blew between the worlds. In three minutes the race would begin, yet now John Merton felt more relaxed, more at peace, than at any time for the past year. Whatever happened when the Commodore gave the starting signal, whether *Diana* carried him to victory or defeat, he had achieved his ambition. After a lifetime spent in designing ships for others, now he would sail his own.

"T minus two minutes," said the cabin radio. "Please confirm your readiness."

One by one, the other skippers answered. Merton recognized all the voices—some tense, some calm—for they were the voices of his friends and rivals. On the four inhabited worlds, there were scarcely twenty men who could sail a sun-yacht; and they were all here, on the starting-line or aboard the escort vessels, orbiting twenty-two thousand miles above the equator.

"Number One, *Gossamer*—ready to go."

"Number Two, *Santa Maria*—all O.K."

"Number Three, *Sunbeam*—O.K."

"Number Four, *Woomera*—all systems go."

Merton smiled at that last echo from the early, primitive days of astronautics. But it had become part of the tradition of space; and there were times when a man needed to evoke the shades of those who had gone before him to the stars.

"Number Five, *Lebedev*—we're ready."

"Number Six, *Arachne*—O.K."

Now it was his turn, at the end of the line; strange to think that the words he was speaking in this tiny cabin were being heard by at least five billion people.

"Number Seven, *Diana*—ready to start."

"One through Seven acknowledged." The voice from the judge's launch was impersonal. "Now T minus one minute."

Merton scarcely heard it; for the last time, he was checking the tension in the rigging. The needles of all the dynamometers were steady; the immense sail was taut, its mirror surface sparkling and glittering gloriously in the sun.

To Merton, floating weightless at the periscope, it seemed to fill the sky. As well it might—for out there were fifty million square feet of sail, linked to his capsule by almost a hundred miles of rigging. All the canvas of all the tea-clippers that had once raced like clouds across the China seas, sewn into one gigantic sheet, could not match the single sail that *Diana* had spread beneath the sun. Yet it was little more substantial than a soap-bubble; that two square miles of aluminized plastic was only a few millionths of an inch thick.

"T minus ten seconds. All recording cameras *on.*"

Something so huge, yet so frail, was hard for the mind to grasp. And it was harder still to realize that this fragile mirror could tow them free of Earth, merely by the power of the sunlight it would trap.

". . . Five, four, three, two, one, *cut!*"

Seven knife-blades sliced through the seven thin lines tethering the yachts to the motherships that had assembled and serviced them.

Until this moment, all had been circling Earth together in a rigidly held formation, but now the yachts would begin to disperse, like dandelion seeds drifting before the breeze. And the winner would be the one that first drifted past the Moon.

Aboard *Diana,* nothing seemed to be happening. But Merton knew better; though his body would feel no thrust, the instrument board told him he was now accelerating at almost one thousandth of a gravity. For a rocket, that figure would have been ludicrous—but this was the first time any solar yacht had attained it. *Diana*'s design was sound; the vast sail was living up to his calculations. At this rate, two circuits of the Earth would build up his speed to escape velocity—then he could head out for the Moon, with the full force of the Sun behind him.

The full force of the Sun. He smiled wryly, remembering all his attempts to explain solar sailing to those lecture audiences back on Earth. That had been the only way he could raise money, in those early days. He might be Chief Designer of Cosmodyne Corporation, with a whole string of successful spaceships to his credit, but his firm had not been exactly enthusiastic about his hobby.

"Hold your hands out to the Sun," he'd said. "What do you feel? Heat, of course. But there's pressure as well—though you've never noticed it, because it's so tiny. Over the area of your hands, it only comes to about a millionth of an ounce.

"But out in space, even a pressure as small as that can be important—for it's acting all the time, hour after hour, day after day. Unlike rocket fuel, it's free and unlimited. If we want to, we can use it; we can build sails to catch the radiation blowing from the Sun."

At that point, he would pull out a few square yards of sail material and toss it towards the audience. The silvery film would coil and twist like smoke, then drift slowly to the ceiling in the hot-air currents.

"You can see how light it is," he'd continue. "A square mile weighs only a ton, and can collect five pounds of radiation pressure. So it will start moving—and we can let it tow us along, if we attach rigging to it.

"Of course, its acceleration will be tiny—about a thousandth of a g. That doesn't seem much, but let's see what it means.

"It means that in the first second, we'll move about a fifth of an inch. I suppose a healthy snail could do better than that. But after a minute, we've covered sixty feet, and will be doing just over a mile an hour. That's not bad, for something driven by pure sunlight! After an hour, we're forty miles from our starting point, and will be moving at eighty miles an hour. Please remember that in space there's no friction, so once you start anything moving, it will keep going forever. You'll be surprised when I tell you what our thousandth-of-a-g sailing boat will be doing at the end of a day's run. *Almost two thousand miles an hour!* If it starts from orbit—as it has to, of course—it can reach escape velocity in a couple of days. And all without burning a single drop of fuel!"

Well, he'd convinced them, and in the end he'd even convinced Cosmodyne. Over the last twenty years, a new sport had come into being. It had been called the sport of billionaires, and that was true—but it was beginning to pay for itself in terms of publicity and television coverage.

The prestige of four continents and two worlds was riding on this race, and it had the biggest audience in history.

Diana had made a good start; time to take a look at the opposition. Moving very gently. Though there were shock absorbers between the control capsule and the delicate rigging, he was determined to run no risks. Merton stationed himself at the periscope.

There they were, looking like strange silver flowers planted in the dark fields of space. The nearest, South America's *Santa Maria,* was only fifty miles away; it bore a resemblance to a boy's kite—but a kite more than a mile on its side. Farther away, the University of Astrograd's *Lebedev* looked like a Maltese cross; the sails that formed the four arms could apparently be tilted for steering purposes. In contrast, the Federation of Australasia's *Woomera* was a simple parachute, four miles in circumference. General Spacecraft's *Arachne,* as its name suggested, looked like a spider-web—and had been built on the same principles, by robot shuttles spiralling out from a central point. Eurospace Corporation's *Gossamer* was an identical design, on a slightly smaller scale. And the Republic of Mars' *Sunbeam* was a flat ring, with a half-mile-wide hole in the center, spinning slowly so that centrifugal force gave it stiffness. That was an old idea, but no one had ever made it work. Merton was fairly sure that the colonials would be in trouble when they started to turn.

That would not be for another six hours, when the yachts had moved along the first quarter of their slow and stately twenty-four hour orbit. Here at the beginning of the race, they were all heading directly away from the Sun—running, as it were, before the solar wind. One had to make the most of this lap, before the boats swung round to the other side of Earth and then started to head back into the Sun.

Time for the first check, Merton told himself, while he had no navigational worries. With the periscope, he made a careful examination of the sail, concentrating on the points where the rigging was attached to it. The shroud-lines—narrow bands of unsilvered plastic film—would have been completely invisible had they not been coated with fluorescent paint. Now they were taut lines of colored light, dwindling away for hundreds of yards towards that gigantic sail. Each had its own electric windlass, not much bigger than a game-fisherman's reel. The little windlasses were continually turning, playing lines in or out, as the autopilot kept the sail trimmed at the correct angle to the Sun.

The play of sunlight on the great flexible mirror was beautiful to watch. It was undulating in slow, stately oscillations, sending multiple images of the Sun marching across the heavens, until they faded away at the edges of the sail. Such leisurely vibrations were to be expected in this vast and flimsy structure; they were usually quite harmless, but Merton watched them carefully. Sometimes they could build up to the catastrophic undulations known as the wriggles, which could tear a sail to pieces.

When he was satisfied that everything was shipshape, he swept the periscope around the sky, rechecking the positions of his rivals. It was as he had hoped; the weeding-out process had begun, as the less efficient boats fell astern. But the real test would come when they passed into the shadow of the Earth; then maneuverability would count as much as speed.

It seemed a strange thing to do, now that the race had just started, but it might be a good idea to get some sleep. The two man crews on the other boats could take it in turns, but Merton had no one to relieve him. He must rely on his physical resources—like that other solitary seaman Joshua Slocum, in his tiny *Spray*. The American skipper had sailed *Spray* single-handed round the world; he could never have dreamt that, two centuries later, a man would be sailing single-handed from Earth to Moon—inspired, at least partly, by his example.

Merton snapped the elastic bands of the cabin seat around his waist and legs, then placed the electrodes of the sleep-inducer on his forehead. He set the timer for three hours, and relaxed.

Very gently, hypnotically, the electronic pulses throbbed

in the frontal lobes of his brain. Colored spirals of light expanded beneath his closed eyelids, widening outwards to infinity. Then—nothing. . . .

The brazen clamor of the alarm dragged him back from his dreamless sleep. He was instantly awake, his eyes scanning the instrument panel. Only two hours had passed—but above the accelerometer, a red light was flashing. Thrust was falling; *Diana* was losing power.

Merton's first thought was that something had happened to the sail; perhaps the antispin devices had failed, and the rigging had become twisted. Swiftly, he checked the meters that showed the tension in the shroud-lines. Strange, on one side of the sail they were reading normally—but on the other, the pull was dropping slowly even as he watched.

In sudden understanding, Merton grabbed the periscope, switched to wide-angle vision, and started to scan the edge of the sail. Yes—there was the trouble, and it could have only one cause.

A huge, sharp-edged shadow had begun to slide across the gleaming silver of the sail. Darkness was falling upon *Diana*, as if a cloud had passed between her and the Sun. And in the dark, robbed of the rays that drove her, she would lose all thrust and drift helplessly through space.

But, of course, there were no clouds here, more than twenty thousand miles above Earth. If there was a shadow, it must be made by man.

Merton grinned as he swung the periscope towards the Sun, switching in the filters that would allow him to look full into its blazing face without being blinded.

"Maneuver 4a," he muttered to himself. "We'll see who can play best at *that* game."

It looked as if a giant planet was crossing the face of the Sun. A great black disc had bitten deep into its edge. Twenty miles astern, *Gossamer* was trying to arrange an artificial eclipse—especially for *Diana*'s benefit.

The maneuver was a perfectly legitimate one; back in the days of ocean racing, skippers had often tried to rob each other of the wind. With any luck, you could leave your rival becalmed, with his sails collapsing around him —and be well ahead before he could undo the damage.

Merton had no intention of being caught so easily. There was plenty of time to take evasive action; things happened very slowly, when you were running a solar sailingboat. It would be at least twenty minutes before *Gossamer* could slide completely across the face of the Sun, and leave him in darkness.

Diana's tiny computer—the size of a matchbox, but the equivalent of a thousand human mathematicians—considered the problem for a full second and then flashed the answer. He'd have to open control panels three and four, until the sail had developed an extra twenty degrees of tilt; then the radiation pressure would blow him out of *Gossamer*'s dangerous shadow, back into the full blast of the Sun. It was a pity to interfere with the auto-pilot, which had been carefully programmed to give the fastest possible run—but that, after all, was why he was here. This was what made solar yachting a sport, rather than a battle between computers.

Out went control lines one to six, slowly undulating like sleepy snakes as they momentarily lost their tension. Two miles away, the triangular panels began to open lazily, spilling sunlight through the sail. Yet, for a long time, nothing seemed to happen. It was hard to grow accustomed to this slow motion world, where it took minutes for the effects of any action to become visible to the eye. Then Merton saw that the sail was indeed tipping towards the Sun—and that *Gossamer*'s shadow was sliding harmlessly away, its cone of darkness lost in the deeper night of space.

Long before the shadow had vanished, and the disc of the Sun had cleared again, he reversed the tilt and brought *Diana* back on course. Her new momentum would carry her clear of the danger; no need to overdo it, and upset his calculations by side-stepping too far. That was another rule that was hard to learn. The very moment you had started something happening in space, it was already time to think about stopping it.

He reset the alarm, ready for the next natural or man-made emergency; perhaps *Gossamer,* or one of the other contestants, would try the same trick again. Meanwhile, it was time to eat, though he did not feel particularly hungry. One used little physical energy in space, and it was easy to forget about food. Easy—and dangerous; for when an emergency arose, you might not have the reserves needed to deal with it.

He broke open the first of the meal packets, and inspected it without enthusiasm. The name on the label— SPACETASTIES—was enough to put him off. And he had grave doubts about the promise printed underneath. Guaranteed Crumbless. It had been said that crumbs were a greater danger to space vehicles than meteorites. They could drift into the most unlikely places, causing short circuits, blocking vital jets and getting into instruments that were supposed to be hermetically sealed.

Still, the liverwurst went down pleasantly enough; so did the chocolate and the pineapple puree. The plastic coffeebulb was warming on the electric heater when the outside world broke in on his solitude. The radio operator on the Commodore's launch routed a call to him.

"Dr. Merton? If you can spare the time, Jeremy Blair would like a few words with you." Blair was one of the more responsible news commentators, and Merton had been on his program many times. He could refuse to be interviewed, of course, but he liked Blair, and at the moment he could certainly not claim to be too busy. "I'll take it," he answered.

"Hello, Dr. Merton," said the commentator immediately. "Glad you can spare a few minutes. And congratulations—you seem to be ahead of the field."

"Too early in the game to be sure of that," Merton answered cautiously.

"Tell me, doctor—why did you decide to sail *Diana* yourself? Just because it's never been done before?"

"Well, isn't that a very good reason? But it wasn't the only one, of course." He paused, choosing his words carefully. "You know how critically the performance of a sun-yacht depends on its mass. A second man, with all his supplies, would mean another five hundred pounds. That

could easily be the difference between winning and losing."

"And you're quite certain that you can handle *Diana*
alone?"

"Reasonably sure, thanks to the automatic controls
I've designed. My main job is to supervise and make de-
cisions."

"But—two square miles of sail! It just doesn't seem
possible for one man to cope with all that!"

Merton laughed.

"Why not? Those two square miles produce a maximum pull of just ten pounds. I can exert more force with
my little finger."

"Well, thank you, doctor. And good luck."

As the commentator signed off, Merton felt a little
ashamed of himself. For his answer had been only part
of the truth; and he was sure that Blair was shrewd
enough to know it.

There was just one reason why he was here, alone in
space. For almost forty years he had worked with teams
of hundreds or even thousands of men, helping to design
the most complex vehicles that the world had ever seen.
For the last twenty years he had led one of those teams,
and watched his creations go soaring to the stars. (But
there were failures that he could never forget, even
though the fault had not been his.) He was famous, with
a successful career behind him. Yet he had never done
anything by himself; always he had been one of an army.

This was his very last chance of individual achievement, and he would share it with no one. There would
be no more solar yachting for at least five years, as the
period of the quiet Sun ended and the cycle of bad
weather began, with radiation storms bursting through
the Solar System. When it was safe again for these frail,
unshielded craft to venture aloft, he would be too old.
If, indeed, he was not too old already. . . .

He dropped the empty food containers into the waste
disposal, and turned once more to the periscope. At first,
he could find only five of the other yachts; there was no
sign of *Woomera*. It took him several minutes to locate

her—a dim, star-eclipsing phantom, neatly caught in the shadow of *Lebedev*. He could imagine the frantic efforts the Australasians were making to extricate themselves, and wondered how they had fallen into the trap. It suggested that *Lebedev* was unusually maneuverable; she would bear watching, though she was too far away to menace *Diana* at the moment.

Now the Earth had almost vanished. It had waned to a narrow, brilliant bow of light that was moving steadily towards the Sun. Dimly outlined within that burning bow was the night side of the planet, with the phosphorescent gleams of great cities showing here and there through gaps in the clouds. The disc of darkness had already blanked out a huge section of the Milky Way; in a few minutes, it would start to encroach upon the Sun.

The light was fading. A purple, twilight hue—the glow of many sunsets, thousands of miles below—was falling across the sail, as *Diana* slipped silently into the shadow of Earth. The Sun plummeted below that invisible horizon. Within minutes, it was night.

Merton looked back along the orbit he had traced now a quarter of the way around the world. One by one he saw the brilliant stars of the other yachts wink out, as they joined him in the brief night. It would be an hour before the Sun emerged from that enormous black shield, and through all that time they would be completely helpless, coasting without power.

He switched on the external spotlight and started to search the now darkened sail with its beam. Already, the thousands of acres of film were beginning to wrinkle and become flaccid; the shroud-lines were slackening, and must be wound in lest they become entangled. But all this was expected; everything was going as planned.

Forty miles astern, *Arachne* and *Santa Maria* were not so lucky. Merton learnt of their troubles when the radio burst into life on the emergency circuit.

"Number Two, Number Six—this is Control. You are on a collision course. Your orbits will intersect in sixty-five minutes! Do you require assistance?"

There was a long pause while the two skippers digested this bad news. Merton wondered who was to blame; perhaps one yacht had been trying to shadow the other, and had not completed the maneuver before they were both caught in darkness. Now there was nothing that either could do; they were slowly but inexorably converging, unable to change course by a fraction of a degree.

Yet, sixty-five minutes! That would just bring them out into sunlight again, as they emerged from the shadow of the Earth. They still had a slim chance, if their sails could snatch enough power to avoid a crash. There must be some frantic calculations going on, aboard *Arachne* and *Santa Maria*.

Arachne answered first; her reply was just what Merton had expected.

"Number Six calling Control. We don't need assistance, thank you. We'll work this out for ourselves."

I wonder, thought Merton. But at least it will be interesting to watch. The first real drama of the race was approaching—exactly above the line of midnight on the sleeping Earth.

For the next hour, Merton's own sail kept him too busy to worry about *Arachne* and *Santa Maria*. It was hard to keep a good watch on that fifty million square feet of dim plastic out there in the darkness, illuminated only by his narrow spotlight and the rays of the still distant Moon. From now on, for almost half his orbit round the Earth, he must keep the whole of this immense area edge-on to the Sun. During the next twelve or fourteen hours, the sail would be a useless encumbrance; for he would be heading into the Sun, and its rays could only drive him backwards along his orbit. It was a pity that he could not furl the sail completely, until he was ready to use it again. But no one had yet found a practical way of doing this.

Far below, there was the first hint of dawn along the edge of the Earth. In ten minutes, the Sun would emerge from its eclipse; the coasting yachts would come to life again as the blast of radiation struck their sails. That would be the moment of crisis for *Arachne* and *Santa Maria*—and, indeed, for all of them.

Merton swung the periscope until he found the two dark shadows drifting against the stars. They were very close together—perhaps less than three miles apart. They might, he decided, just be able to make it. . . .

Dawn flashed like an explosion along the rim of Earth, as the Sun rose out of the Pacific. The sail and shroud-lines glowed a brief crimson, then gold, then blazed with the pure white light of day. The needles of the dynamometers began to lift from their zeros—but only just. *Diana* was still almost completely weightless, for with the sail pointing towards the Sun, her acceleration was now only a few millionths of a gravity.

But *Arachne* and *Santa Maria* were crowding on all the sail they could manage, in their desperate attempt to keep apart. Now, while there was less than two miles between them, their glittering plastic clouds were unfurling and expanding with agonizing slowness, as they felt the first delicate push of the Sun's rays. Almost every TV screen on Earth would be mirroring this protracted drama; and even now, at this very last minute, it was impossible to tell what the outcome would be.

The two skippers were stubborn men. Either could have cut his sail, and fallen back to give the other a chance; but neither would do so. Too much prestige, too many millions, too many reputations, were at stake. And so, silently and softly as snowflakes falling on a winter night, *Arachne* and *Santa Maria* collided.

The square kite crawled almost imperceptibly into the circular spider's-web; the long ribbons of the shroud-lines twisted and tangled together with dreamlike slowness. Even aboard *Diana,* busy with his own rigging, Merton could scarcely tear his eye away from this silent, long drawn out disaster.

For more than ten minutes the billowing, shining clouds continued to merge into one inextricable mass. Then the crew capsules tore loose and went their separate ways, missing each other by hundreds of yards. With a flare of rockets, the safety launches hurried to pick them up.

That leaves five of us, thought Merton. He felt sorry for the skippers who had so thoroughly eliminated each other, only a few hours after the start of the race; but they were young men, and would have another chance.

Within minutes, the five had dropped to four. From the very beginning, Merton had had doubts about the slowly rotating *Sunbeam*. Now he saw them justified.

The Martian ship had failed to tack properly; her spin had given her too much stability. Her great ring of a sail was turning to face the Sun, instead of being edge-on to it. She was being blown back along her course at almost her maximum acceleration.

That was about the most maddening thing that could happen to a skipper—worse even than a collision, for he could blame only himself. But no one would feel much sympathy for the frustrated colonials, as they dwindled slowly astern. They had made too many brash boasts before the race, and what had happened to them was poetic justice.

Yet it would not do to write off *Sunbeam* completely. With almost half a million miles still to go, she might still pull ahead. Indeed, if there were a few more casualities, she might be the only one to complete the race. It had happened before.

However, the next twelve hours were uneventful, as the Earth waxed in the sky from new to full. There was little to do while the fleet drifted round the unpowered half of its orbit, but Merton did not find the time hanging heavily on his hands. He caught a few hours' sleep, ate two meals, wrote up his log, and became involved in several more radio interviews. Sometimes, though rarely, he talked to the other skippers, exchanging greetings and friendly taunts. But most of the time he was content to float in weightless relaxation, beyond all the cares of Earth, happier than he had been for many years. He was —as far as any man could be in space—master of his own fate, sailing the ship upon which he had lavished so much skill, so much love, that she had become part of his very being.

The next casualty came when they were passing the

line between Earth and Sun, and were just beginning the powered half of the orbit. Aboard *Diana*, Merton saw the great sail stiffen as it tilted to catch the rays that drove it. The acceleration began to climb up from the micro-gravities, though it would be hours yet before it would reach its maximum value.

It would never reach it for *Gossamer*. The moment when power came on again was always critical, and she failed to survive it.

Blair's radio commentary, which Merton had left running at low volume, alerted him with the news: "Hullo, *Gossamer* has the wriggles!" He hurried to the periscope, but at first could see nothing wrong with the great circular disc of *Gossamer*'s sail. It was difficult to study it, as it was almost edge-on to him and so appeared as a thin ellipse; but presently he saw that it was twisting back and forth in slow, irresistible oscillations. Unless the crew could damp out these waves, by properly timed but gentle tugs on the shroud-lines, the sail would tear itself to pieces.

They did their best, and after twenty minutes it seemed that they had succeeded. Then, somewhere near the center of the sail, the plastic film began to rip. It was slowly driven outwards by the radiation pressure, like smoke coiling upwards from a fire. Within a quarter of an hour, nothing was left but the delicate tracery of the radial spars that had supported the great web. Once again there was a flare of rockets, as a launch moved in to retrieve the *Gossamer*'s capsule and her dejected crew.

"Getting rather lonely up here, isn't it?" said a conversational voice over the ship-to-ship radio.

"Not for you, Dimitri," retorted Merton. "You've still got company back there at the end of the field. I'm the one who's lonely, up here in front." It was not an idle boast. By this time *Diana* was three hundred miles ahead of the next competitor, and his lead should increase still more rapidly in the hours to come.

Aboard *Lebedev*, Dimitri Markoff gave a good-natured

chuckle. He did not sound, Merton thought, at all like a man who had resigned himself to defeat.

"Remember the legend of the tortoise and the hare," answered the Russian. "A lot can happen in the next quarter-million miles."

It happened much sooner than that, when they had completed their first orbit of Earth and were passing the starting line again—though thousands of miles higher, thanks to the extra energy the Sun's rays had given them. Merton had taken careful sights on the other yachts, and had fed the figures into the computer. The answer it gave for *Woomera* was so absurd that he immediately did a recheck.

There was no doubt of it—the Australasians were catching up at a fantastic rate. No solar yacht could possibly have such an acceleration, unless—

A swift look through the periscope gave the answer. *Woomera*'s rigging, pared back to the very minimum of mass, had given way. It was her sail alone, still maintaining its shape, that was racing up behind him like a handkerchief blown before the wind. Two hours later it fluttered past, less than twenty miles away. But long before that, the Australasians had joined the growing crowd aboard the Commodore's launch.

So now it was a straight fight between *Diana* and *Lebedev*—for though the Martians had not given up, they were a thousand miles astern and no longer counted as a serious threat. For that matter, it was hard to see what *Lebedev* could do to overtake *Diana*'s lead. But all the way round the second lap—through eclipse again, and the long, slow drift against the Sun, Merton felt a growing unease.

He knew the Russian pilots and designers. They had been trying to win this race for twenty years and after all, it was only fair that they should, for had not Pyotr Nikolayevich Lebedev been the first man to detect the pressure of sunlight, back at the very beginning of the Twentieth Century? But they had never succeeded.

And they would never stop trying. Dimitri was up to something—and it would be spectacular.

Aboard the official launch, a thousand miles behind the racing yachts, Commodore van Stratten looked at the radiogram with angry dismay. It had travelled more than a hundred million miles, from the chain of solar observatories swinging high above the blazing surface of the Sun, and it brought the worst possible news.

The Commodore—his title, of course, was purely honorary—back on Earth he was Professor of Astrophysics at Harvard—had been half expecting it. Never before had the race been arranged so late in the season; there had been many delays, they had gambled and now, it seemed they might all lose.

Deep beneath the surface of the Sun, enormous forces were gathering. At any moment, the energies of a million hydrogen bombs might burst forth in the awesome explosion known as a solar flare. Climbing at millions of miles an hour, an invisible fireball many times the size of Earth would leap from the Sun, and head out across space.

The cloud of electrified gas would probably miss the Earth completely. But if it did not, it would arrive in just over a day. Spaceships could protect themselves, with their shielding and their powerful magnetic screen. But the lightly-built solar yachts, with their paper-thin walls, were defenseless against such a menace. The crews would have to be taken off, and the race abandoned.

John Merton still knew nothing of this as he brought *Diana* round the Earth for the second time. If all went well, this would be the last circuit, both for him and for Russians. They had spiralled upwards by thousands of miles, gaining energy from the Sun's rays. On this lap, they should escape from Earth completely—and head outwards on the long run to the Moon. It was a straight race now. *Sunbeam*'s crew had finally withdrawn, exhausted, after battling valiantly with their spinning sail for more than a hundred thousand miles.

Merton did not feel tired; he had eaten and slept well, and *Diana* was behaving herself admirably. The autopilot, tensioning the rigging like a busy little spider, kept

the great sail trimmed to the Sun more accurately than
any human skipper. Though by this time, the two square
miles of plastic sheet must have been riddled by hundreds
of micrometeorites, the pinhead-sized punctures had produced no falling off to thrust.

He had only two worries. The first was shroud-line
Number Eight, which could no longer be adjusted properly. Without any warning, the reel had jammed; even
after all these years of astronautical engineering, bearings
sometimes seized up in vacuum. He could neither lengthen
nor shorten the line, and would have to navigate as best
he could with the others. Luckily, the most difficult ma-
neuvers were over. From now on, *Diana* would have the
Sun behind her as she sailed straight down the solar wind.
And as the old-time sailors often said, it was easy to handle a boat when the wind was blowing over your shoulder.

His other worry was *Lebedev,* still dogging his heels
three hundred miles astern. The Russian yacht had shown
remarkable maneuverability, thanks to the four great
panels that could be tilted around the central sail. All her
flip-overs as she rounded Earth had been carried out with
superb precision; but to gain maneuverability she must
have sacrificed speed. You could not have it both ways.
In the long, straight haul ahead, Merton should be able
to hold his own. Yet he could not be certain of victory
until, three or four days from now, *Diana* went flashing
past the far side of the Moon.

And then, in the fiftieth hour of the race, near the end
of the second orbit around Earth, Markoff sprang his little
surprise.

"Hello, John," he said casually, over the ship-to-ship
circuit. "I'd like you to watch this. It should be interesting."

Merton drew himself across to the periscope and turned
up the magnification to the limit. There in the field of
view, a most improbable sight against the background of
the stars, was the glittering Maltese cross of *Lebedev,*
very small but very clear. And then, as he watched, the

four arms of the cross slowly detached themselves from the central square and went drifting away, with all their spars and rigging, into space.

Markoff had jettisoned all unnecessary mass, now that he was coming up to escape velocity and need no longer plod patiently around the Earth, gaining momentum on each circuit. From now on, *Lebedev* would be almost un-steerable—but that did not matter. All the tricky naviga-tion lay behind her. It was as if an old-time yachtsman had deliberately thrown away his rudder and heavy keel —knowing that the rest of the race would be straight downwind over a calm sea.

"Congratulations, Dimitri," Merton radioed. "It's a neat trick. But it's not good enough—you can't catch up now."

"I've not finished yet," the Russian answered. "There's an old winter's tale in my country, about a sleigh being chased by wolves. To save himself, the driver has to throw off the passengers one by one. Do you see the anal-ogy?"

Merton did, all too well. On this final straight lap, Dimitri no longer needed his co-pilot. *Lebedev* could real-ly be stripped down for action.

"Alexis won't be very happy about this," Merton re-plied. "Besides, it's against the rules."

"Alexis isn't happy, but I'm the captain. He'll just have to wait around for ten minutes until the Commodore picks him up. And the regulations say nothing about the size of the crew—you should know that."

Merton did not answer. He was too busy doing some hurried calculations, based on what he knew of *Lebedev*'s design. By the time he had finished, he knew that the race was still in doubt. *Lebedev* would be catching up with him at just about the time he hoped to pass the Moon.

But the outcome of the race was already being de-cided, ninety-two million miles away.

On Solar Observatory Three, far inside the orbit of Mercury, the automatic instruments recorded the whole history of the flare. A hundred million square miles of

the Sun's surface suddenly exploded in such blue-white
fury that, by comparison, the rest of the disc paled to a
dull glow. Out of that seething inferno, twisting and turning like a living creature in the magnetic fields of its own
creation, soared the electrified plasma of the great flare.
Ahead of it, moving at the speed of light, went the warning flash of ultra-violet and X-rays. That would reach
Earth in eight minutes, and was relatively harmless. Not
so the charged atoms that were following behind at their
leisurely four million miles an hour—and which, in just
over a day, would engulf *Diana, Lebedev,* and their accompanying little fleet in a cloud of lethal radiation.

The Commodore left his decision to the last possible
minute. Even when the jet of plasma had been tracked
past the orbit of Venus, there was a chance that it might
miss the Earth. But when it was less than four hours
away, and had already been picked up by the Moon-based
radar network, he knew that there was no hope. All solar
sailing was over for the next five or six years until the
Sun was quiet again.

A great sigh of disappointment swept across the Solar
System. *Diana* and *Lebedev* were halfway between Earth
and Moon, running neck and neck—and now no one
would ever know which was the better boat. The enthu-
siasts would argue the result for years; history would
merely record: Race cancelled owing to solar storm.

When John Merton received the order, he felt a bit-
terness he had not known since childhood. Across the
years, sharp and clear, came the memory of his tenth
birthday. He had been promised an exact scale model of
the famous spaceship *Morning Star,* and for weeks had
been planning how he would assemble it, where he would
hang it up in his bedroom. And then, at the last moment,
his father had broken the news. "I'm sorry, John—it
costs too much money. Maybe next year. . . ."

Half a century and a successful lifetime later, he was
a heart-broken boy again.

For a moment, he thought of disobeying the Commodore. Suppose he sailed on, ignoring the warning? Even
if the race were abandoned, he could make a crossing to

the Moon that would stand in the record books for generations.

But that would be worse than stupidity. It would be suicide—and a very unpleasant form of suicide. He had seen men die of radiation poisoning, when the magnetic shielding of their ships had failed in deep space. No—nothing was worth that. . . .

He felt sorry for Dimitri Markoff as for himself; they both deserved to win, and now victory would go to neither. No man could argue with the Sun in one of its rages, even though he might ride upon its beams to the edge of space.

Only fifty miles astern now, the Commodore's launch was drawing alongside *Lebedev,* preparing to take off her skipper. There went the silver sail, as Dimitri—with feeling that he would share—cut the rigging. The tiny capsule would be taken back to Earth, perhaps to be used again—but a sail was spread for one voyage only.

He could press the jettison button now, and save his rescuers a few minutes of time. But he could not do so. He wanted to stay aboard to the very end, on the little boat that had been for so long a part of his dreams and his life. The great sail was spread now at right angles to the Sun, exerting its utmost thrust. Long ago it had torn him clear of Earth—and *Diana* was still gaining speed.

Then, out of nowhere, beyond all doubt or hesitation, he knew what must be done. For the last time, he sat down before the computer that had navigated him halfway to the Moon.

When he had finished, he packed the log and his few personal belongings. Clumsily—for he was out of practice, and it was not an easy job to do by oneself—he climbed into the emergency survival suit.

He was just sealing the helmet when the Commodore's voice called over the radio. "We'll be alongside in five minutes, Captain. Please cut your sail so we won't foul it."

John Merton, first and last skipper of the sun-yacht *Diana,* hesitated for a moment. He looked for the last time round the tiny cabin, with its shining instruments and its neatly arranged controls, now all locked in their final positions. Then he said to the microphone: "I'm abandoning ship. Take your time to pick me up. *Diana* can look after herself."

There was no reply from the Commodore, and for that he was grateful. Professor van Stratten would have guessed what was happening—and would know that, in these final moments, he wished to be left alone.

He did not bother to exhaust the airlock, and the rush of escaping gas blew him gently out into space; the thrust he gave her then was his last gift to *Diana*. She dwindled away from him, sail glittering splendidly in the sunlight that would be hers for centuries to come. Two days from now she would flash past the Moon; but the Moon, like the Earth, could never catch her. Without his mass to slow her down, she would gain two thousand miles an hour in every day of sailing. In a month, she would be travelling faster than any ship that man had ever built.

As the Sun's rays weakened with distance, so her acceleration would fall. But even at the orbit of Mars, she would be gaining a thousand miles an hour in every day. Long before then, she would be moving too swiftly for the Sun itself to hold her. Faster than any comet that had ever streaked in from the stars, she would be heading out into the abyss.

The glare of rockets, only a few miles away, caught Merton's eye. The launch was approaching to pick him up at thousands of times the acceleration that *Diana* could ever attain. But engines could burn for a few minutes only, before they exhausted their fuel—while *Diana* would still be gaining speed, driven outwards by the Sun's eternal fires, for ages yet to come.

"Good-bye, little ship," said John Merton. "I wonder what eyes will see you next, how many thousand years from now?"

At last he felt at peace, as the blunt torpedo of the launch nosed up beside him. He would never win the race to the Moon; but his would be the first of all man's ships to set sail on the long journey to the stars.

THE BETTER MAN

Ray Russell

The ubiquitous Ray Russell, whose latest book-length opus, The Colony, *is a sharp, funny, ferocious, and altogether wild novel of Hollywood, here returns to the short-short form of which he is a master. Who else but Russell could provide not one but three surprise endings in one science fiction miniature—which might be described as sharp, funny, ferocious, and altogether wild?*

SHE WAS LOVELY and graceful and serene, but it wouldn't have mattered if she were none of these. All that mattered was that she was female. And that mattered very much indeed, for she was said to be the last woman.

As such, she was the hope of the earth, a prize to be fought over. Her two suitors—the last of their sex—stood now in the twilight of their world, prepared to duel to the death. The winner would become a new Adam, in an Eden of ashes and rubble.

"Put away your weapons," she said. "There has been enough dying. Let us decide by reason which of you is the better man."

"My name is John," said the one who limped and was bald, "and I am the better man. It is true that I am no kid, as they say, and my sight is no longer what it should be, and I am deaf in one ear, and I seem to have developed this cough, and my teeth are false, and I really cannot say to what extent my genes may be affected by radiation, but I am educated, skilled in many crafts and, I hope, wise with the experience of my years."

"Thank you, John," she said sweetly. "And you, young man?"

"My name is Nine," said the other one, who was tall and handsome, "and I am not a man at all. My full name is Nine Four Six Three Seven, decimal, Zero Zero Five Two Eight. I am an android. But *I* am the better man."

John laughed. "Better man! A thing of plastic bones and chemical blood and artificial flesh? Ridiculous!"

She asked, "Why do you say you are the better man, Nine?"

Nine cleared his throat. "I won't bore you with the history of robots and androids," he began.

"Please don't." John interjected.

"But I'm sure both of you are aware," Nine continued, "of the refinements that have gone into the manufacture of androids during the past few centuries?"

John shrugged. "Eyes that work like eyes instead of like television cameras."

"Hair and nails that grow," she said.

"Waste-disposal systems like our own," John grunted, and gallantly added, "Excuse me, miss."

"Laughter," she said. "Tears." And she smiled.

Nine smiled back at her. "That's right," he said. "As we were made more efficient, we naturally were made more human, because the human body and brain are still the most efficient machines there are. You might almost say that, while you folks were becoming more and more false-toothed and nose-jobbed and bustplastied, and more and more warped and mutated by radiation, more and more *dehumanized,* we androids were becoming more and more human. Kind of ironic."

"Very," said John, stifling a yawn.

Nine said, "The point being, John, that you're getting old and infirm, while this body of mine—ersatz though it may be—will last another hundred years or so, with care. I'm stronger than you, also, and have better sight and hearing and quicker reflexes, all of which will be vital in building the new world. So you see," he concluded, spreading his hands, "there's no contest."

Smugly, John said, "You're forgetting one thing."

"No, I'm not," said Nine. "We androids used to be put together in laboratories and on assembly lines, I grant you, but not anymore. Too expensive. It's not generally known, but for quite a while now it's been cheaper and simpler for androids to be so constructed that we can reproduce ourselves. In fact, it's been proven in certain top-secret lab experiments that, theoretically at least, we can even, er, intermarry with humans."

John sputtered and stammered. "But that's—indecent and—unheard of and—you mean *mate?* Produce offspring? A human and an android? That's absurd!"

"It is, isn't it?" reflected Nine. "But it's also true."

Their beautiful prize looked long at the handsome, muscular Nine, then turned to the squinting, coughing John. "He's right, I'm afraid, John," she said, sorrowfully. "He *is* the better . . . man."

John sighed but said nothing. He crept slowly away into the jagged shadows. In a few moments, they heard a single shot and the sound of a frail body crumpling to the ground.

"Poor John," she said. "I felt so sorry for him."

"So did I," said Nine, "but that's life." He led her toward the hovel that would be their home. "You know," he said, "I was really afraid John's education and skill and wisdom and all that might tip the scales in his favor . . ."

"It did, almost."

"Yes, I could tell. That's why I made up that little fib about being an android. My name's not Nine, it's Bill, and I'm one hundred percent human."

"Just as I thought," said John triumphantly, emerging from the shadows. "Not only a liar but stupid as well. Stupid enough to be taken in by my simple sound effects a moment ago." John turned to the lovely object of their rivalry. "Is this the kind of mate you deserve, my dear? A man without principles? A muscle-bound clod both morally corrupt and mentally deficient? Is he indeed the better man?"

She wavered, but for only an instant. "No, John. The father of the new race should be a man of honor and intelligence. You are the better man."

John turned to Bill. "In the absence of judges and juries, I take it upon myself to pronounce sentence upon you for mendacity, opacity, and crimes to future humanity. The sentence is death." John shot Bill through the head, and the younger suitor fell, lifeless.

"Now, wife," said John, with a gleam in his eye, "let us not waste any more precious time in getting that new race started. I am, admittedly, neither as young nor as handsome as the late Bill, but I think you'll find there is life in the old boy yet."

"Are *you* an android, by any chance?" she asked.

John said, "It just so happens that Bill was entirely correct about the, er, compatibility of humans and androids. I put up a fuss about it only because I didn't want to lose you. So, actually, it wouldn't make any difference if I *were* an android. However, I assure you I am quite human, if it matters."

She smiled prettily and took his arm. "How nice," she said. "If it matters, I'm not." And silenced his expression of surprise with an admirably genuine kiss.

CARRIER

Robert Sheckley

Locating a meaty, never-anthologized Sheckley science fiction novelet is no easy task. When this editor discovered "Carrier" in a yellowing issue of If, *the sensation was directly comparable to finding a loose twenty-dollar bill in the front yard.*

Here is prime Sheckley—a story which is fresh, suspenseful and gaudily imaginative, dealing in cool and meaningful terms with an evolving society in which a man who cannot fly becomes a hunted rebel.

EDWARD ECKS awoke, yawned, and stretched. He squinted at the sunlight pouring in through the open east wall of his one-room apartment, and ordered his clothes to come to him.

They didn't obey! He wiped sleep from his eyes and ordered again. But the closet door remained stubbornly shut, and not a garment stirred.

Thoroughly alarmed, Ecks swung out of bed and walked over to the closet. He began to phrase the mental command again, but stopped himself. He must not become panicky. If the clothes didn't obey, it was because he was still half asleep.

Deliberately he turned and walked to the east wall. He

had rolled it up during the night and now he stood, bare toes gripping the edge, where the floor met the outside wall of the building, looking out at the city.

It was early. The milkmen were out, soaring up to the terraces to deposit their milk. A man in full evening dress passed, flying like a wounded bird. Drunk, Ecks decided, noting how uncertain the man's levitation sense was. The man banked, narrowly missing a building, dodged a milkman, misjudged the ground and fell the last two feet. Miraculously he held his balance, shook his head and continued on foot.

Ecks grinned, watching him weave down the street. That was the safest place for him. No one ever used the streets, except the Normals, or psis who *wanted* to walk for some reason. But levitating in his condition, he might get clipped by a teleported bale, or break his neck against a building.

A newsboy floated past the window, goggles dangling from his hip pocket. The boy caught his breath and shot up, straight and true, to a twentieth floor penthouse.

Ecks craned his neck to watch the boy land his paper on the sunny terrace and sweep on. A penthouse, Ecks thought. That was the life. He lived on the third floor of an ancient building—so old that it still had stairway and elevator. But once he had finished his courses at Mycrowski University—once he had his degree—

There was no time for dreaming. Mr. Ollen didn't like him to be late; and his job at Mr. Ollen's store enabled him to attend the University.

Ecks walked back, opened the closet and dressed. Then, thoroughly calm, he ordered the bed to make itself.

A blanket half-lifted, wavered, and fell back on the bed. He ordered again, angrily. The sheets sluggishly straightened, the blankets slowly crawled into place. The pillow wouldn't move.

On the fifth order the pillow dragged itself to the head of the bed. It had taken him almost five minutes to make the bed—a task he usually finished in seconds.

A shocking realization struck him, and his knees buckled; he sat down on the edge of the bed. He wasn't even able to handle simple motor-response teleportation.

And that, he knew, was how people discovered they had The Disease.

But why? How had it begun? He didn't have any unexplained tensions, any vital, unresolved problems. At twenty-six life was just beginning for him. His studies at the University were going well. His general psi rating was in the upper tenth, and his sensitivity rating approached the all-time high set by The Sleeper.

Why should it happen to him? Why should he catch the only disease left on Earth?

"I'll be damned, I don't feel sick," he said out loud, wiping perspiration from his face. Quickly he commanded the wall to close, just to see if it would. And it did! He turned on a faucet by mental command, levitated a glass, filled it and brought it to him, without spilling a drop.

"Temporary blockage," he told himself. "A fluke." Perhaps he had been studying too hard. More social life, that was what he needed.

He sent the glass back to the sink, watching the sunlight glint from it as it swooped through the air.

"I'm as good as I ever was," he said.

The glass dropped to the floor, shattering.

"Just a little shaky," he reassured himself. Of course, he should go to Psi-Health for an examination. If there is any impairment of your psi abilities, don't wait. Don't infect others. Get an examination.

Well, should he? Yes, he probably should.

But the Psi-Health agents were a jumpy bunch. If he showed his face they'd probably isolate him. Give him a few years of solitary rehabilitation, just to play safe.

That would be the end of him. Highly extroverted, Ecks knew himself well enough to realize that he could never stand solitary. His psi abilities would be completely wrecked that way.

Nuts, he said, and walked to the wall. Opening it, he looked out on the three story drop, steeled himself, and jumped.

For a horrible moment, he thought he had forgotten even the basic skill of levitation. Then he caught it, and soared toward Mr. Ollen's store. Weaving slightly, like a wounded bird.

Psi-Health Headquarters on the eighty-second floor of the Aerinon Building hummed with activity. Messengers levitated in and out the great windows, flying across the room to drop their reports on the Receiving desk. Other reports were teleped in, recorded by Psi-Grade Three telepathic-sensitive office girls. Samples were teleported through the windows, recorded, and shuttled downstairs by Grade Two Polters. A skinny Grade Four psi girl collected the typed reports and levitated them across the room in a steady stream to the file clerks.

Three messengers swept in through a single window, laughing, barely clearing the jambs, and shot across the room. One, misjudging his arc, intercepted the path of reports.

"Why don't you look where you're going?" the Grade Four girl asked angrily. Her bridge of papers was scattered across the floor. She levitated them again.

"Sorry, honey," the messenger said, grinning and handing his report to the Receiving desk. He winked at her, looped over the white stream, and shot out the window.

"Some nerve," the girl murmured, watching him streak into the sky. Without her attention, the papers began to scatter again.

The end-product of all the activity was funneled to the orderly black desk of Senior Health Officer Paul Marrin.

"Anything wrong, chief?" Marrin looked up and nodded to his assistant, Joe Leffert. Silently he handed him five file cards.

They were breakdown reports. Leffert scanned the first one rapidly.

"Jane Martinelli, waitress, Silver Cow, 4543 Broadway. Subject: Loss of psi ability. Observations: Discoordination of psi motor functions. Diagnosis: Acute loss of confidence. Infectious. Recommended: Quarantine, indefinite period."

The other reports were about the same.

"Quite a few," Leffert said, his tone perfectly even.

Another pile of cards was dropped on the black desk. Marrin leafed through them rapidly, his face impassive. The impassivity was mental as well. Not a thought leaked out of his rigidly held mind.

"Six more." He turned to a large map behind his desk and pinpointed the new locations. They formed an irregular pattern across almost a third of New York.

Leffert didn't have to speak. Even undirected, his teleped thought was strong enough for Marrin to catch.

Epidemic!

"Keep that to yourself," Marrin said in his normal low voice. He walked slowly back to his desk, considering the implications of eleven cases in a single day, when their average was one a week.

"Get me the full reports on these people," Marrin said, handing Leffert the file cards. "I want a list of everyone they've been in contact with over the past two weeks. And keep quiet about it." Leffert hurried away.

Marrin thought for a moment, then teleped Krandall, chief of The Sleeper project. Normally, teleped messages were handled through a series of telepathic-sensitive girls; there were just too many minds for most people to make contact easily, without auxiliary guidance. But Marrin's psi abilities were of unusual strength. Also, he was strongly attuned to Krandall, having worked with him for many years.

"What's up?" Krandall asked, and the accompanying identity-image had the full, indescribable flavor of the man.

Quickly Marrin outlined the situation.

"I want you to find out if it's a random scattering, or if we've got a carrier to deal with," Marrin finished.

"That'll cost you a supper," Krandall teleped. From the peripheral thoughts, Marrin knew that he was sitting on a pier at Sag Harbor, fishing. "A supper at The Eagles."

"Fine. I'll have all the data. Is five-thirty all right?"

"Please, my boy! Make it six-thirty. A man of my—ah —dimensions—shouldn't levitate too rapidly." The accompanying visual was of an overstuffed sausage.

"At six-thirty, then." They broke contact. Marrin sat back and arranged the papers on his desk into still neater piles. At the moment he wished he were a health officer in some earlier age, with a nice fat germ to hunt down.

The source of The Disease was more subtle.

Diagnosis: Acute Loss of Confidence. Try putting that under your microscope.

He thought momentarily about the waitress, the first case on the files. Perhaps she had been stacking plates on a shelf. A doubt planted in her mind hours before, minutes before, blossomed. The plates fell. And a girl was seriously sick, horribly infected with mankind's last disease. *Loss of motor-coordination.* So she had to go into solitary, in order not to infect anyone else. For how long? A day, a year. A life.

But in the meantime, perhaps some of the customers had caught it from her. And spread it to their wives . . .

He sat upright and teleped his wife. Her answering thought was quick and warm.

"Hello, Paul!"

He told her he would be working late.

"All right," she said, but her accompanying thoughts were confused with a strong desire to know why, and the knowledge that she couldn't ask.

"Nothing serious," he said in reply to the unspoken question, and regretted it instantly. Lies, untruths, half-truths—even little white lies—didn't telep well. Nevertheless, he didn't retract it.

"All right Paul," his wife said, and they broke contact.

Five o'clock, and the office staff put away their papers and headed for the windows, flying to their homes in Westchester, Long Island and New Jersey.

"Here's the stuff, chief," Leffert said, flying up to the desk with a thick briefcase. "Anything else?"

"I'd like you to stand by," Marrin said, taking the briefcase. "Telep a few more agents, also."

"Right. Do you think something might break?"

"I don't know. Better get some supper." Leffert nodded.

His eyes grew blank, and Marrin knew he was teleping his wife in Greenwich, telling her he wouldn't be home tonight.

Leffert left, and Marrin was left alone in the room, staring at the sunset. Out of the west window he could see the great red disk of the sun, and flitting across it were the black silhouettes of commuters, levitating home.

Marrin felt very much alone. Just him and a probable epidemic.

At exactly six-twenty, Marrin picked up the briefcase and levitated to The Eagles.

The Eagles restaurant was two thousand feet above New York, suspended on the backs of 200 men. The men were Grade One Psi laborers, government-tested for load capacity. As Marrin approached, he saw them under the base of the building. The restaurant floated above them, easily supported by their enormous combined psi strength.

Marrin landed on the main guest desk and was greeted by the head waiter.

"How's everything, Mr. Marrin?" the waiter asked, leading him to a terrace.

"Fine," Marrin said, as he always did.

"You should try our other place some time, Mr. Marrin. If you're ever near Miami, there's an Eagles there. Same high-quality food."

And high-quality prices, Marrin thought, ordering a martini. The owner of the Eagles was making a fortune. Airborne restaurants were common now, but Eagles had been the first and was still the most popular. The owner didn't even have to pay a New York property tax; when he wasn't open, he parked his restaurant in a pasture in Pennsylvania.

The terraces were starting to fill up when Krandall arrived out of wind and perspiring.

"My God," he gasped, sitting down. "Why aren't there any more airplanes? Bucked a head wind all the way in. Scotch on the rocks."

The waiter hurried away.

"Why do you have your emergencies on my day off?"

Krandall asked, teleping the question. "Long distance flights are for the strong young apes. I am a mental worker. How is your wife?"

"The same," Marrin said. His face, schooled for years into a health officer's blank mask, refused to smile now. He ordered his dinner, and handed Krandall the briefcase.

"Hmmm." Krandall bent over the pages, scanning them rapidly. His broad, good-natured face grew abstracted as he memorized the information.

Marrin looked across the terrace while Krandall absorbed the data. The sun was almost gone, and most of the land was in shadow. Beneath him, the lights of New York were winking on in the shaded areas. Above, the stars snapped on.

Krandall ignored his soup, flipping the pages quickly. Before the soup was cold, he was through.

"That's that," he said. "What shall we talk about?" Krandall was the finest psi calculator in the business. He had to be to head the important Sleeper project. Like all calculators, he let his unconscious do the work. Once the data was committed, he ignored it. Unconsciously, the information was assimilated, examined, compared, synthesized. In a few minutes or hours he would have an answer. Krandall's great talent was compensated for in other ways, though. He couldn't pass a newsboy's test for levitation, and teleportation or telekinetic manifestations were almost out of the question for him.

"Is there anything new with The Sleeper?" Marrin asked.

"Still sleeping. Some of the boys cooked up a subconscious-infiltration technique. They're trying that in a few days."

"Do you think it will work?"

Krandall laughed. "I give them a one-point-one probability. That's high, compared with some of the stuff they've tried."

Krandall's brook trout was served, teleported fresh from the stream. Marrin's steak followed.

"Do you think anything will work?" Marrin asked.

"No." Krandall's face was serious as he looked at the lean, impassive health officer. "I don't believe The Sleeper will ever awaken."

Marrin frowned. The Sleeper was one of Psi's most important projects, and its least successful. It had started about thirty years ago.

Psi had been standard, but still unpredictable. It had come a long way in two hundred years from Rhine's halting experiments in extra-sensory perception, but it still had a long way to go.

Mycrowski took a lot of the wild-talent aspect from psi. Classified as an extreme sensitive with genius-level psi abilities, Mycrowski was the outstanding man of his age.

With men like Krandall, Myers, Blacenck, and others, Mycrowski led the telekinesis projects, explored projection techniques, theorized on instantaneous transfer in teleportation, and examined the possibilities of new, undiscovered psi abilities.

In his spare time he worked on his own pet ideas, and founded the School for Parapsychological Research, later changed to Mycrowski University.

What *really* happened to him was argued for years. One day, Krandall and Blacenck found him lying on a couch with a bare whisper of pulse to show that he was alive. They were unable to revive him.

Mycrowski had always believed that the mind was a separate and distinct entity from the body. It was believed that he had discovered a separation-projection technique for the mind.

But the mind never returned.

Others argued that his mind had simply snapped from too much strain, leaving him in a catatonic state. In any case, periodic attempts were made to awaken him, without success. Krandall, Myers, and a few others had kept the project alive, but in a few years they had all the help they needed. The rare quality of Mycrowski's genius was recognized.

The tomb where the living body of Mycrowski, The Sleeper, vegetated, became a tourists' shrine.

"Haven't *you* any idea what he was looking for?" Marrin asked.

"I don't think he did himself," Krandall said, starting his cherry jubilee. "Oddest damned man in the world. Didn't like to talk about anything until he could throw it in your face as done. None of us had any reason to think anything was going to happen. We were sure that the stars were right around the corner and immortality was following that." He shook his head. "Ah, youth, youth."

Over the coffee Krandall looked up, pursed his lips and frowned. The assimilated data had synthesized. His conscious mind had the answer in a manner once called intuitive, until psi research pinned down the hidden factor as subconscious reasoning.

"You know, Marrin, you've definitely got a growing epidemic on your hands. There's no random scattering of cases."

Marrin felt his chest contract. He teleped the question tightly. "Is there a carrier?"

"There is." Mentally, Krandall checked the names on his list. His subconscious had correlated the frequency factors, tabulated probabilities and sent up a "hunch." "His name is Edward Ecks. He is a student, living at 141 Fourth Avenue."

Marrin teleped Leffert immediately and told him to pick up Ecks.

"Hold it," Krandall said. "I don't believe you'll find him there. Here's a probability-course of his movements." He teleped the information to Leffert.

"Try his apartment first," Marrin told Leffert. "If he's not there, try the next probability. I'll meet you downtown, in case we have to hunt him." He broke contact and turned to Krandall. "For the extent of the emergency you'll work with me?" It was hardly a question.

"Of course," Krandall said. "Health has top priority, and The Sleeper isn't going to be doing much moving. But I doubt if you'll have much trouble picking up Ecks. He should be completely crippled by this time."

Upon landing, Ecks lost his balance and fell heavily to his knees. He got up at once, brushed himself off, and started walking. A sloppy levitation, he told himself. So even that was going!

The crumbling streets of the lower New York slums were scattered with Normals, people who had never mastered the basic psi power. This mass of land-borne people was a sight never seen in the more respectable uptown areas. Ecks moved into the crowd, feeling safer.

He discovered, suddenly, that he was hungry. He went into a luncheonette, sat down at the empty counter and ordered a hamburger. The cook had one all ready. Expertly he teleported it to a plate and, without watching, made the plate loop in the air and drop lightly in front of Ecks.

Ecks cursed the man's casual ability and reached for the ketchup. He expected the bottle to slide toward him, but it didn't. He looked at it for a moment, blankly, then stretched his arm. He'd have to watch his step, making a mistake like that.

Ecks was beginning to discover what it was like to be a cripple.

Finished, he held out his hand, palm up, expecting the change in his pocket to come. But of course, it didn't. He cursed silently. He was so used to it—it didn't seem possible that he could have lost all his faculties at once.

But he had, he knew. His unconscious had decided, and no amount of surface assurance would help.

The cook was looking at him oddly, so he reached quickly in his pocket, found the change, and paid. He tried to smile at the cook, then hurried out the door.

"Queer guy," the cook thought. He dismissed it, but down deep in his mind an appraisal was going on. Inability to command a bottle . . . Inability to command coins . . .

Ecks walked down the crowded, grimy streets. His legs began to ache. He had never walked so much in his life. Around him were mixed groups of Normals and psis. The Normals walked naturally, as they had all their lives. The psis were awkward, unaccustomed to long stretches on foot. With relief they soared into their natural element, the air. People landed and took off, and the air was filled with teleported objects.

Looking back, Ecks saw a well-dressed man drop out of the air and stop one of the walking psis. He talked to him for a moment, then moved on.

A health-agent! Ecks knew he had been traced.

He twisted around a corner and started to run.

The street lights became fewer as Ecks moved on, pushing his aching legs. He tried to levitate, but couldn't get off the ground.

In panic he tried to telep his friends. Useless. His telepathic sense had no power.

The shock broke over him like an ocean wave, and he stumbled against a lamp post and hung on. The full realization came.

In a world where men flew, he was landbound.

In a world of telepathic contact, he was reduced to clumsy words at face-to-face distance.

In a world where artificial light was unnecessary, he could see only when his eyes were stimulated.

Crippled. Blind, deaf, and dumb.

He walked on, into narrower streets, dingy, damp alleys. His numbed mind started working again. He had one advantage. His blunted mind could no longer broadcast a strong identity-pattern. That would make him more difficult to find.

What he needed, he decided, was a sanctuary. Some place where he wouldn't infect anyone, and where the health officers couldn't find him. Perhaps he could find a Normal boarding house. He could stay there and study, find out what was wrong with him; treat himself. And he wouldn't be alone. Normals were better than no people at all.

He came to the end of an alley, where the streets branched off. Automatically he pushed out his location sense, to find out what was ahead.

Useless. It was paralyzed, as dead as the rest of him. But the right-hand turn seemed the safest. He started for it.

"Don't!"

Ecks whirled, alarmed at the spoken word. A girl had come out of a doorway. She ran to him.

"They're waiting for me?" Ecks asked, his heart pounding like a triphammer.

"The health officers. They figured you'd take the right turn. Something about your right-hand tropism, I couldn't hear it all. Take the street on your left."

Ecks looked at her closely. At first he thought she was about fifteen years old, but he revised his estimate to twenty. She was small, slender with large dark eyes in a bony face.

"Why are you helping me?" he asked.

"My uncle told me to," the girl said. "Hurry!"

There was no time to argue. Ecks walked in the alley, following the girl. She ran ahead, and Ecks had trouble keeping up with her.

She was a Normal, to judge by her sure stride. But how had she overheard the health-officer's conversation? Almost certainly they had teleped on a tight beam.

Her uncle, perhaps?

The alley opened into a courtyard. Ecks raced in, and stopped. From the tops of the buildings men floated down. They dropped quickly, surrounding him.

The health officers!

He looked around, but the girl had darted back into the alley. The way was blocked for him. He backed against a building, wondering how he could have been so stupid. Of course! This was how they liked to take people. Quietly, so no one else would become infected.

That damned girl! He tightened his aching legs, to run for it . . .

Just as Krandall predicted, Marrin thought. "Take his arms and legs." Hovering fifty feet in the air, he supervised the operation.

Without pity, he watched. The agents moved in cautiously. They didn't want to use the force of their minds against him if they could help it.

After all, the man was a cripple.

They had almost reached him, when—

Ecks started to fade. Marrin dropped closer, unable to believe his eyes. Ecks was dissolving into the wall, becoming a part of it, disappearing.

Then he was gone.

"Look for a door!" Marrin teleped. "Examine the pavement!"

While his agents were looking, Marrin considered what he had seen. After the initial surprise, he didn't doubt it. The search for a door was an excuse for his agents. If they thought the man had disappeared through a hidden door, good. It wouldn't help their confidence—their sanity—to believe what had actually happened.

The cripple, Ecks, merging with the wall.

Marrin ordered a search of the building. But there wasn't a trace of Ecks' thought pattern. He was gone, as though he had never been.

But how, Marrin asked himself. Did someone help him? Who?

Who would help a carrier?

The first thing Ecks saw when he returned to consciousness was the cracked, stained plaster wall in front of him. He stared at it for a long time, watching dust motes floating in the sunlight, across the bed's torn brown blanket.

The bed! Ecks sat up and looked around. He was in a dingy little room. Long cracks ran across the ceiling. Aside from the bed, the only other piece of furniture was a plain wooden chair, set near the half-open door.

But what was he doing here? He remembered the events of last night; it must have been last night, he decided. The blank wall, the health officers. He must have been rescued. But how?

"How do you feel?" A girl's voice asked from the door. Ecks turned, and recognized the pale, sensitive face. It was the girl who had warned him last night.

"I feel all right," Ecks said. "How did I get here?"

"My uncle brought you," the girl said, coming into the room. "You must be hungry."

"Not especially," Ecks said.

"You should eat," she told him. "My uncle tells me that

dematerialization is quite a strain on the nervous system. That's how he rescued you from the psis, you know." She paused. "I can give you some very nice broth."

"He *dematerialized* me?" Ecks asked.

"He can do things like that," the girl said serenely. "The power came to him afterwards." She walked over and opened the window. "Shall I get the broth?"

Ecks frowned at her. The situation was becoming unreal, at a time when he needed his fullest grasp on reality. This girl seemed to consider it perfectly normal to have an uncle with the power of dematerialization—although psi science had never discovered it.

"Shall I get the broth?" she asked again.

"No," Ecks said. He wondered what the repeated emphasis on food might mean. There was nothing in the girl's face to tell him. She was handsome enough, even in a cheap, unbecoming dress. She had unusually dark eyes, and an unusually calm expression. Or lack of expression, really.

He filed his suspicions for the moment, and asked, "Is your uncle a psi?"

"No," the girl said. "My uncle doesn't hold with psi powers. His strength is spiritual."

"I see," Ecks said, and he thought he had the answer. Throughout history, people had preferred to believe that their natural psi gifts were the product of demon intervention. Strange powers were the devil's gift until psi regularized and formularized them. And even in this day there were gullible Normals, people who preferred to believe that their occasional flashes of supernormal power were spirit-guided. Evidently the uncle fell into this category.

"Has your uncle been able to do this sort of thing long?" Ecks asked.

"Only for about five years," she said. "Only since he died."

"Perfectly correct," a voice said. Ecks looked around quickly. The voice seemed to come from behind his shoulder.

"Don't look for me," the voice said. "All that there is

of me in this room is a voice. I am the spirit of Cari's Uncle John."

Ecks had a quick moment of panic before he realized the trick. It was a teleped voice, of course; cleverly focused and masked to give the effect of speech. A teleped voice meant only one thing; this was a psi passing himself off as a spirit.

"Mr. Ecks," the voice said, cleverly simulating the effects of spoken words, "I have rescued you by the intervention of my powers. You are a crippled psi, a carrier. Capture and isolation are, I believe, distasteful to you. Is that not true?"

"Perfectly," Ecks said. He probed with his blunted senses for the source of the voice. The imitation was perfect; not a single image leaked, to show the telepathic-human source.

"You feel, perhaps, a certain gratitude toward me?" the voice asked.

Ecks looked at the girl. Her face was still expressionless. "Of course I do," he said.

"I know your desires," Uncle John told him. "You wish sanctuary for a sufficient time to restore your powers. And you shall have it, Edward Ecks. You shall have it."

"I'm very grateful," Ecks said. His mind was working quickly, trying to decide upon a course of action. Was he expected to keep up the pretense of believing in this spirit? Surely the teleping psi knew that no university-trained person was going to accept something like that. On the other hand, he might be dealing with a neurotic, playing spirit for his own reasons. He decided to play along. After all, he wasn't interested in the man's pretensions. What mattered was the sanctuary.

"You would not, I am certain, object to doing me a small favor," Uncle John said.

"What do you want me to do?" Ecks asked, immediately on his guard.

"I sense your thought," the voice said. "You think there may be danger involved. I assure you, such is not the case. Although I am not omnipotent, I have certain powers unknown to you—or to psi science. Accept that fact. Surely your rescue proves it. And accept that I have your best interests at heart."

"When do I find out about this errand?" Ecks asked.

"When the time is right. For now, goodbye, Edward Ecks." The voice was gone.

Ecks sat down in the chair. He had had two possible explanations before; that the "uncle" was a psychotic, or a psi. Now he had another.

What if the uncle was a mutant psi? The next evolution in the procession. What then?

Cari left and returned with a bowl of soup.

"What was your uncle like?" Ecks asked the girl. "What sort of man was he—when he was alive?"

"Oh, he was a very nice man," she said, holding the steaming soup carefully. "He was a shoemaker. He raised me when my father died."

"Did he ever show any signs of psi power? Or supernatural power?"

"No," Cari said. "He led a quiet life. It was only after he died—"

Ecks looked at the girl with pity. She was the saddest part of the whole thing. The psi had undoubtedly read her mind, found the dead uncle—and the gullibility. And used her as his pawn. A cruel game.

"Please eat the soup," she said. He reached for it automatically, glancing at her face. Then he pulled back his hand.

"You eat it," he said. The first tinge of color came into her cheeks.

With an apology, she started on the soup, spilling some in her eagerness.

The sailboat heeled sharply, and Marrin let out a foot of mainsail to steady it. His wife, seated on the bow, waved to him, enjoying the plunging motion.

Below, he could see a bank of thunderheads, a storm in the making.

"Let's have our picnic on those clouds over there," Myra said, pointing to a wispy cirrus formation, bright and sunny above the thunderheads. Marrin changed course. Myra lay back on the bow, her feet propped against the mast.

Marrin was holding the entire weight of the boat himself, but he scarcely noticed it. The light rig weighed less than two hundred pounds, sail and all. His and Myra's combined weight added about two hundred and sixty pounds more, but Marrin's tested levitation capacity was over two tons.

And the wind did most of the work. All the operator of the boat did was to supply enough power to keep it in the air. The wind drove it, a twisting white feather.

Marrin couldn't get his mind off the carrier. How in hell had Ecks disappeared? Dematerialization—impossible! And yet there it was.

Ecks, into the wall. And gone, without a thought-trace.

"Stop thinking," Myra said. "Your doctor told you not to think about anything but me today." He knew that his thoughts hadn't leaked; nor had his face changed. But Myra was sensitive to his moods. He didn't have to grimace for her to know he was happy, or cry to demonstrate sadness.

Marrin brought the light, flat boat to a stop in the clouds, and, heading into the wind, dropped the sail. They spread their picnic on the bow of the boat. Marrin did most of the levitating, although Myra was trying . . . gallantly.

As she had been trying for seven years, since her partial infection by a carrier. Although her psi faculties never left her completely, they were spasmodic.

Another reason for hunting down Ecks.

The sandwiches Myra made were very like herself; small and decorative. And tasty, Marrin thought, teleping the thought.

"Beast," Myra said out loud. The warm sun beat down on them, and Marrin felt wonderfully lazy. The two of them stretched out on the deck of the boat, Marrin holding it up by reflex. He was more relaxed than he had been in weeks.

"Marrin!"

Marrin started, awakened out of near-sleep by the teleped voice.

"Look, I'm awfully sorry, boy." It was Krandall, embarrassed and apologetic.

"I hate breaking in on your day, but I've got a lead, and a pretty damned good one. Evidently someone doesn't like our carrier. I've just been told where he'll be in about four hours. Of course, it may be a crank, but I knew you'd want to know—"

"I'm coming," Marrin said. "We can't afford to pass up anything." He broke contact and turned to his wife. "I'm terribly sorry, dear."

She smiled, and her eyes were clear with understanding. She hadn't been included in Krandall's tight-beam message, but she knew what it meant.

"Can you take it down yourself?" Marrin asked.

"Of course. Good hunting." Marrin kissed her and jumped off the boat. He watched for a few seconds, to see that she had it under control; then he teleped the rental service.

"My wife's bringing it in," he told them. "I wish you'd keep an eye on her." They promised. Now, even if she went out of control there'd be no danger.

Marrin hurled himself down. He was so busy calculating the rate of disease increase that he barely saw the dagger in time.

It flashed past him, then turned, twenty feet away, and came again. Marrin reached out for it mentally, but the telekineticized knife broke free. He barely deflected it, grappled, and had it in his hand. Quickly he tried to trace the wielder, but he was gone without a trace.

Not quite without a trace. Marrin was able to catch the tail end of an identity thought, the hardest kind to control. He puzzled over it, trying to place the image. Then he had it.

Ecks!

Ecks, the cripple. Blind Ecks, the carrier, who vanished into walls. And who, evidently, could polter a dagger.

Or had someone do it for him.

Grimly, with the growing awareness that it was turning into a personal affair, Marrin levitated into the Psi-Health Offices.

In the darkened room, Edward Ecks lay on the tattered brown blanket. His eyes were lightly closed, his body passive. Little muscles in his legs jumped. He willed them to relax.

"Relaxation is one of the keys to psi power. Complete relaxation calls forth confidence; fears disappear, tensions evaporate. Relaxation is vital to psi." Ecks told himself this, breathing deeply.

Don't think about the disease. There is no disease. There is only rest, and relaxation.

The leg muscles slackened. Ecks concentrated on his heart, ordering it to pump more easily. He sent orders to his lungs, to breathe deeply and slowly.

Uncle John? He hadn't heard from him for almost two days now. But he mustn't think of him. Not now. An unexplained factor, Uncle John would be resolved in time. The awareness of deception, Ecks told himself, is the first step in finding out what the deception is.

And what about the pale, hungry, attractive niece? Don't think about her, either.

The unsettling memories sponged away as his breathing deepened. Next, the eyes. It was hard to relax the eyes. After-images danced across his retina. Sunlight. Darkness, a building, a disappearance.

No. Don't think.

"My eyes are so heavy," he told himself. "My eyes are made of lead. They want to sink—to sink—"

Then his eye-muscles relaxed. His thoughts seemed calm, but just under the surface was a crazy welter of images and impressions.

A cripple, through dim streets. A ghost that wasn't. A hungry niece. Hungry for what? A turmoil of sense-impressions, flashes of red and purple, memories of classes in Mycrowski University, tele-wrestling at the Palladium, a date at Skytop.

All had to be smoothed down. "Relaxation is the first

step toward reintegration." Ecks told himself that every-thing was blue. All thoughts were swallowed in a vast blue abyss.

Slowly, he succeeded in calming his mind. A deep peace started to seep into him, slowly, soothingly—

"Edward Ecks."

"Yes?" Ecks opened his eyes at once; the relaxation had been that superficial. He looked around and realized that it was the uncle's voice.

"Take this." A small sphere darted into the room, and came to rest in front of Ecks. He picked it up and exam-ined it. The sphere seemed to be made of some shiny, solid plastic.

"What is it?" he asked.

"You will place this sphere inside the Cordeer Build-ing," the voice of Uncle John told him, ignoring the ques-tion. "Leave it on a desk, behind a door, in an ashtray, anywhere. Then return directly here."

"What will the sphere do?" Ecks asked.

"That is not your concern," the voice told him. "The sphere is the apex of a psychic triangle of forces which you do not understand. Suffice it to say that it will harm no one and will greatly aid me."

"Every officer in the city is looking for me," Ecks said. "I'll be picked up if I go back to the main part of the city."

"You have forgotten my powers, Ecks. You will be safe, if you keep to the route I map out for you."

Ecks hesitated. He wanted to know more about the un-cle, and his game. Above all, why was he masquerading as a spirit?

Or was he?

After all, what would a spirit have to do with Earth? The classic yarns of demons seeking temporal power were just so much muggy anthropomorphizing.

"Will I be left alone after I get back?" Ecks wanted to know.

"You have my word. Do this to my satisfaction and you will receive all the sanctuary you need. Now go. Cari

has the route drawn up for you. She is waiting at the door."

The voice was gone. Even with his blunted senses, Ecks could feel the withdrawn contact.

With the sphere in his hand, he walked to the door. Cari was waiting.

"Here are the instructions," she said.

Ecks looked at her sharply. He wished he had some psi-abilities left. He would have given a good deal to know what was going on behind that quiet, pretty face. Psis never bothered to read faces; the affective aura surrounding every individual was a far better indicator.

If one had normal psi-sensitivity to read it.

"Have you eaten?" he asked.

"Oh, yes," she said, following him outside. The sunlight was momentarily blinding, after two days in the little room. Ecks blinked and looked around automatically. There was no one in sight.

They walked in silence for a while, following Uncle John's instructions. Ecks glanced right and left, pitifully aware of his vulnerability, on the lookout for detection. The instructions laid out a devious, meaningless pattern for Ecks to walk; doubling back on streets, circling others. They approached West Broadway, moving out of the slums into psi territory.

"Has your uncle ever told you what he wishes to do?" Ecks asked.

"No," Cari said. They walked in silence for a while longer. Ecks tried not to look at the sky, out of which he expected the psi officers to fall, like avenging angels.

"Sometimes I'm afraid of Uncle John," Cari volunteered, after a few moments. "He's so strange, sometimes."

Ecks nodded absently. Then he thought about the girl's position. Actually, she was worse off than he was. He knew the score. She was being used for some unknown purpose. She might well be in danger, although he didn't know why that should concern him.

"Look," he said, "if anything happens, do you know the Angler's Bar on Sixth and Bleeker?"

"No, but I could find it."

"Meet me there, if anything goes wrong."

"All right," she said. "Thank you."

Ecks smiled wryly. How idiotic of him to offer her protection! When he couldn't even protect himself. At least, he told himself, it was an understandable urge. Even if he didn't quite understand it himself.

They walked several more blocks. Then the girl looked at Ecks nervously.

"There's one thing I don't understand," she said.

"What's that?"

"Well," she began, "I sometimes can see things that are going to be. I never know when, but just sometimes I have a picture of something. Then in a little while it happens."

"That's interesting," Ecks said. "You're probably an undeveloped clairvoyant. You should go to Mycrowski University. They're always looking for people like you."

"So far, everything I've seen has turned out right," she said.

"That's a nice record," Ecks told her. He wondered what the girl was driving at. Did she want praise? She couldn't be naive enough to believe that she was the only person in the world with latent clairvoyance.

"So far my uncle has been right in everything he's said, too," she told him.

"Very commendable," Ecks said acidly. He was in no mood for a family panegyric. They were approaching Fourteenth Street, and the air was thick with psis. A few people were walking—but very few.

The Cordeer Building was three blocks ahead.

"What I'm wondering is," she said, "if I see something happening one way, and my uncle sees it happening the other way, which of us will be right?"

"What do you mean?" Ecks said, taking her arm as they crossed a street filled with jagged rocks.

"My uncle said you'd be safe," she said, "and I just don't understand."

"What?" He stopped.

"I think they're going to try to capture you."

"When?"

"Now," she said. Ecks stared at her, then stiffened. He didn't need psi power to know that the trap was sprung.

The health men weren't being gentle this time. Telekinetic force jerked him off his feet. He looked for Cari, but the girl was gone. Then his head was forced painfully down, his hands and feet seized.

Physically, not a hand had touched him yet.

Ecks fought wildly, in blind panic. *Capture* seemed to touch off some ultimate instability in his personality. He tried desperately to snap the telekinetic bonds.

He almost did. Power came. He freed an arm and managed to throw himself into the air. Frantically he tried for height.

He was smashed to the pavement.

Again he tried, a supreme effort—

And passed out.

His last conscious thought was a realization that he had been tricked. The uncle—he determined to kill him, if the opportunity ever presented itself.

And then there was blackness.

A meeting of World-Health was called at once. Marrin, in Psi headquarters in New York, opened the special channel. Chiefs in Rio, London, Paris, Canton, came into emergency circuit.

Marrin's tightly organized information was flashed around the world in less than a minute. At once he received a question.

"I would like to know," the Health Chief from Barcelona asked, "how this Ecks person escaped you *twice*." The thought carried its inevitable identity pattern. The Barcelona chief's face was dimly apparent; long, sad, moustached. Not his true face, of course. Identity patterns were always idealized in the manner the particular mind viewed itself. Actually, the Barcelonan might be short, fat and clean shaven.

"The second escape was in broad daylight, was it not?" the Berlin chief asked, and the other chiefs glimpsed his broad, powerful, idealized face.

"It was," Marrin replied. "I cannot explain it." Marrin was seated at his black desk in Psi-Health. Around him hummed the normal activity of the day. He was unaware of it.

"Here is the complete sequence." It took longer to telep the scene-by-scene breakdown of the attempted rescue.

After the attack by the poltered dagger, Marrin had assembled his men around the point where Krandall's informant said Ecks would appear.

"This informant. Who——"

"Later. Let him complete the sequence."

Fifty agents covered the area. Ecks appeared on time, and in the indicated place. He was restrained with little difficulty, at first. Fighting, he showed a slight surge of latent strength; then he collapsed.

At that moment his energy potential took an explosive, exponential jump. Ecks vanished.

With Marrin's permission, his recollection of the moment was broken down and scrutinized more closely. The picture remained clear. One moment Ecks was there, the next, he was gone.

The images were slowed to one a half second. In this running there was a blur of energy around Ecks just before he vanished. The energy was on so high a band that it was almost indetectable.

There was no known explanation for it.

The impressions of the participating agents, as recorded by Marrin, were combed, with no positive result.

"Would the Health-Chief from New York care to give his theories?"

"Since Ecks is a cripple," Marrin said, "I can only assume that someone is helping him."

"There is another possibility," the Warsaw Chief said. His idealized identity came through with the thought; slim, white-haired, gay. "Ecks may have stumbled on some undiscovered form of psi power."

"That would appear to be beyond the realm of probability," the sad-eyed Barcelonan teleped.

"Not at all. Consider the emergence of the original psi

faculties. They began as wild talents. Couldn't the next mutation begin in a wild talent stage?"

"There are tremendous implications in that," the London Chief said. "But if so, why hasn't Ecks utilized it to greater advantage?"

"He is probably unaware of it. But he has an inherent protection system, perhaps, which shunts him out of danger at stress moments." "I don't know," Marrin said dubiously. "It is a possibility, of course. We are well aware that there are many untouched secrets of the mind. Still . . ."

"An argument against *your* theory," the Warsaw Chief broke in, teleping directly to Marrin, "is the fact that anyone helping Ecks would necessarily have this extra-psi power. They would have to, to effect an almost instantaneous disappearance. If they did have it, wouldn't they have more of a plan—less randomness—"

"Or seeming randomness," the Londoner said. "It could be a test of strength. By dangling Ecks in front of Marrin, such a group could determine a good deal about his capabilities and, by extrapolation, the capabilities of all psis. The repeated inability to capture Ecks would be meaningful."

"It's a possibility," Marrin said cautiously. Academically, he found the discussion interesting. But it didn't seem to be serving any practical good.

"What about Krandall's informant?" the Barcelonan teleped. "Has he been questioned?"

"He has never been found," Marrin said. "The sender was able to block all identity-thoughts and he left no trace to follow."

"What do you plan to do?"

"First," Marrin said, "to alert you. That is the purpose of the meeting, since the carrier might well get out of New York. Also, the disease rate here has passed the minimum epidemic level. It can be expected to spread, even though I'm closing the city." He paused and wiped his forehead.

"Second, I'm going to trace Ecks myself, working on a

new set of probability locations supplied by Krandall.
Working alone, I'll be able to avoid all thought haze and
deflection. It's just possible one may do what many cannot."

Marrin discussed it with them for half an hour longer,
then broke contact. He sat for a few moments, moodily
sorting papers. Then he shrugged off his mood of despair
and went to see Krandall.

Krandall was in his office at the tomb of The Sleeper.
He grunted hello when Marrin levitated in and motioned
him to a chair.

"I'd like to see those probability locations," Marrin
said.

"Right," Krandall said. The end-product was quite simple: a list of streets and times. But to get that information, Krandall had correlated the total amount of data
available. The locations of Ecks' disappearances, his reap-
pearances, his psychological index, plus the added corre-
lates of suitable hiding spots in the city where a cripple
could stay undetected.

"I think you stand a pretty good chance of finding
him," Krandall said. "Of course, holding him is something
else again."

"I know," Marrin said. "I've come to a decision about
that." He looked away from Krandall. "I'm going to have
to kill Ecks."

"I know," Krandall said.

"What?"

"You can't risk having him loose any more. Your infection rate is still rising."

"That's right. The policy of the Health Board is to
quarantine diseased persons. But this is a matter of public
safety."

"You don't have to justify it to me," Krandall said.

"What do you mean?" Marrin got halfway to his feet,
then sat down again and shook his head. "You're right.
Evidently Ecks can't be captured. We'll see if he can be
killed."

"Good hunting," Krandall said. "I hope you have better luck on *your* project."

"The Sleeper?"

"The latest attempt flopped. Not a stir out of him."

Marrin frowned. That was bad news. If they ever needed Mycrowski's intellect, it was now. Mycrowski was the man to resolve these events into a related whole.

"Would you like to see him?" Krandall asked.

Marrin glanced at the probability list and saw that the first time-street fix was almost an hour off. He nodded, and followed Krandall. They went down a dim corridor to an elevator, and then through another corridor.

"You haven't ever been here, have you?" Krandall asked, at the end of the corridor.

"No. But I helped draw up plans for the remodeling ten years ago."

Krandall unlocked and opened the last door.

In the brightly lighted room The Sleeper rested. Tubes ran into his arms, carrying the nutrient solutions that kept him alive. The bed he lay on slowly massaged The Sleeper's flabby muscles. The Sleeper's face was blank and expressionless, as it had been for thirty years. The face of a dead man, still living.

"That's enough," Marrin said. "I'm depressed enough."

They went back upstairs.

"Those streets I gave you are in the slums," Krandall said. "Watch your step. Asociality is still present in such places."

"I'm feeling pretty asocial myself," Marrin said, and left.

He levitated to the fringe of the slums, and dropped to the street. His sensitive, trained mind was keyed for stimulation. He walked, sorting impressions as he went, searching for the dull, almost obliterated throb of the carrier's mind. Marrin's web extended for blocks, sifting, feeling, sorting.

If Ecks was alive and conscious he would find him.

And kill him.

"You fool! You incompetent! You imbecile!" The disembodied voice roared at Ecks.

Blurrily, Ecks realized that he was back in Cari's house, in the slums.

"I gave you a course to follow," Uncle John screamed, his voice bouncing against the walls. "You took the wrong turn!"

"I did not," Ecks said, getting to his feet. He wondered vaguely how long he had been unconscious.

"Don't contradict me! You did. And you must do it again!"

"Just a minute," Ecks said evenly. "I don't know what your game is, but I followed your instructions to the letter. I turned down every street you wrote down."

"You didn't!"

"Stop this farce!" Ecks shouted back. "Who in hell are you?"

"Get out!" Uncle John roared. "Get out—or I'll kill you."

"Be reasonable," Ecks said. "Just tell me what you want. Tell me what I'm supposed to do. Explain it. I don't work well in a mystery."

"Get out," the voice said ominously.

"I can't," Ecks said in despair. "Why don't you drop this spirit pose and tell me what it is you want? I'm a normal person. Health officers are everywhere. They will kill me too. I must first regain my abilities. But I can't—"

"Are you going?" the voice asked.

Ecks didn't answer.

Invisible hands were at Ecks' throat. He jerked back. The grip tightened. Force battered him against the wall, chopping down at him. Ecks rolled, trying to escape the merciless beating. The air was alive with energy, hurling itself at him, crushing him, smothering him.

Marrin sensed the increase in energy output at once. He traced it, got a fix and levitated toward the location, sifting through the energy manifestations for some identity pattern.

Ecks!

Marrin crashed through a flimsy wooden door, and stopped. He saw Ecks' crumpled body.

Berserk force was alive in the room, undirected now. Suddenly, Marrin found himself fighting for his life. Shielding, he smashed against the telekinetic power that surged around him.

A chair was swept up and thrown at him. He deflected it, and was struck from behind by a pitcher. A bed tried to crush him against the wall. Avoiding it, he was struck in the back by a poltered table. A lamp shattered on the wall above his head, spraying him with fragments. A broom caught him behind the knees.

Marrin shielded and located the psi power source.

In the basement of the building.

He sent a tremendous wave rippling across it, poltering chairs and tables with it. The attack stopped abruptly. The place was a shambles of broken furniture.

Marrin looked around. Ecks was gone again. He searched for his identity pattern, but couldn't locate it.

The man in the cellar?

Also gone. But a trace was left behind!

Marrin went through a window, following the trace thought. Trained for this work, he held contact with the attenuated, stifled thought as its owner shot into the city. He followed it through a twisting maze of buildings, and out into open air.

One part of his mind was still able to probe for Ecks. No luck.

But he had Ecks' accomplice, if he could hold him.

He shortened the distance by fractions. Ecks' helper—and attacker—shot out of the city, heading West.

Marrin followed.

"A glass of beer, please," Ecks said, trying hard to catch his breath. It had been a long run. Luckily, the bartender was a Normal, and a phlegmatic one at that. He moved stolidly to the tap.

Ecks saw Cari at the end of the bar, leaning against the wall. Thank God she had remembered. He paid for his beer and carried it to where she was.

"What happened?" she asked, looking at his bruised face.

"Your nice uncle tried to kill me," Ecks said wryly. "A health-officer came bursting in, and I let them fight it out." Ecks had slipped out the door during the fight. He had counted on the insensitivity of his thought pattern to conceal him. Crippled, he was hardly able to broadcast an identity thought. For once, the loss of telepathic power was an asset.

Cari shook her head sadly. "I just don't understand it," she said. "You may not believe this, but Uncle John was always a good man. He was the most harmless person I ever knew. I just don't understand—"

"Simple," Ecks said. "Try to understand this. That was not Uncle John. Some highly developed psi has been masquerading as him."

"But why?" she asked.

"I don't know," Ecks said. "He saves me, tries to get me captured again, then tries to kill me. It doesn't make sense."

"What now?" she asked.

Ecks finished his beer. "Now, the end," he said.

"Isn't there some place we can go?" she asked. "Some place we can hide?"

"I don't know of any," Ecks said. "You'd better go on your own. I'm a risky person to be with."

"I'd rather not," Cari said.

"Why not?" Ecks wanted to know.

She looked away. "I'd just rather not."

Even without telepathy, Ecks had an intimation of what she meant. Mentally, he cursed. He didn't like the idea of having the responsibility of her. Psi-Health must be getting desperate. They wouldn't pull any punches this time, and she might get hurt.

"Go away," he said firmly.

"No!"

"Well, come on," he said. "We'll just have to get by as well as we can. The only thing I can think of is getting out of the city. I should have done that at first, instead of playing spirit." Now it was undoubtedly too late. The psi officers would be checking everyone on foot.

"Can you use that clairvoyance of yours?" he asked. "Is there anything you can see?"

"No," she said sadly. "The future's a blank to me."

That was how Ecks saw it, too.

Marrin sensed that he had greater inherent strength than the man he was pursuing. He detected the signs of weakening and pushed harder.

The fugitive was visible now, a mile ahead of him doubling back toward the city. As he got closer, Marrin threw his telekinetic strength, pulling the man down.

He clung doggedly. The man was slowing, fighting spasmodically. Marrin overhauled him, brought him down and pinned him to the ground. Coming down himself, he probed for an identity thought.

And found one.

Krandall!

For a moment all he could do was stare.

"Did you get Ecks?" Krandall teleped. The exertion had drained the big man of everything. He lay, face down, fighting for breath.

"No. You were his backer all along. Is that right?"

Krandall's thought was affirmative.

"How could you! What were you thinking of? You know what the disease means!"

"I'll explain later," Krandall panted.

"Now!"

"No time. You have to find Ecks."

"I know that," Marrin said. "But why did you help him?"

"I didn't," the fat man said. "Not really. I tried to kill him. *You* must kill him." He dragged himself to his feet. "He's a far greater menace than you think. Believe me, Marrin. Ecks must be killed!"

"Why did you rescue him?" Marrin asked.

"In order to put him back into danger," Krandall gasped. "I couldn't let you capture and isolate him. He must be killed."

"Go on," Marrin said.

"Not now," Krandall said. "I poltered the dagger at you, to make you consider Ecks a personal menace. I had to goad you to the point where you would kill him."

"What is he?"

"Not now! Get him!"

"Another thing," Marrin said. "You couldn't handle that amount of telekinetic power. Who was doing it?"

"The girl," Krandall said, swaying on his feet. "The girl Cari. I was posing as her uncle's spirit. She's in back of it all. You must kill her, too." He wiped his streaming face.

"I'm sorry I had to play it this way, Paul. You'll hear the whole story at the right time. Just take my word for it now."

Krandall tightened his hands into fists and shook them at Marrin.

"You must kill those two! Before they kill everything you stand for!"

The teleped thought had the ring of truth. Marrin took to the air again, contacting his agents. Briefly he gave his instructions.

"Kill both of them," he said. "And pick up Krandall and hold him."

Ecks turned down streets at random, hoping the lack of a plan would confuse the psis. Every shadow seemed to have a meaning of its own. He waited for the mental bolt that would drop him.

Why had the uncle tried to kill him? Impossible to answer. Why was he so seemingly important? Another unanswerable question. And the girl?

Ecks watched her out of the corner of his eye. Cari walked silently beside him. Her face had some color now, and some animation. She seemed almost gay; perhaps freedom from the uncle was the reason for that. What other reason could there be?

Because she was with him?

The air was thick with the usual day's traffic. A load of ore was being brought in, tons of it, expertly shepherded by a dozen workers. Other cargoes were being flown in from Southern ports; fruit and vegetables from Brazil, meat from Argentina.

And psi officers. Ecks wasn't especially surprised. The city was being watched too thoroughly for a fly to escape, much less a crippled man.

The psi officers dropped down, forming a tight mental linkage.

"All right," Ecks called. "The hell with it, I give up." He decided that it was time he bowed to the inevitable. He had the girl to consider also. The psis were probably tired of playing; this time, if he tried to escape, they might play for keeps.

A bolt of energy sheered him off his feet.

"I said I give up!" he shouted. Beside him, Cari fell also. Energy swept over them, twisting them across the courtyard, increasing, building.

"Stop it!" Ecks shouted. "You'll hurt—" He had time —an infinitesimal fraction of a second—to realize fully his own feeling about the girl. He couldn't let anything happen to her. Ecks didn't have time to consider how or why; the feeling was there.

A sad, bitter sensation of love.

Ecks tried to get to his feet. The linked mental energy smashed him down again. Stones and rocks were poltered at him.

Ecks realized that he wasn't going to be allowed to surrender. They were going to kill him.

And Cari.

At first, it seemed as though it were a dream. He had become used to the possibility of death in the last few days. He tried to shield, aware of his nakedness, tried to cover Cari. She doubled up as a poltered rock caught her in the stomach. Rocks hummed around them.

Seeing Cari struck, Ecks could have burst with rage. He struggled to his feet and swayed two steps forward, hands outstretched.

He was knocked down again. A section of wall started to collapse, pushed by psi force. He tried to drag Cari out of the way. Too late. The wall fell—

In that moment Ecks bridged the gap. His tortured,

overstrained mind performed the energy leap into the new
potential. In that instant, contact and comprehension
flooded his mind.

The wall thundered down. But Ecks and Cari weren't
under it.

"Marrin!"

Dully, the psi chief raised his head. He was back at
his desk in Psi-Health. Again it had happened.

"Marrin!"

"Who is it?" the psi chief asked.

"Ecks."

Nothing could surprise him now. That Ecks was capable of tight-beam telepathy just didn't matter.

"What do you want?" he asked.

"I want to meet you. Name a place."

"Wherever you wish," Marrin said, with the calmness of
despair. Then curiosity overcame him. "How are you able
to telep?"

"All psis can telep," Ecks said mockingly.

"Where did you go?" Marrin asked. He tried to get a
location on the message. But Ecks was easily managing
the tight beam, allowing only the direct message to go
through.

"I want a little quiet," Ecks said. "So I'm in the tomb
of The Sleeper. Would you care to meet me there?"

"Coming," Marrin said, and broke contact. "Leffert,"
he said aloud.

"Yes, Chief?" his assistant said, coming over.

"I want you to take over until I get back. If I get
back."

"What *is* Ecks?" Leffert asked.

"I don't know," Marrin said. "I don't know what powers he has. I don't know why Krandall wanted to kill him,
but I concur in the judgment."

"Could we bomb the tomb?" Leffert asked.

"There's nothing faster than thought," Marrin answered. "Ecks has discovered some form of near-instan-
taneous transportation. He could be away before the
bombs were dropped." He paused. "There is a way, but

I'm not going to say any more. He might be listening in on this conversation."

"Impossible!" Leffert said. "This is direct-talk. He couldn't—"

"He couldn't escape," Marrin reminded him wearily. "We're through underestimating Mr. Ecks. Hereafter, consider him capable of anything."

"Right," Leffert said dubiously.

"Have you got the latest figures on the contagion rate?" Marrin asked, walking to the window.

"They're way past epidemic. And the disease has jumped as far as the Rockies."

"It can't be checked now," Marrin said. "We've been pushed off the cliff—on the wrong side. In a year we'll be lucky if there are a thousand psis left in the world." He tightened his hands into fists. "For that alone I could cut Ecks into little pieces."

He levitated out the window.

The first thing Marrin saw when he entered The Sleeper's chamber was Mycrowski himself, still unconscious. Ecks and the girl were standing beside him.

Marrin walked forward.

"I'd like you to meet Cari," Ecks said, smiling.

Marrin ignored the dazed-looking girl. "I'd like an explanation," he said.

"Of course," Ecks said. "Would you like to know what I am, to begin with?"

"Yes," Marrin said.

"I am the stage after psi. The para-psi."

"I see. And this came—"

"When you tried to kill Cari."

"We'd better start somewhere else," Marrin said. He decided to hear the explanation first before taking the final step. "Why have you removed the nutrient pipes from The Sleeper?"

"Because Mycrowski won't need them any more," Ecks said. He turned to The Sleeper, and the room suddenly hummed with energy.

"Good work, Ecks." For a moment Marrin thought it was the girl who had teleped. Then he realized that it was Mycrowski!

"He won't be fully conscious for a while," Ecks said. "Let me start at the beginning. As you know, thirty years ago Mycrowski was searching for the extra-psi powers. He split mind and body to find them. Then, having the knowledge, he was unable to get back in his body. It required a leap into a higher energy level to do that and, without a nervous system at his command, he couldn't gather that power. No ordinary psi could help him, either. To attain the new level, all normal channels must be blocked and redirected, and a terrific strain is placed on the whole nervous system.

"That is, essentially, the same method by which the first true psis got their power."

Marrin looked puzzled for a moment, then asked, "Then you're not a mutation?"

"Mutations have nothing to do with this. Let me go on. Mycrowski couldn't bridge the gap unaided. He had to have a para-psi bridge the gap for him. That's where I come in."

"It is also where *you* come in." Mycrowski, conscious now, teleped to Marrin. "And the girl, and Krandall. I was in telepathic contact with Krandall. Together we chose Ecks for the experiment. It couldn't be Krandall himself, because his nervous system was not suitable. Ecks was picked for his temperament and sensitivity. And, I might add, for his selfishness and suggestibility. Everything was predicted, including Cari's role."

Marrin listened coldly. Let them explain. He had an answer of his own. A final one.

"First, the rechanneling. Ecks' psi senses were blocked. Then he was put in a position of stress; incipient capture and isolation, both repugnant to his nature. When he failed to bridge the gap, Krandall rescued him, with my help. With Krandall posing as Cari's Uncle John we threatened his life, increasing the stress."

"So that's what Krandall meant," Marrin said.

"Yes. Krandall told you that you had to kill Ecks. That

was true. You had to try. He told you that the girl was the key to the whole thing. And that was true also. Because when Ecks' life and the girl's were threatened, it was the greatest stress we could bring to bear. He bridged the gap to the higher potential. Comprehension followed immediately."

"And he gave you back your body," Marrin added.

"And he gave me back my body," Mycrowski agreed.

Marrin knew what he had to do, and he thanked God for the foresight of Psi-Health. Nevertheless, he delayed for a moment.

"Then if I understand correctly, all this—the infection of Ecks, his miraculous rescues, all the deviousness you used, was designed to create a force great enough to get you back in your body?"

"That's a part of it," Mycrowski said. "Another part is the creation, in Ecks, of another para-psi."

"Very well," Marrin said. "It will interest you to know that Psi-Health has always considered, as one possibility, the return of The Sleeper—insane. Against that eventuality, this room is wired for atomic explosion. All four walls, ceiling, and roof are keyed to me. Atomic explosions are not instantaneous, I realize." He smiled humorlessly. "But then, I doubt if para-psi transit is, either.

"My thought-processes are as fast as yours. I am going to explode this place."

"You health men *are* a suspicious lot," Mycrowski said. "But why on earth would you want to do a thing like that?" Marrin noticed that he seemed genuinely surprised.

"*Why?* Do you realize what you have done? You have regained your body. But the disease is uncontrollable now. Psi science and all it stands for is destroyed, because of your selfishness." Mentally, Marrin reached for the key.

"Wait!" Ecks said. "Evidently you don't understand. There'll be a temporary disturbance, true. But it won't affect everyone at once. Diseased persons can be trained."

"Trained? To what?"

"Para-psi, of course," Ecks said. "A complete rechanneling is necessary to reach the next para-psychological step. The disease is the initial point. The present level of psi is unstable, anyhow. If I didn't set it off, someone else would in a few years."

"It'll be easier when we get a few more people to bridge the gap," Mycrowski said. "As in the first development of psi, the rest is relatively easy after the initial gain has been made."

Marrin shook his head. "How can I believe you?"

"How? *Look!*"

Telepathy transmits delicate shades of meaning quite lost in spoken language. A 'true' statement, teleped, reveals immediately how 'true' the sender believes it to be. There are an infinite number of gradations to the 'truth.'

As Ecks had, Marrin read Mycrowski's belief in the para-psi—read it clear down to the subconscious level. An unimaginably 'true' truth! There was no possible argument.

Suddenly Cari smiled. She had had one of her flash premonitions—a pleasant one.

"Help me up," Mycrowski said to Marrin. "Let me outline my training program." Marrin walked over to help him.

Then Ecks grinned. He had just read Cari's premonition.

THE CASTAWAY

Charles E. Fritch

As Ray Bradbury examined the life of a man alone on Mars, so Charles Fritch deals with a similar spaceman, cast on an alien shore to survive or die. The protagonist, Jordan, is a dreamer, a man whose life flowers only in a star-filled universe. His struggle to embrace that universe forms the theme of this unusual story.

Having turned to other areas of writing, Charles E. Fritch no longer works within the SF field. "The Castaway," printed in 1963 in the second issue of Gamma, is one of his last science fictional efforts. It is also one of his best.

HE DIDN'T KNOW how long he had been here. In this world of eternal day there was no way of telling the passage of time. The spaceship's chronometer was dead, as the spaceship itself was dead, as someday he would be dead. The rocket had crashed on this oxygen planet, breathed its last mechanical sigh, and died.

Jordan—that was his name; that much he knew. He'd forgotten a great many things during the long years, but those things didn't matter. Jordan was his name, and he clung to the identity with the grasp of a dying man.

A dying man, he thought. How long? How long?

Between the twin suns the planet rotated slowly, warmed and illuminated first by one sun and then by the other. There was no need for clothing, for the air was warm, and besides, all his clothing had crumbled into dust long ago. How long? Months, years, decades?

Ageless and yet aging. He found himself growing old without the discomforts of growing old. After a while, he didn't even mind being alone. It was terrible at first. If only the radio had worked, even if only the receiver, so he could hear a human voice; but the twin suns blocked communication. And after a while, after a long while, he forgot about it.

He remembered the crash and the darkness that followed. He recalled approaching this planet with his spaceship wobbling, bursting spasmodic jets of flame through torn tubes, frantically working controls that wouldn't respond as they should, forcing him toward the twin suns, toward the single planet between the twin suns. His heart held no hope; he had expected to die.

But he was alive. He remembered sitting up and feeling his bones and stretching and wondering at this miracle. Fifty yards away the spaceship lay, a broken metal hulk that should have been his coffin. Great gaping wounds stood from it like evil sores, and mechanical veins sprouted lifeless from the holes. It was a miracle he had lived. A second miracle that the planet contained an atmosphere he could breathe without discomfort.

But greater miracles were forthcoming.

He took small handweapons from the spaceship and explored the planet. It was very much like his Earth, but much smaller. The gravity was similar. There was green grass and there were evergreen trees and there were small ponds and rivers which reflected the sky and the great yellow suns and there was even a small ocean. He stood at the edge of this ocean and wondered what lay beyond. Years—or was it decades?—later he found out. He wandered across the face of the planet, occasionally building crude but serviceable rafts to navigate bodies of water, and found the world the same as it was where he had crashed. There were no intelligent creatures to be found.

There were animals which looked like squirrels, others which resembled deer; the waters held a multicolored fish not too unlike those of Earth. This offered some consolation. He even made friends with one squirrel-like animal, calling it "Friday."

If any ships flew near the planet they might see the crashed rocket and investigate; that was his hope. Often he shaded his eyes from the glare of the sun and gazed into the bright sky, searching for a gleam of metal, but he found none.

Food was everywhere. Fruits and berries could be had for the reaching, and small animals could easily be caught. But he wasn't hungry. At first this puzzled him. After the crash he'd taken inventory of his rations aboard the spaceship, mentally calculating how long they'd last. After several days—or what he considered to be several days—he tried to force rations down his throat, thinking he would starve if he didn't. But the food was repugnant, and he felt worse for having tried to eat it.

He looked into the cracked mirror aboard the spaceship at his smooth young features. I'm twenty-six now, he thought; how old will I be when I'm rescued—or will I spend the rest of my life here?

At that thought, he angrily picked up a stool and smashed his only mirror into fragments. He had cause to regret that, for later when he looked into ponds of clear water that bore his reflection he tried to see what lines lay in his features to calculate how long he had been on this planet. After a while, he forgot about it.

He forgot about most things. Most things, but not all. At first, he strained and fretted and cursed and glanced a thousand times at the empty sky. But calmness returned. His mind grew placid and reasonably content. Only one thing remained to torment him.

Space. Its cool reaches out there just beyond that sun, out in that yellowness that becomes black as the blackest velvet, with the stars like blazing diamonds. He was twenty-six, and all of space lay before him like a great challenge, like a beckoning finger, inviting.

"No one could ever know what it meant to me," he told Friday. "It was an obsession. I remember when I was in my 'teens, the way I used to stand and stare at the stars. I'd spend the whole night just standing there and watching the stars whirling about the heavens, looking at the universe as though it were a great celestial circus. And I'd say to myself, 'Someday, I'm going out there. Someday I'm going out there and take apart some of those flaming pinwheels and see what they're made of. I'll go farther than anyone has ever gone before, and then farther than that. I'll discover suns and worlds no one has ever known existed, and I'll find out if the universe is round after all, and if it is I'll find out what's on the outside of it.' "

Jordan laughed. Friday sat on a nearby rock contemplating the Earthman with large round eyes that looked thoughtful.

"It was a good dream, Friday, but only a dream. You'll never know how I felt about it. This is your world, your planet. You can climb the highest tree on it and look down on the world and know you've accomplished what you've set out to do. Not me."

He looked up and shrugged. "And yet I haven't seen a star or the night sky in—how long has it been?"

Friday looked up at him sympathetically. Jordan laughed and reached out to pet the animal.

"You're a good friend," Jordan said. "Not many friends would be so patient."

It was good to have someone to talk to. Jordan was grateful. And then, suddenly—or *was* it suddenly?—the time came when the animal was gone. Jordan found him dead a short distance from his tree home.

Jordan cried unashamedly, remembering the times they'd spent together, with the Earthman tossing a berry for the animal to scamper for, with Friday occasionally making some small chattering noise.

But death was real, and came without regard for friendship.

He buried Friday beneath the tree that was his home, and then stood for a moment, eyes misted, staring at the grave. A sudden chattering brought his eyes upward, to the crotch of a tree, where another animal squatted on its haunches and regarded him with frank curiosity.

"Friday," Jordan breathed.

No, that was impossible. There were differences, even among the animals. A subtle difference in the placement of colors on the fur, a tapering to the ears and the bushy tail, an individual idiosyncrasy even in the automatic twitching of the nose.

Jordan turned away sadly and went back to the rocket. The spaceship was a skeleton now, almost toppling beneath its own weight. He didn't look at it. He sat down in the sunlight.

The animal leaped upon a nearby rock, as Friday used to do, and regarded the Earthman.

"I wonder if you knew Friday," he said to the animal. "Maybe you were relatives. Perhaps a cousin. That's it, you look like you might be a cousin. He used to sit there just the way you're doing, and I used to tell him about the other worlds in this universe. He never complained about being limited to this planet. I wish I could be as content."

In the days that followed, Jordan grew to like the small furry animal. He called it Friday; he knew that Friday wouldn't mind, and at times it seemed to the Earthman that Friday actually lived in this animal.

"That's the advantage of a family," Jordan said. "Through offspring you achieve immortality, passing a part of yourself on from generation to generation, so that in a sense you actually live on after death. But what of my death?"

He didn't like to think of that. Not because he was afraid, because he wasn't. But there were so many things he had wanted to do, so many places out there in the universe to see, so much that it would take a million lifetimes to see only a small part of it.

At least, he thought, there should be night.

But there wasn't the slightest inkling that such a thing

could exist. The planet rotated at an even pace between
the two suns. When one sun was not in the sky, the other
was; when one left, the other appeared. And there was
no twilight period, no brief instant when a faint pinpoint
of starlight might pierce the atmosphere. Yet Jordan never
ceased to look for it.

During all the years, no spaceship came. His own ship
was red dust now. It takes a long time for metal to become dust. How long?

He looked into the quiet pools of water at his reflection
gazing back at him. It was an ancient face, wrinkled and
incredibly old. He looked at his hands, and at his naked
body, and found them the color and texture of burned
leather, with the bones showing through.

Dozens of Fridays had sat upon the rocks and patiently
listened to his story. He had forgotten many things, but
he never forgot the blackness of space and the stars that
might have shared his destiny. He buried each animal
tenderly, weeping for the friend he had lost. And each
time Friday came reincarnated to listen to him, to keep
him company during the long lonely vigil.

"I'm an old man," he said. "An old, old man."

He walked across the fields and among the trees and
down to the ocean. Soon he would not be able to do this.
He felt a gradual lessening of strength, an overall weakness that slowly crept over him. Now he remained in the
vicinity of the rocket crash, near the last few fragments.
He sat beneath a tree near the edge of the clearing.

"And here I'll die," he thought. The only regret he felt
was at not seeing the stars again. He sat quietly in the
shade. If he had required food, he would have starved,
for he lacked the strength to move. The animal often sat
nearby, a quizzical look on its squirrel features, as though
wondering why no sound came from the lips of this
strange creature that had once talked to it.

Jordan sat there thinking silently to himself. Jordan—
that was all that there was left now, the identity, the
name. How long would it be, he wondered, before even
consciousness left?

He waited.

He waited patiently while the planet rotated on its axis and the twin suns chased each other across the sky. He waited, dying, while the forest grew on around him, and animals came to stare at him and wonder. He waited, and his body grew brittle, until it seemed the skin would crack open like a dry riverbed baked in the sun. It seemed his bones were dry powder within him, as though his blood had ceased flowing.

When a gentle breeze came he could feel his body tremble like a leaf in a windstorm, as though it were a pattern of dust that would scatter in a meaningless cloud. He stared straight ahead with eyes that grew weak and weaker, staring at the empty stretch of clearing and the forest that lay beyond. He sat, not moving because he could not move, and thought of the stars he would never see.

He waited, while the years passed uncounted.

And one day the spaceship came.

It came down out of the yellow sky, all silver and flame, and settled in the clearing. It was a new ship, like a freshly minted coin, sturdy and powerful, with a promise of lightning velocities in its proud lines. Two men descended a ladder to the ground, tall Earthmen in spacesuits.

The Earthmen stopped by the rust fragments that were once a spaceship and looked down at them wondering. They walked cautiously about the clearing.

They don't see me, Jordan thought wildly, they don't see me sitting here by the tree. Here! Over here! I've been waiting for you!

But no sound came.

The two Earthmen returned to their spaceship, climbed the ladder. Jordan watched them enter the rocket, saw the airlock door swing shut. His last chance, about to blast off on wings of flame, forever.

He struggled. He tried to raise an arm, a leg, tried to move his lips, his head. He could feel his ancient body shudder gently under the strain, feel the very particles shake from a precarious balance.

And then, suddenly, he was free. He ran to the edge of

the forest, into the clearing, to the great silver ship. He stood beneath it and shouted, "Here, here I am! Look! Look down here! Don't take off yet! I've been waiting for you! Down here!"

But the rocket grumbled, and great sheets of golden flame swept down over him, blinding him, cutting off all sight of the grass and the trees and the sky.

The spaceship was gone, a dot that became less than a dot and then nothing, a memory, a dream. Sadly, Jordan turned away. At the foot of the tree where he had sat was a pattern of dust; he looked at it, puzzled for a moment, wondering.

He felt weightless. He felt he could fly. Experimentally, he rose from the ground. He flew. Below him, the forest grew small, the world became a round ball, with rivers and ponds and oceans in one vast panoramic view.

What did it mean? he wondered. What did it mean?

His body had grown old, and older, and then older still. It had grown so old that it had disintegrated at a movement, but that was not really death. And if it did not really die, but merely aged until it could age no longer—what would prevent the mind, the consciousness, from continuing on?

Jordan knew the answer: he was no longer planet bound, no longer prisoner to gravity. He knew it as he left the planet far, far below him, wrapped in its haze of atmosphere, as he swept past the nearest golden sun, brushing it with a mental finger. And then he was clear.

Night burst upon him like a velvet mantle, cool with ice-crystal patterns of stars. He hung poised for a brief moment, centuries of emotion flooding through him. He whirled excitedly then, looking this way and that.

Here were the stars, and the constellations, and the island universes, and the nebulae that curved and spiraled and stretched in great gaseous bands across the heavens like fiery jewels in some vast showcase. And here, and here, and here were the others, all of them, all of them waiting.

Softly, he spoke their names. They were old friends

not seen in too long a time. It would take a million lifetimes to visit only a small number of them, but he had
that and more.

"Which way first?" he wondered. "Which way?"

Around him, patiently, the universe waited.

GHETTO

Poul Anderson

Poul Anderson offers solid proof that quantity does not always affect quality. (At least in the case of a truly talented writer!) Anderson is one of the most prolific of science fiction wordsmiths, having turned out some 175 stories in the 1951–1965 period alone, many of them of novelet length. Yet his quality level remains high.

"Ghetto," the movingly poetic story chosen for this anthology, was written in the Golden Age of Boucher and McComas' Fantasy and Science Fiction, in the mid-Fifties. In it, Anderson creates a colony of starmen, outcasts on their own home planet, hated by the people they serve, segregated and reduced to second-class citizenship. Here is a truly unique love story, written with sensitivity and compassion, which projects a startling group portrait of tomorrow's far space voyagers.

THE MONORAIL set them off at Kith Town, on the edge of the great city. Its blaze of light, red and gold and green looped between high slim towers, pulsed in the sky above them, but here it was dark and still, night had come. Kenri Shaun stood for a moment with the others, shifting awkwardly on his feet and wondering what to say. They knew he was going to resign, but the Kithman's rule of privacy kept the words from their lips.

"Well," he said at last, "I'll be seeing you around."

"Oh, sure," said Graf Kishna. "We won't be leaving Earth again for months yet."

After a pause, he added: "We'll miss you when we do go. I—wish you'd change your mind, Kenri."

"No," said Kenri. "I'm staying. But thanks."

"Come see us," invited Graf. "We'll have to get a bunch together for a poker game sometime soon."

"Sure. Sure I will."

Graf's hand brushed Kenri's shoulder, one of the Kith gestures which said more than speech ever could. "Goodnight," he spoke aloud.

"Goodnight."

Words murmured in the dimness. They stood there for an instant longer, half a dozen men in the loose blue doublets, baggy trousers, and soft shoes of the Kith in Town. There was a curious similarity about them, they were all of small and slender build, dark-complexioned, but it was the style of movement and the expression of face which stamped them most. They had looked on strangeness all their lives, out between the stars.

Then the group dissolved and each went his own way. Kenri started toward his father's place. There was a thin chill in the air, the northern pole was spinning into autumn, and Kenri hunched his shoulders and jammed his hands into his pockets.

The streets of the Town were narrow concrete strips, nonluminous, lit by old-style radiant globes. These threw a vague whiteness on lawns and trees and the little half-underground houses set far back from the roads. There weren't many people abroad: an elderly officer, grave in mantle and hood; a young couple walking slowly, hand in hand; a group of children tumbling on the grass; small lithe forms filling the air with their laughter, filling themselves with the beauty and mystery which were Earth. They might have been born a hundred years ago, some of those children, and looked on worlds whose very suns were invisible here, but always the planet drew men home again. They might cross the Galaxy someday, but always they would return to murmurous forests and galloping seas, rain and wind and swift-footed clouds, through all space and time they would come back to their mother.

Most of the hemispheres Kenri passed were dark, tended only by machines while their families flitted somewhere beyond the sky. He passed the home of a friend, Jong Errifrans, and wondered when he would see him again. The *Golden Flyer* wasn't due in from Betelgeuse for another Earth century, and by then the *Fleetwing*, Kenri's own ship, might well be gone—*No, wait, I'm staying here. I'll be a very old man when Jong comes back, still young and merry, still with a guitar across his shoulders and laughter on his lips. I'll be an Earthling then.*

The town held only a few thousand houses, and most of its inhabitants were away at any given time. Only the *Fleetwing*, the *Flying Cloud*, the *High Barbaree*, the *Our Lady*, and the *Princess Karen* were at Sol now: their crews would add up to about 1200, counting the children. He whispered the lovely, archaic names, savoring them on his tongue. Kith Town, like Kith society, was changeless; it had to be. When you traveled near the speed of light and time shrank so that you could be gone a decade and came back to find a century flown on Earth—And here was home, where you were among your own kind and not a tommy who had to bow and wheedle the great merchants of Sol, here you could walk like a man. It wasn't true what they said on Earth, that tommies were rootless, without planet or history or loyalty. There was a deeper belongingness here than the feverish rise and warring and fall of Sol could ever know.

"—Good evening, Kenri Shaun."

He stopped, jerked out of his reverie, and looked at the young woman. The pale light of a street globe spilled across her long dark hair and down her slim shape. "Oh —" He caught himself and bowed. "Good evening to you, Theye Barinn. I haven't seen you in a long time. Two years, isn't it?"

"Not quite so long for me," she said. "The *High Barbaree* went clear to Vega last trip. We've been in orbit here about an Earth-month. The *Fleetwing* got in a couple of weeks ago, didn't she?"

Covering up, not daring to speak plainly. He knew she knew almost to the hour when the great spaceship had arrived from Sirius and taken her orbit about the home planet.

"Yes," he said, "but our astrogation computer was burned out and I had to stay aboard with some others and get it fixed."

"I know," she answered. "I asked your parents why you weren't in Town. Weren't you—impatient?"

"Yes," he said, and a thinness edged his tone. He didn't speak of the fever that had burned in him, to get away, get downside, and go to Dorthy where she waited for him among the roses of Earth. "Yes, of course, but the ship came first, and I was the best man for the job. My father sold my share of the cargo for me; I never liked business anyway."

Small talk, he thought, biting back the words, chatter eating away the time he could be with Dorthy. But he couldn't quite break away, Theye was a friend. Once he had thought she might be more, but that was before he knew Dorthy.

"Things haven't changed much since we left," she said. "Not in twenty-five Earth-years. The Star Empire is still here, with its language and its genetic hierarchy—a little bigger, a little more hectic, a little closer to revolt or invasion and the end. I remember the Africans were much like this, a generation or two before they fell."

"So they were," said Kenri. "So were others. So will still others be. But I've heard the Stars are clamping down on us."

"Yes." Her voice was a whisper. "We have to buy badges now, at an outrageous price, and wear them everywhere outside the Town. It may get worse. I think it will."

He saw that her mouth trembled a little under the strong curve of her nose, and the eyes turned up to his

were suddenly filmed with a brightness of tears. "Kenri—
is it true what they're saying about you?"

"Is what true?" Despite himself, he snapped it out.

"That you're going to resign? Quit the Kith—become
an . . . Earthling?"

"I'll talk about it later." It was a harshness in his
throat. "I haven't time now."

"But Kenri—" She drew a long breath and pulled her
hand back.

"Goodnight, Theye. I'll see you later. I have to hurry."

He bowed and went on, quickly, not looking back. The
lights and the shadows slid their bars across him as he
walked.

Dorthy was waiting, and he would see her tonight. But
just then he couldn't feel happy about it, somehow.

He felt like hell.

*She had stood at the vision port, looking out into a
dark that crawled with otherness, and the white light of
the ship's walls had been cool in her hair. He came softly
behind her and thought again what a wonder she was.
Even a millennium ago, such tall slender blondes had
been rare on Earth. If the human breeders of the Star
Empire had done nothing else, they should be remembered with love for having created her kind.*

*She turned around quickly, sensing him with a keenness
of perception he could not match. The silver-blue eyes
were enormous on him, and her lips parted a little, half
covered by one slim hand. He thought what a beautiful
thing a woman's hand was. "You startled me, Kenri
Shaun."*

"I am sorry, Freelady," he said contritely.

*"It—" She smiled with a hint of shakiness. "It is noth-
ing. I am too nervous—don't know interstellar space at
all."*

*It can be . . . unsettling, I suppose, if you aren't used
to it, Freelady," he said. "I was born between the stars,
myself."*

*She shivered faintly under the thin blue tunic. "It is
too big," she said. "Too big and old and strange for us,*

Kenri Shaun. I thought traveling between the planets was something beyond human understanding, but this—" Her hand touched his, and his fingers closed on it, almost against his own will. *"This is like nothing I ever imagined."*

"When you travel nearly at the speed of light," he said, covering his shyness with pedantry, "you can't expect conditions to be the same. Aberration displaces the stars, and Doppler effect changes the color. That's all, Freelady."

The ship hummed around them, as if talking to herself. Dorthy had once wondered what the vessel's robot brain thought—what it felt like to be a spaceship, forever a wanderer between foreign skies. He had told her the robot lacked consciousness, but the idea had haunted him since. Maybe only because it was Dorthy's idea.

"It's the time shrinking that frightens me most, perhaps," she said. Her hand remained in his, the fingers tightening. He sensed the faint wild perfume she wore, it was a heady draught in his nostrils. "You—I can't get over the fact that you were born a thousand years ago, Kenri Shaun. That you will still be traveling between the stars when I am down in dust."

It was an obvious opening for a compliment, but his tongue was locked with awkwardness. He was a spacefarer, a Kithman, a dirty slimy tommy, and she was Star-Free, unspecialized genius, the finest flower of the Empire's genetic hierarchy. He said only: "It is no paradox, Freelady. As the relative velocity approaches that of light, the measured time interval decreases, just as the mass increases; but only to a 'stationary' observer. One set of measurements is as 'real' as another. We're running with a tau factor of about 33 this trip, which means that it takes us some four months to go from Sirius to Sol; but to a watcher at either star, we'll take almost eleven years." His mouth felt stiff, but he twisted it into a smile. "That's not so long, Freelady. You'll have been gone, let's see, twice eleven plus a year in the Sirian System— twenty-four years. Your estates will still be there."

"Doesn't it take an awful reaction mass?" she asked. A

fine line appeared on the broad forehead as she frowned, trying to understand.

"No, Freelady. Or, rather, it does, but we don't have to expel matter as an interplanetary ship must. The field drive reacts directly against the mass of local stars—theoretically the entire universe—and converts our mercury 'ballast' into kinetic energy for the rest of the ship. It acts equally on all mass, so we don't experience acceleration pressure and can approach light-speed in a few days. In fact, if we didn't rotate the ship, we'd be weightless. When we reach Sol, the agoratron will convert the energy back into mercury atoms and we'll again be almost stationary with respect to Earth."

"I'm afraid I never was much good at physics," she laughed. "We leave that to Star-A and Norm-A types on Earth."

The sense of rejection was strangling in him. Yes, he thought, brain work and muscle work are still just work. Let the inferiors sweat over it, Star-Frees need all their time just to be ornamental. *Her fingers had relaxed, and he drew his hand back to him.*

She looked pained, sensing his hurt, and reached impulsively out to touch his cheek. "I'm sorry," she said quietly. "I didn't mean to . . . I didn't mean what you think."

"It is nothing, Freelady," he said stiffly, to cover his bewilderment. That an aristocrat should apologize—!

"But it is much," she said earnestly. "I know how many people there are who don't like the Kith. You just don't fit into our society, you realize that. You've never really belonged on Earth." *A slow flush crept up her pale cheeks, and she looked down. Her lashes were long and smoky black.* "But I do know a little about people, Kenri Shaun. I know a superior type when I meet it. You could be a Star-Free yourself, except . . . we might bore you."

"Never that, Freelady," he said thickly.

He had gone away from her with a singing in him. Three months, he thought gloriously, three ship-months yet before they came to Sol.

A hedge rustled dryly as he turned in at the Shaun gate. Overhead, a maple tree stirred, talking to the light wind, and fluttered a blood-colored leaf down on him. *Early frost this year,* he thought. The weather-control system had never been rebuilt after the Mechanoclasts abolished it, and maybe they had been right there. He paused to inhale the smell of the wind. It was cool and damp, full of odors from mould and turned earth and ripened berries. It struck him suddenly that he had never been here during a winter. He had never seen the hills turn white and glittering, or known the immense hush of snowfall.

Warm yellow light spilled out to make circles on the lawn. He put his hand on the doorplate, it scanned his pattern and the door opened for him. When he walked into the small, cluttered living room, crowded with half a dozen kids, he caught the lingering whiff of dinner and regretted being too late for it. He'd eaten on shipboard, but there was no cook in the Galaxy quite like his mother.

He saluted his parents as custom prescribed, and his father nodded gravely. His mother was less restrained, she hugged him and said how thin he had gotten. The kids said hello and went back to their books and games and chatter. They'd seen their older brother often enough, and were too young to realize what his decision of resigning meant.

"Come, Kenri, I will fix a sandwich for you at least—" said his mother. "It is good to have you back."

"I haven't time," he said. Helplessly: "I'd like to, but —well—I have to go out again."

She turned away. "Theye Barinn was asking about you," she said, elaborately casual. "The *High Barbaree* got back an Earth-month ago."

"Oh, yes," he said. "I met her on the street."

"Theye is a nice girl," said his mother. "You ought to go call on her. It's not too late tonight."

"Some other time," he said.

"The *High Barbaree* is off to Tau Ceti in another two months," said his mother. "You won't have much chance to see Theye, unless—" Her voice trailed off. *Unless you marry her. She's your sort, Kenri. She would belong well on the* Fleetwing. *She would give me strong grandchildren.*

"Some other time," he repeated. He regretted the brusqueness in his tone, but he couldn't help it. Turning to his father: "Dad, what's this about a new tax on us?"

Volden Shaun scowled. "A damned imposition," he said. "May all their spacesuits spring leaks. We have to wear these badges now, and pay through the nose for them."

"Can . . . can I borrow yours for tonight? I have to go into the city."

Slowly, Volden met the eyes of his son. Then he sighed and got up. "It's in my study," he said. "Come along and help me find it."

They entered the little room together. It was filled with Volden's books—he read on every imaginable subject, like most Kithmen—and his carefully polished astrogation instruments and his mementos of other voyages. It all meant something. That intricately chased sword had been given him by an armorer on Procyon V, a many-armed monster who had been his friend. That stereograph was a view of the sharp hills on Isis, frozen gases like molten amber in the glow of mighty Osiris. That set of antlers was from a hunting trip on Loki, in the days of his youth. That light, leaping statuette had been a god on Dagon. Volden's close-cropped gray head bent over the desk, his hands fumbling among the papers.

"Do you really mean to go through with this resignation?" he asked quietly.

Kenri's face grew warm. "Yes," he said. "I'm sorry, but —Yes."

"I've seen others do it," said Volden. "They even prospered, most of them. But I don't think they were ever very happy."

"I wonder," said Kenri.

"The *Fleetwing's* next trip will probably be clear to Rigel," said Volden. "We won't be back for more than a thousand years. There won't be any Star Empire here. Your very name will be forgotten."

"I heard talk about that voyage." Kenri's voice thickened a little. "It's one reason I'm staying behind."

Volden looked up, challengingly. "What's so good about the Stars?" he asked. "I've seen twelve hundred years of human history, good times and bad times. This is not one of the good times. And it's going to get worse."

Kenri didn't answer.

"That girl is out of your class, son," said Volden. "She's a Star-Free. You're just a damn filthy tommy."

"The prejudice against us isn't racial," said Kenri, avoiding his father's gaze. "It's cultural. A spaceman who goes terrestrial is . . . all right by them."

"So far," said Volden. "It's beginning to get racial already, though. We may all have to abandon Earth for a while."

"I'll get into her class," said Kenri. "Give me that badge."

Volden sighed. "We'll have to overhaul the ship to raise our tau factor," he said. "You've got a good six months yet. We won't leave any sooner. I hope you'll change your mind."

"I might," said Kenri, and knew he lied in his teeth.

"Here it is." Volden held out a small yellow loop of braided cords. "Pin it on your jacket." He took forth a heavy wallet. "And here is a thousand decards of your money. You've got fifty thousand more in the bank, but don't let this get stolen."

Kenri fastened the symbol on. It seemed to have weight, like a stone around his neck. He was saved from deeper humiliation by the automatic reaction of his mind. Fifty thousand decards . . . what to buy? A spaceman necessarily invested in tangible and lasting property—

Then he remembered that he would be staying here. The money ought to have value during his lifetime, at least. And money had a way of greasing the skids of prejudice.

"I'll be back . . . tomorrow, maybe," he said. "Thanks, Dad. Goodnight."

Volden's gaunt face drew into tighter lines. His voice was toneless, but it caught just a little.

"Goodnight, son," he said.

Kenri went out the door, into the darkness of Earth.

The first time, neither of them had been much impressed. Captain Seralpin had told Kenri: "We've got us another passenger. She's over at Landfall, on Ishtar. Want to pick her up?"

"Let her stay there till we're ready to leave," said Kenri. "Why would she want to spend a month on Marduk?"

Seralpin shrugged: "I don't know or care. But she'll pay for conveyance here. Take Boat Five," he said.

Kenri had fueled up the little interplanetary flitter and shot away from the Fleetwing, *grumbling to himself. Ishtar was on the other side of Sirius at the moment, and even on an acceleration orbit it took days to get there. He spent the time studying Murinn's* General Cosmology, *a book he'd never gotten around to before though it was a good 2500 years old. There had been no basic advance in science since the fall of the African Empire, he reflected, and on Earth today the conviction was that all the important questions had been answered. After all, the universe was finite, so the scientific horizon must be too; after several hundred years during which research turned up no phenomenon not already predicted by theory, there would naturally be a loss of interest which ultimately became a dogma.*

Kenri wasn't sure the dogma was right. He had seen too much of the cosmos to have any great faith in man's ability to understand it. There were problems in a hundred fields—physics, chemistry, biology, psychology, history, epistemology—to which the Nine Books gave no quantitative answer; but when he tried to tell an Earthling that, he got a blank look or a superior smile. . . . No, science was a social enterprise, it couldn't exist when the society didn't want it. But no civilization lasts forever. Someday there would again be a questioning.

Most of the Fleetwing's *passengers were time-expired engineers or planters returning home. Few of the big ships had ever transported a Star aristocrat. When he* came down to Landfall, in a spuming rain, and walked through the hot wet streets and onto the bowered veran- dah of the town's hostel, it was a shock to find that his cargo was a young and beautiful woman. He bowed to her, crossing arms on breast as prescribed, and felt the stiffness of embarrassment. He was the outsider, the in- ferior, the space tramp, and she was one of Earth's own- ers.

"I hope the boat will not be too uncomfortable for you, Freelady," he mumbled, and hated himself for the obse- quiousness of it. He should have said, you useless brainless bitch, my people keep Earth alive and you ought to be kneeling to me in thanks. But he bowed again instead, and helped her up the ladder into the cramped cabin.

"I'll make out," she laughed. She was too young, he guessed, to have taken on the snotty manners of her class. The fog of Ishtar lay in cool drops in her hair, like small jewels. The blue eyes were not unfriendly as they rested on his sharp dark face.

He computed an orbit back to Marduk. "It'll take us four-plus days, Freelady," he said. "I hope you aren't in too much of a hurry."

"Oh, no," she said. "I just wanted to see that planet too, before leaving." He thought of what it must be cost- ing her, and felt a vague sense of outrage that anyone should throw good money around on mere tourism; but he only nodded.

They were in space before long. He emerged from his curtained bunk after a few hour's sleep to find her already up, leafing through Murinn. "I don't understand a word of it," she said. "Does he ever use one syllable where six will do?"

"He cared a great deal for precision, Freelady," said Kenri as he started breakfast. Impulsively, he added: "I would have liked to know him."

Her eyes wandered around the boat's library, shelf on shelf of microbooks and full-sized volumes. "You people do a lot of reading, don't you?" she asked.

Not too much else to do on a long voyage, Freelady," he said. "There are handicrafts, of course, and the preparation of goods for sale—things like that—but there's still plenty of time for reading."

"I'm surprised you have such big crews," she said. "Surely you don't need that many people to man a ship."

"No, Freelady," he replied. "A ship between the stars just about runs herself. But when we reach a planet, a lot of hands are needed."

"There's company, too, I suppose," she ventured. "Wives and children and friends."

"Yes, Freelady." His voice grew cold. What business of hers was it?

"I like your Town," she said. "I used to go there often. It's so—quaint? Like a bit of the past, kept alive all these centuries."

Sure, he wanted to say, sure, your sort come around to stare. You come around drunk, and peer into our homes, and when an old man goes by you remark what a funny little geezer he is, without even lowering your voices, and when you bargain with a shopkeeper and he tries to get a fair price it only proves to you that all tommies think of nothing but money. Oh, yes, we're very glad to have you visit us. "Yes, Freelady."

She looked hurt, and said little for many hours. After a while she went back into the space he had screened off for her, and he heard her playing a violin. It was a very old melody, older than man's starward wish, unbelievably old, and still it was young and tender and trustful, still it was everything which was good and dear in man. He couldn't quite track down the music, what was it—? After a while, she stopped. He felt a desire to impress her. The Kith had their own tunes. He got out his guitar and strummed a few chords and let his mind wander.

Presently he began to sing.

He sensed her come quietly out and stand behind him, but pretended not to be aware of her. His voice lilted between the thrumming walls, and he looked out toward cold stars and the ruddy crescent of Marduk.

He ended the song with a crash of strings and looked around and got up to bow.

"No . . . sit down," she said. *"This isn't Earth. What was that song?"*

"Jerry Clawson, Freelady," he replied. *"It's ancient—in fact, I was singing a translation from the original English. It goes clear back to the early days of interplanetary travel."*

Star-Frees were supposed to be intellectuals as well as esthetes. He waited for her to say that somebody ought to collect Kith folk ballads in a book.

"I like it," she said. *"I like it very much."*

He looked away. "Thank you, Freelady," he said. *"May I make bold to ask what you were playing earlier?"*

"Oh . . . that's even older," she said. *"A theme from the* Kreutzer Sonata. *I'm awfully fond of it."* She smiled slowly. *"I think I would have liked to know Beethoven."*

They met each other's eyes, then, and did not look away or speak for what seemed like a long time.

The Town ended as sharply as if cut off by a knife. It had been like that for 3000 years, a sanctuary from time: sometimes it stood alone on open windy moors, with no other work of man in sight except a few broken walls; sometimes it was altogether swallowed by a roaring monster of a city; sometimes, as now, it lay on the fringe of a great commune; but always it was the Town, changeless and inviolate.

No—not so. There had been days when war swept through it, pockmarking walls and sundering roofs and filling its streets with corpses; there had been murderous mobs looking for a tommy to lynch; there had been haughty swaggering officers come to enforce some new proclamation. They could return. Through all the endless turmoil of history, they would. Kenri shivered in the wandering autumn breeze and started off along the nearest avenue.

The neighborhood was a slum at the moment, gaunt crumbling tenements, cheerless lanes, aimlessly drifting crowds. They wore doublets and kilts of sleazy gray, and they stank. Most of them were Norms, nominally free—

which meant free to starve when there wasn't work to be had. The majority were Norm-Ds, low-class manual laborers with dull heavy faces, but here and there the more alert countenance of a Norm-C or B showed briefly in the glare of a lamp, above the weaving, sliding shadows. When a Standard pushed through, gay in the livery of the state or his private owner, something flickered in those eyes. A growing knowledge, a feeling that something was wrong when slaves were better off than freemen—Kenri had seen that look before, and knew what it could become: the blind face of destruction. And elsewhere were the men of Mars and Venus and the Jovian moons, yes, the Radiant of Jupiter had ambitions and Earth was still the richest planet. . . . No, he thought, the Star Empire wouldn't last much longer.

But it ought to last his and Dorthy's lifetime, and they could make some provision for their children. That was enough.

An elbow jarred into his ribs. "Outta the way, tommy!"

He clenched his fists, thinking of what he had done beyond the sky, what he could do here on Earth—silently, he stepped off the walk. A woman, leaning fat and blowsy from an upstairs window, jeered at him and spat. He dodged the fleck of spittle, but he could not dodge the laughter that followed him.

They hate, he thought. *They still don't dare resent their masters, so they take it out on us. Be patient. It cannot endure another two centuries.*

It still shook in him, though. He grew aware of the tautness in his nerves and belly, and his neck ached with the strain of keeping his face humbly lowered. Though Dorthy was waiting for him in a garden of roses, he needed a drink. He saw the winking neon bottle and turned in that door.

A few sullen men were slumped at tables, under the jerky obscenity of a live mural that must be a hundred years old. The tavern owned only half a dozen Standard-D girls, and they were raddled things who must have been bought third hand. One of them gave Kenri a mechanical smile, saw his face and dress and badge, and turned away with a sniff.

He made his way to the bar. There was a live tender who showed him a glazed stare. "Vodzan," said Kenri. "Make it a double."

"We don't serve no tommies here," said the bartender.

Kenri's fingers whitened on the bar. He turned to go, but a hand touched his arm. "Just a minute, spaceman." To the attendant: "One double vodzan."

"I told you—"

"This is for me, Wilm. And I can give it to anyone I want. I can pour it on the floor if I so desire." There was a thinness in the tone, and the bartender went quickly off to his bottles.

Kenri looked into a white, hairless face with a rakish cast to its skull structure. The lean gray-clad body was hunched over the bar, one hand idly rolling dice from a cup. There were no bones in the fingers, they were small delicate tentacles; and the eyes were colored like ruby.

"Thank you," said Kenri. "May I pay—"

"No. It's on me." The other accepted the glass and handed it over. "Here."

"Your health, sir." Kenri lifted the glass and drank. The liquor was pungent fire along his throat.

"Such as it is," said the man indifferently. "No trouble to me. What I say here goes." He was probably a petty criminal of some sort, perhaps a member of the now out-lawed Assassins' Guild. And the body type was not quite human. He must be a Special-X, created in the genetic labs for a particular job or for study or for amusement. Presumably he had been set free when his owner was done with him, and had made a place for himself in the slums.

"Been gone long?" he asked, looking at the dice.

"About twenty-three years," said Kenri. "Sirius."

"Things have changed," said the X. "Anti-Kithism is growing strong again. Be careful you aren't slugged or robbed, because if you are, it'll do you no good to appeal to the city guards."

"It's nice of you to—"

"Nothing." The slim fingers scooped up the dice and rattled the cup again. "I like somebody to feel superior to."

"Oh." Kenri set the glass down. For a moment, the smoky room blurred. "I see. Well—"

"No, don't go off." The ruby eyes lifted up to his, and he was surprised to see tears in them. "I'm sorry. You can't blame me for being bitter. I wanted to sign on myself, once, and they wouldn't have me."

Kenri said nothing.

"I would, of course, give my left leg to the breastbone for a chance to go on just one voyage," said the X dully. "Don't you think an Earthling has his dreams now and then—we too? But I wouldn't be much use. You have to grow up in space, damn near, to know enough to be of value on some planet Earth never heard of. And I suppose there's my looks too. Even the underdogs can't get together any more."

"They never could, sir," said Kenri.

"I suppose you're right. You've seen more of both space and time than I ever will. So I stay here, belonging nowhere, and keep alive somehow; but I wonder if it's worth the trouble. A man isn't really alive till he has something bigger than himself and his own little happiness, for which he'd gladly die. Oh, well." The X rolled out the dice. "Nine. I'm losing my touch." Glancing up again: "I know a place where they don't care who you are if you've got money."

"Thank you, sir, but I have business elsewhere," said Kenri awkwardly.

"I thought so. Well, go ahead, then. Don't let me stop you." The X looked away.

"Thank you for the drink, sir."

"It was nothing. Come in whenever you want, I'm usually here. But don't yarn about the planets out there. I don't want to hear that."

"Goodnight," said Kenri.

As he walked out, the dice clattered across the bar again.

Dorthy had wanted to do some surface traveling on Marduk, get to see the planet. She could have had her pick of the colony for escorts, but she chose to ask Kenri. One did not say no to a Star, so he dropped some promising negotiations for pelts with a native chief, hired a groundcar, and picked her up at the time she set.

They rode quietly for a while, until the settlement was lost behind the horizon. Here was stony desert, flamboyantly colored, naked crags and iron hills and low dusty thorn-trees sharp in the thin clear air. Overhead, the sky was a royal blue, with the shrunken disc of Sirius A and the brilliant spark of its companion spilling harsh light over the stillness.

"This is a beautiful world," she said at last. Her tones came muffled through the tenuous air. "I like it better than Ishtar."

"Most people don't, Freelady," he answered. "They call it dull and cold and dry."

"They don't know," she said. Her fair head was turned from him, looking at the fantastic loom of a nearby scarp, gnawed rocks and straggling brush, tawny color streaked with the blue and red lightning of mineral veins.

"I envy you, Kenri Shaun," she said at last. "I've seen a few pictures, read a few books—everything I could get hold of, but it isn't enough. When I think of all you have seen that is strange and beautiful and wonderful, I envy you."

He ventured a question: "Was that why you came to Sirius, Freelady?"

"In part. When my father died, we wanted someone to check on the family's Ishtarian holdings. Everyone assumed we'd just send an agent, but I insisted on going myself, and booked with the Temeraire. *They all thought I was crazy. Why, I'd come back to new styles, new slang, new people . . . my friends would all be middle-aged, I'd be a walking anachronism . . . you know." She sighed. "But it was worth it."*

He thought of his own life, the grinding sameness of the voyages, weeks slipping into months and years within a pulsing metal shell; approach, strangeness, the savage hostility of cruel planets—he had seen friends buried under landslides, spitting out their lungs when helmets cracked open in airlessness, rotting alive with some alien sickness; he had told them goodbye and watched them go off into a silence which never gave them back and had wondered how they came to die; and on Earth he was a ghost, not belonging, adrift above the great river of time, on Earth he felt somehow unreal. "I wonder, Freelady," he said.

"Oh, I'll adjust," she laughed.

The car ground its way over high dunes and down tumbling ravines, it left a track in the dust which the slow wind erased behind them. That night they camped near the ruins of a forgotten city, a place which must once have been a faerie spectacle of loveliness. Kenri set up the two tents and started a meal on the glower while she watched. "Let me help," she offered once.

"It isn't fitting, Freelady," he replied. And you'd be too clumsy anyway, you'd only make a mess of it. *His hands were deft on the primitive skillet. The ruddy light of the glower beat against darkness, etching their faces red in windy shadows. Overhead, the stars were high and cold.*

She looked at the sputtering meal. "I thought you . . . people never ate fish," *she murmured.*

"Some of us do, some don't, Freelady," *he said absently. Out here, it was hard to resent the gulf between them.* "It was originally tabooed by custom in the Kith back when space and energy for growing food on shipboard were at a premium. Only a rich man could have afforded an aquarium, you see; and a tight-knit group of nomads has to ban conspicuous consumption to prevent ill feeling. Nowadays, when the economic reason has long disappeared, only the older people still observe the taboo."

She smiled, accepting the plate he handed her. "It's funny," *she said.* "One just doesn't think of your people as having a history. You've always been around."

"Oh, we do, Freelady. We've plenty of traditions—more than the rest of mankind, perhaps."

A hunting marcat screamed in the night. She shivered. "What's that?"

"Local carnivore, Freelady. Don't let it worry you." He slapped his slug-thrower, obscurely pleased at a chance to show—what? Manliness? "No one with a weapon has to fear any larger animals. It's other things that make the danger—occasionally a disease, more often cold or heat or poison gases or vacuum or whatever hell the universe can brew for us." He grinned, a flash of teeth in the dark lean face. "Anyway, if it ate us it would die pretty quickly. We're as poisonous to it as it is to us."

"Different biochemistry and ecology," she nodded. "A billion or more years of separate evolution. It would be strange, wouldn't it, if more than a very few planets had developed life so close to Earth's that we could eat it. I suppose that's why there never was any real extrasolar colonization—just a few settlements for mining or trading or extracting organic chemicals."

"That's partly it, Freelady," he said. "Matter of economics, too. It was much easier—in money terms, cheaper —for people to stay at home; no significant percentage of them could ever have been taken away in any event— human breeding would have raised the population faster than emigration could lower it."

She gave him a steady look. When she spoke, her voice was soft. "You Kithmen are a brainy lot, aren't you?"

He knew it was true, but he made the expected disclaimer.

"No, no," she said. "I've read up on your history a little. Correct me if I'm wrong, but since the earliest times of space travel the qualifications have been pretty rigid. A spaceman just had to be of high intelligence, with quick reactions and stable personality both. And he couldn't be too large, physically; but he had to be tough. And a dark complexion must be of some small help, now and then, in strong sunlight or radiation. . . . Yes, that was how it was. How it still is. When women began going to space too, the trade naturally tended to run in families. Those spacemen who didn't fit into the life, dropped out; and the recruits from Sol were pretty similar in mind and body to the people they joined. So eventually you got the Kith— almost a separate race of man; and it evolved its own *ways of living. Until at last you had a monopoly on space traffic."*

"No, Freelady," he said. "We've never had that. Anyone who wants to build a spaceship and man it himself, can do so. But it's an enormous capital investment; and after the initial glamour had worn off, the average Solarian just wasn't interested in a hard and lonely life. So today, all spacemen are Kithmen, but it was never planned that way."

"That's what I meant," she said. Earnestly: "And your being different naturally brought suspicion and discrimination. . . . No, don't interrupt, I want to say this through. . . . Any conspicuous minority which offers competition to the majority is going to be disliked. Sol has to have the fissionables you being from the stars, we've used up our own; and the unearthly chemicals you bring are often of great value, and the trade in luxuries like furs and jewels is brisk. So you are essential to society, but you still don't really belong in it. You are too proud, in your own way, to ape your oppressors. Being human, you naturally charge all the traffic will bear, which gives you the reputation of being gougers; being able to think better and faster than the average Solarian, you can usually best him in a deal, and he hates you for it. Then there's the tradition handed down from Mechanoclastic times, when technology was considered evil and only you maintained a high level of it. And in the puritan stage of the Martian conquest, your custom of wife trading—oh, I know you do it just to relieve the endless monotony of the voyages, I know you have more family life than we do—Well, all those times are gone, but they've left their legacy. I wonder why you bother with Earth at all. Why you don't all just wander into space and let us stew in our own juice.".

"Earth is our planet too, Freelady," he said, very quietly. After a moment: "The fact that we are essential gives us some protection. We get by. Please don't feel sorry for us."

"A stiff-necked people," she said. "You don't even want pity."

"Who does, Freelady?" he asked.

On the edge of the slum, in a zone bulking with the tall warehouses and offices of the merchant families, Kenri took an elevator up to the public skyway going toward the address he wanted. There was no one else in sight at that point; he found a seat and lowered himself into it and let the strip hum him toward city center.

The skyway climbed fast, until he was above all but the highest towers. Leaning an arm on the rail, he looked down into a night that was alive with radiance. The streets and walls glowed, strings of colored lamps flashed and flashed against a velvet dark, fountains leaped white and gold and scarlet, a flame display danced like molten rainbows at the feet of a triumphal statue. Star architecture was a thing of frozen motion, soaring columns and tiers and pinnacles to challenge the burning sky; high in that airy jungle, the spaceman could hardly make out the river of vehicles and humanity below him.

As he neared the middle of town, the skyway gathered more passengers. Standards in bright fantastic livery, Norms in their tunics and kilts, an occasional visitor from Mars or Venus or Jupiter with resplendent uniform and greedy smoldering eyes—yes, and here came a party of Frees, their thin garments a swirling iridescence about the erect slender forms, a hard glitter of jewels, the men's beards and the women's hair elaborately curled. Fashions had changed in the past two decades. Kenri felt acutely aware of his own shabbiness, and huddled closer to the edge of the strip.

Two young couples passed his seat. He caught a woman's voice: "Oh, look, a tommy!"

"He's got a nerve," mumbled one of the men. "I've half a mind to—"

"No, Scanish." Another feminine voice, gentler than the first. "He has the right."

"He shouldn't have. I know these tommies. Give 'em a finger and they'll take your whole arm." The four were settling into the seat behind Kenri's. "My uncle is in Transsolar Trading. He'll tell you."

"Please, no, Scanish, he's listening!"

"And I hope he—"

"Never mind, dear. What shall we do next? Go to Halgor's?" She attempted a show of interest.

"Ah, we've been there a hundred times. What is there to do? How about getting my rocket and shooting over to China? I know a place where they got techniques you never—"

"No. I'm not in the mood. I don't know what I want to do."

"My nerves have been terrible lately. We bought a new doctor, but he says just the same as the old one. They don't any of them know which end is up. I might try this new Beltanist religion, they seem to have something. It would at least be amusing."

"Say, have you heard about Marla's latest? You know who was seen coming out of her bedroom last ten-day?"

Kenri grabbed hold of his mind and forced it away from listening. He didn't want to. He wouldn't let the weariness and sickness of spirit which was the old tired Empire invade him.

Dorthy, he thought. *Dorthy Persis from Canda. It's a beautiful name, isn't it? There's music in it. And the from Candas have always been an outstanding family. She isn't like the rest of the Stars.*

She loves me, he thought with a singing in him. *She loves me. There is a life before us. Two of us, one life, and the rest of the Empire can rot as it will. We'll be together.*

He saw the skyscraper ahead of him now, a thing of stone and crystal and light that climbed toward heaven in one great rush. The insigne of the from Candas burned on its façade, an ancient and proud symbol. It stood for 300 years of achievement.

But that's less than my own lifetime. No, I don't have to be ashamed in their presence. I come of the oldest and best line of all humanity. I'll fit in.

He wondered why he could not shake off the depression that clouded him. This was a moment of glory. He should be going to her as a conqueror. But—

He sighed and rose as his stop approached.

Pain stabbed at him. He jumped, stumbled, and fell to

one knee. Slowly, his head twisted around. The young
Star grinned in his face, holding up a shockstick. Kenri's
hand rubbed the pain, and the four people began to laugh.
So did everyone else in sight. The laughter followed him
off the skyway and down to the ground.

*There was no one else on the bridge. One man was
plenty to stand watch, here in the huge emptiness between suns. The room was a hollow cavern of twilight,
quiet except for the endless throbbing of the ship. Here
and there, the muted light of instrument panels glowed,
and the weird radiance of the distorted stars flamed in the
viewport. But otherwise there was no illumination, Kenri
had switched it off.*

She came through the door and paused, her gown white
in the dusk. His throat tightened as he looked at her, and
when he bowed, his head swam. There was a faint sweet
rustling as she walked closer. She had the long swinging
stride of freedom, and her unbound hair floated silkily
behind her . . .

"I've never been on a bridge before," she said. "I didn't
think passengers were allowed there."

"I invited you, Freelady," he answered, his voice catching.

"It was good of you, Kenri Shaun." Her fingers fluttered
across his arm. "You have always been good to me."

"Could anyone be anything else, to you?" he asked.

Light stole along her cheeks and into the eyes that
turned up at his. She smiled with a strangely timid curve
of lips. "Thank you," she whispered.

"Ah, I, well—" He gestured at the viewport, which
seemed to hang above their heads. "That is precisely on
the ship's axis of rotation, Freelady," he said. "That's why
the view is constant. Naturally, 'down' on the bridge is
any point at which you are standing. You'll note that the
desks and panels are arranged in a circle around the inner
wall, to take advantage of that fact." His voice sounded
remote and strange to his ears. "Now here we have the
astrogation computer. Ours is badly in need of overhauling

*just now, which is why you see all those books and cal-
culations on my desk—"*

Her hand brushed the back of his chair. "This is yours,
Kenri Shaun? I can almost see you working away on it,
with that funny tight look on your face, as if the problem
were your personal enemy. Then you sigh, and run your
fingers through your hair, and put your feet on the desk
to think for a while. Am I right?"

"How did you guess, Freelady?"

"I know. I've thought a great deal about you, lately."
She looked away, out to the harsh blue-white stars clus-
ered in the viewport.

Suddenly her fists gathered themselves. "I wish you
didn't make me feel so futile," she said.

"You—"

"This is life, here." She spoke swiftly, blurring the
words in her need to say them. "You're keeping Earth
alive, with your cargoes. You're working and fighting and
thinking about—about something real. Not about what to
wear for dinner and who was seen where with whom and
what to do tonight when you're too restless and unhappy
to stay quietly at home. You're keeping Earth alive, I
said, and a dream too. I envy you, Kenri Shaun. I wish I
were born into the Kith."

"Freelady—" It rattled in his throat.

"No use." She smiled, without self-pity. "Even if a ship
would have me, I could never go. I don't have the training, or the inborn strength, or the patience, or— No! Forget it." There were tears in the ardent eyes. "When I get
home, knowing now what you are in the Kith, will I even
try to help you? Will I work for more understanding of
your people, kindness, common decency? No. I'll realize
it's useless even to try. I won't have the courage."

"You'd be wasting your time, Freelady," he said. "No
one person can change a whole culture. Don't worry
about it."

"I know," she replied. "You're right, of course. You're
always right. But in my place, you would try!"

They stared at each other for a long moment.

That was the first time he kissed her.

The two guards at the soaring main entrance were giants, immobile as statues in the sunburst glory of their uniforms. Kenri had to crane his neck to look into the face of the nearest. "The Freelady Dorthy Persis is expecting me," he said.

"*Huh?*" Shock brought the massive jaw clicking down.

"That's right." Kenri grinned and extended the card she had given him. "She said to look her up immediately."

"But—there's a party going on—"

"Never mind. Call her up."

The guardsman reddened, opened his mouth, and snapped it shut again. Turning, he went to the visiphone booth. Kenri waited, regretting his insolence. *Give 'em a finger and they'll take your whole arm.* But how else could a Kithman behave? If he gave deference, they called him a servile bootlicker; if he showed his pride, he was an obnoxious pushing bastard; if he dickered for a fair price, he was a squeezer and bloodsucker; if he spoke his own old language to his comrades, he was being secretive; if he cared more for his skyfaring people than for an ephemeral nation, he was a traitor and coward; if—

The guard returned, shaking his head in astonishment. "All right," he said sullenly. "Go on up. First elevator to your right, fiftieth floor. But watch your manners, tommy."

When I'm adopted into the masters, thought Kenri savagely, *I'll make him eat that word.* Then, with a new rising of the unaccountable weariness: *No. Why should I? What would anyone gain by it?*

He went under the enormous curve of the door, into a foyer that was a grotto of luminous plastic. A few Standard servants goggled at him, but made no move to interfere. He found the elevator cage and punched for fifty. It rose in a stillness broken only by the sudden rapid thunder of his heart.

He emerged into an anteroom of red velvet. Beyond an arched doorway, he glimpsed colors floating, a human blaze of red and purple and gold; the air was loud with music and laughter. The footman at the entrance stepped

in his path, hardly believing the sight. "You can't go in
there!"

"The hell I can't." Kenri shoved him aside and strode
through the arch. The radiance hit him like a fist, and he
stood blinking at the confusion of dancers, servants, on-
lookers, entertainers—there must be a thousand people in
this vaulted chamber.

"Kenri! Oh, Kenri—"

She was in his arms, pressing her mouth to his, drawing his head down with shaking hands. He strained her
close, and the misty cloak she wore whirled about to
wrap them in aloneness.

One moment, and then she drew back breathlessly,
laughing a little. It wasn't quite the merriment he had
known, there was a thin note to it, and shadows lay under
the great eyes. She was very tired, he saw, and pity lifted
in him. "Dearest," he whispered.

"Kenri, not here . . . Oh, darling, I hoped you would
come sooner, but—No, come with me now, I want them
all to see the man I've got me." She took his hand and
half dragged him forward. The dancers were stopping,
pair by pair as they noticed the stranger, until at last
there were a thousand faces stiffly turned to his. Silence
dropped like a thunderclap, but the music kept on. It
sounded tinny in the sudden quiet.

Dorthy shivered. Then she threw back her head with a
defiance that was dear to him and met the eyes. Her arm
rose to bring the wristphone to her lips, and the ceiling
amplifiers boomed her voice over the room: "Friends, I
want to announce . . . Some of you already know . . .
well, this is the man I'm going to marry—"

It was the voice of a frightened little girl. Cruel to
make it loud as a goddess talking.

After a pause which seemed to last forever, somebody
performed the ritual bow. Then somebody else did, and
then they were all doing it, like jointed dolls. There were
a few scornful exceptions, who turned their backs.

"Go on!" Dorthy's tones grew shrill. "Go on dancing.
Please! You'll all—later—" The orchestra leader must
have had a degree of sensitivity, for he struck up a noisy

tune and one by one the couples slipped into a figure dance.

Dorthy looked hollowly up at the spaceman. "It's good to see you again," she said.

"And you," he replied.

"Come." She led him around the wall. "Let's sit and talk."

They found an alcove, screened from the room by a trellis of climbing roses. It was a place of dusk, and she turned hungrily to him. He felt how she trembled.

"It hasn't been easy for you, has, it?" he asked tonelessly.

"No," she said.

"If you—"

"Don't say it!" There was fear in the words. She closed his mouth with hers.

"I love you," she said after a while. "That's all that matters, isn't it?"

He didn't answer.

"Isn't it?" she cried.

He nodded. "Maybe. I take it your family and friends don't approve of your choice."

"Some don't. Does it matter, darling? They'll forget, when you're one of us."

"One of you—I'm not born to this," he said bleakly. "I'll always stick out like—Well, never mind. I can stand it if you can."

He sat on the padded bench, holding her close, and looked out through the clustered blooms. Color and motion and high harsh laughter—it wasn't his world. He wondered why he had ever assumed it could become his.

They had talked it out while the ship plunged through night. She could never be of the Kith. There was no room in a crew for one who couldn't endure worlds never meant for man. He would have to join her instead. He could fit in, he had the intelligence and adaptability to make a place for himself.

What kind of place? he wondered as she nestled against him. A planner of more elaborate parties, a purveyor of trivial gossip, a polite ear for boredom and stupidity and cruelty and perversion—No, there would be Dorthy, they would be alone in the nights of Earth and that would be enough.

Would it? A man couldn't spend all his time making love.

There were the big trading firms, he could go far in one of them. (Four thousand barrels of Kalian jung oil rec'd pr. acct., and the fierce rains and lightning across the planet's phosphorescent seas. A thousand refined thorium ingots from Hathor, and moonlight sparkling the crisp snow and the ringing winter stillness. A bale of green furs from a newly discovered planet, and the ship had gone racing through stars and splendor into skies no man had ever seen.) Or perhaps the military. (Up on your feet, soldier! Hup, hup, hup, hup! . . . Sir, the latest Intelligence report on Mars . . . Sir, I know the guns aren't up to spec but we can't touch the contractor, his patron is a Star-Free. . . . The General commands your presence at a banquet for staff officers. . . . Now tell me, Colonel Shaun, tell me what you *really* think will happen, you officers are all so *frightfully* close-mouthed. . . . Ready! Aim! Fire! So perish all traitors to the Empire!) Or even the science centers. (Well, sir, according to the book, the formula is . . .)

Kenri's arm tightened desperately about Dorthy's waist. "How do you like being home?" he asked. "Otherwise, I mean."

"Oh—fine. Wonderful!" She smiled uncertainly at him. "I was so afraid I'd be old-fashioned, out of touch, but no, I fell in right away. There's the most terribly amusing crowd, a lot of them children of my own old crowd. You'll love them, Kenri. I have a lot of glamour, you know, for going clear to Sirius. Think how much you'll have!"

"I won't," he grunted. "I'm just a tommy, remember?"

"Kenri!" Anger flicked across her brow. "What a way to talk. You aren't, and you know it, and you won't be unless you insist on thinking like one all the time—" She caught herself and said humbly: "I'm sorry, darling. That was a terrible thing to say, wasn't it?"

He stared ahead of him.

"I've been, well, infected," she said. "You were gone so long. You'll cure me again."

Tenderness filled him, and he kissed her.

"A-hum! Pardon!"

They jerked apart, almost guiltily, and looked up to the two who had entered the alcove. One was a middle-aged man, austerely slender and erect, his night-blue tunic flashing with decorations; the other was younger, pudgy-faced, and rather drunk. Kenri got up. He bowed with his arms straight, as one equal to another.

"Oh, you must meet, I know you'll like each other—" Dorthy was speaking fast, her voice high. "This is Kenri Shaun. I've told you enough about him, haven't I?" A nervous little laugh. "Kenri, my uncle, Colonel from Canda of the Imperial Staff, and my nephew, the Honorable Lord Doms. Fancy coming back and finding you have a nephew your own age!"

"Your honor, sir." The colonel's voice was as stiff as his back. Doms giggled.

"You must pardon the interruption," went on from Canda. "But I wished to speak to . . . to Shaun as soon as possible. You will understand, sir, that it is for the good of my niece and the whole family."

Kenri's palms were cold and wet. "Of course," he said. "Please sit down."

"Thank you." From Canda lowered his angular frame onto the bench, next to the Kithman; Doms and Dorthy sat at opposite ends, the young man slumped over and grinning. "Shall I send for some wine?"

"Not for me, thanks," said Kenri huskily.

The cold eyes were level on his. "First," said the colonel, "I want you to realize that I do not share this absurd race prejudice which is growing up about your people. It is demonstrable that the Kith is biologically equal to the Star families, and doubtless superior to some." His glance flickered contemptuously over to Doms. "There is a large cultural barrier, of course, but if that can be surmounted, I, for one, would be glad to sponsor your adoption into our ranks."

"Thank you, sir." Kenri felt dizzy. No Kithman had

ever gone so high in all history. That it should be *him*—!
He heard Dorthy's happy little sigh as she took his arm,
and something of the frozenness within him began to
thaw. "I'll . . . do my best—"

"But will you? That is what I have to find out." From
Canda leaned forward, clasping his gaunt hands between
his knees. "Let us not mince words. You know as well as
I that there is a time of great danger ahead for the Empire, and that if it is to survive the few men of action left
must stand together and strike hard. We can ill afford the
weaklings among us; we can certainly not afford to have
strong men in our midst who are not wholeheartedly for
our cause."

"I'll be . . . loyal, sir," said Kenri. "What more can I
do?"

"Much," said the colonel. "Considerable of it may be
distasteful to you. Your special knowledge could be of
high value. For example, the new tax on the Kith is not
merely a device to humiliate them. We need the money.
The Empire's finances are in bad shape, and even that
little bit helps. There will have to be further demands, on
the Kith as well as everyone else. You can assist us in
guiding our policy, so that they are not goaded to the
point of abandoning Earth altogether."

"I—" Kenri swallowed. He felt suddenly ill. "You can't
expect—"

"If you won't, then you won't, and I cannot force you,"
said from Canda. There was a strange brief sympathy in
the chill tones. "I am merely warning you of what lies
ahead. You could mitigate the lot of your . . . former . . .
people considerably, if you help us."

"Why not . . . treat them like human beings?" asked
Kenri. "We'll always stand by our friends."

"Three thousand years of history cannot be canceled by
decree," said from Canda. "You know that as well as I."

Kenri nodded. It seemed to strain his neck muscles.

"I admire your courage," said the aristocrat. "You have
started on a hard road. Can you follow it through?"

Kenri looked down.

"Of course he can," said Dorthy softly.

Lord Doms giggled. "New tax," he said. "Slap a new one on fast. I've got one tommy skipper on the ropes already. Bad voyage, debts, heh!"

Red and black and icy blue, and the shriek of lifting winds.

"Shut up, Doms," said the colonel. "I didn't want you along."

Dorthy's head leaned back against Kenri's shoulder. "Thank you, uncle," she said. There was a lilt in her voice. "If you'll be our friend, it will all work out."

"I hope so," said from Canda.

The faint sweet odor of Dorthy's hair was in Kenri's nostrils. He felt the gold waves brushing his cheek, but still didn't look up. There was thunder and darkness in him.

Doms laughed. "I got to tell you 'bout this spacer," he said. "He owes the firm money, see? I can take his daughter under contract if he doesn't pay up. Only his crew are taking up a collection for him. I got to stop that somehow. They say those tommy girls are mighty hot. How about it, Kenri? You're one of us now. How are they, really? Is it true that—"

Kenri stood up. He saw the room swaying, and wondered dimly if he was wobbling on his feet or not.

"Doms," snapped from Canda, "if you don't shut your mouth—"

Kenri grabbed a handful of Lord Doms' tunic and hauled him to his feet. The other hand became a fist, and the face squashed under it.

He stood over the young man, weaving, his arms hanging loose at his sides. Doms moaned on the floor. Dorthy gave a small scream. From Canda leaped up, clapping his hand to a sidearm.

Kenri lifted his eyes. There was a thickness in his words. "Go ahead and arrest me," he said. "Go on, what are you waiting for?"

"K-K-Kenri—" Dorthy touched him with shaking hands.

From Canda grinned and nudged Doms with a boot.

"That was foolish of you, Kenri Shaun," he said, "but the job was long overdue. I'll see that nothing happens to you."

"But this Kith girl——"

"She'll be all right too, I daresay, if her father can raise that money." The hard eyes raked Kenri's face. "But remember, my friend, you cannot live· in two worlds at once. You are not a Kithman any longer."

Kenri straightened. He knew a sudden dark peace, as if all storms had laid themselves to rest. His head felt a little empty, but utterly clear.

It was a memory in him which had opened his vision and shown him what he must do, the only thing he could do. There was a half-human face and eyes without hope and a voice which had spoken: *"A man isn't really alive till he has something bigger than himself and his own little happiness, for which he'd gladly die."*

"Thank you, sir," he said. "But I am a Kithman. I will always be."

"*Kenri*—" Dorthy's tone broke. She held his arms and stared at him with wildness.

His hand stroked her hair. "I'm sorry, dearest," he said gently.

"Kenri, you can't go, you can't, you can't——"

"I must," he said. "It was bad enough that I should give up everything which had been my life for an existence that to me is stupid and dreary and meaningless. For you, I could have stood that. But you are asking me to be a tyrant, or at least to be a friend of tyrants. You're asking me to countenance evil. I can't do it. I wouldn't if I could." He took her shoulders and looked into the unseeing bewilderment of her eyes. "Because that would, in the end, make me hate you, who had so twisted my own self, and I want to go on loving you. I will always love you."

She wrenched away from him. He thought that there were psychological treatments to change her feelings and make her stop caring about him. Sooner or later, she'd take one of those. He wanted to kiss her farewell, but he didn't quite dare.

Colonel from Canda extended a hand. "You will be my enemy, I suppose," he said. "But I respect you for it. I like you, and wish—well, good luck to you, Kenri Shaun."

"And to you, sir . . . Goodbye, Dorthy."

He walked through the ballroom, not noticing the eyes that were on him, and out the door to the elevator. He was still too numb to feel anything, that would come later.

Theye Barinn is a nice girl, he thought somewhere on the edge of his mind. *I'll have to go around and see her soon. We could be happy together.*

It seemed like a long while before he was back in the Town. Then he walked along empty streets, alone within himself, breathing the cool damp night wind of Earth.

HAPPILY EVER AFTER

William F. Nolan

I always wanted to try a simple variation on the Garden of Eden theme. Finally I did. The result is short, direct, and, I sincerely hope, entertaining.

ON THE way back to Level 12, in the spacecab, Donald Spencer couldn't resist the impulse to sing. The android pilot looked curiously at him, and Spencer smiled.

"I'm just happy," he told the android. "Bought a rather expensive wedding present today—to celebrate the end of bachelorhood. I've been a married man for exactly—" He checked his wrist, "—six hours and twenty-seven minutes."

"Congratulations," said the pilot. "I hope that you and your wife will live happily ever after."

Spencer nodded at this ancient response. Feed an android information and the standard clichès emerge. But it *was* something to think about . . . living happily ever after.

Paula Spencer impatiently watched her husband step out of the humming spacecab. He waved a greeting as the Walk brought him swiftly down to her. Then he was in her arms.

"Well . . . where *is* it?" she demanded in mock-anger, stepping back. "You said you were going out to buy us a wedding present."

"And so I did." Spencer pointed skyward. "It's up there."

"What's up where?"

"Our wedding present," he grinned. "I bought us an asteroid."

"Don—you're joking!"

"Twenty thousand credits is no joke," he said. "We are now the legal owners of Asteroid K-157 in the Luani Cluster."

Stunned, Paula blinked at him. "But can we afford it?"

"It's a solid investment, honey," Spencer assured her. "Nobody loses money on asteroids these days. Now, I've arranged everything. We leave tonight for the Cluster. Our living quarters are all set up and waiting . . . so how's about a smile for your rich new husband?"

"Oh, I'll do better than that," Paula said—and brought her lips softly to his.

The trip out to the Cluster was perfect. As their new home swung into sight on the ship's wide viewscreen, Donald Spencer knew that he'd made a shrewd purchase. In ten years an asteroid would fetch at least 50,000 credits on the Earth market. The furiously expanding population guaranteed it. Some of his business friends had been skeptical, warning him against the deal, telling him that no one really knew much about the Luani Cluster, that he might run into trouble there—but Spencer ignored them. They were simply jealous of his business ability. In a few years Luani would be completely settled, and real estate would soar.

"Ready, darling?" he asked.

Paula Spencer nodded excitedly.

The couple shook hands with the Captain, then transferred to their personal landing craft. Spencer raised a hand—and a section of the passenger rocket's outer hull slid back. The small silver craft bulleted toward K-157, leaving the giant ship behind to continue its galactic voyage.

The landing was smooth—and Donald Spencer took his wife's hand after the atomic motor had stilled.

"Happy?"

"You *know* I am, Don."

"Then, c'mon. Meet your asteroid!"

They scrambled out of the ship. The air was heavy, but breathable. In rising waves, the tall blue trees and multicolored vegetation of Asteroid K-157 pressed around them, all but engulfing their tiny space craft.

"I had a section cleared for us," Spencer told his wife. "The house is just beyond those trees."

"I can hardly *wait* to see it!" Paula said, running ahead of him across the springy green soil.

He joined her at the clearing's edge, smiling at her reaction. Paula clapped her hands together in delight.

"Don, it's wonderful . . . all I'd hoped for!" she said, hugging him.

The new house was low and modern, sculptured to the alien soil, a flat plastibrick structure gleaming under double suns. As they approached it, the front door slid silently open for them.

"All the comforts of Earth," said Spencer. "Even a microfilm library."

"Are we . . . alone here?" Paula asked.

"Absolutely. The last of the building crew was due out yesterday. The entire place is ours."

She darted through the house, exclaiming at all the latest electronic marvels. In the bedroom, she turned to face him. "We're going to make this the most *tremendous* honeymoon any couple ever had."

"That," he grinned, "will be a pleasure."

Later that night Donald Spencer awoke to find the bed empty beside him. He got up quickly, calling Paula's name. When she failed to answer he pulled on his robe and rushed outside into the bright moonlight.

"Paula—are you out here?"

Then Spencer saw her, standing at the edge of the clearing, facing the massed line of blue trees.

"Darling, I was worried." He put a hand on her shoulder.

She turned calmly, the moonlight filling her eyes. "I needed some fresh air. The room was stifling."

"Sure you're all right?"

Paula didn't reply, turning slowly away from him. Spencer was puzzled, strangely uneasy, yet nothing seemed to be wrong.

"Let's go back to the house."

"No," the girl said firmly. "I want to stay out here."

"But—"

"You go in if you wish."

Spencer shrugged, a little angry. He walked back, trying to pinpoint the difference he had noticed in Paula. She had somehow changed . . .

"Exactly *how* have I changed, Donald?"

He spun around; she had followed him back. Then he gasped; how had she known—

"—what you were thinking?" She finished his mental question. "Because I can read your mind now, of course."

She stood there in the doorway, framed in soft moonlight, smiling at him as a mother smiles at her child.

"It's true," she said. "I can also move faster than you can. I'm much stronger. In fact, I could easily kill you with one blow. Easily."

"Good God," said Spencer. "What kind of nonsense is this?"

"Not nonsense. Fact. All of it can be yours, too. The trees will accept you, I know they will."

Spencer began to speak, but she raised a silencing hand.

"I walked out for air, earlier, while you slept—but it was really not for air at all. The trees had called me. They wanted me to become part of them, part of this place . . . and so I did."

"Paula, what are you telling me?"

"That this asteroid is alive. That the blue trees are alive, and have mental powers far beyond our own. They called me tonight, and I went out to them, ate the fruit

I found on their branches. Then I was one of them. I'm sure they want you too, Don. Go to them . . ."

"You're just tired. The trip, the new house . . . Maybe in the morning we can—"

"In the morning," she told him, "I won't be here. At least not as you see me. The mutation will be complete by then. This creature you call Paula will be gone; I'll be part of *them*."

She extended a hand. Spencer saw that she held a triangular piece of fruit, which cast a subtle blue glow in the darkness.

"We're in a new Garden of Eden," she said softly. "Eat this and you'll be free, as I am free."

Spencer moved back from her. He believed Paula now; she *had* changed, and something on this asteroid had effected that change. The Luani Cluster was undeveloped, wholly alien; no one could specify exactly what man would encounter here . . . That was one of the risks. He knew he'd made a terrible error in seeking out this place, that because of his error the woman he had loved was lost to him. Paula was no longer his wife—no longer human.

"Well, Don?"

"I—I don't want to join you," he said, watching her cold eyes. "I'll leave in the morning. The house, the asteroid is yours. Everything."

She laughed, and a sudden chill made him shiver beneath his robe.

"You'll never leave. No one can. All the others—the construction crew—they're out . . . with the trees. By morning you'll be one of us."

"Then I won't wait for morning. I'll go now. I can make contact with a passenger ship near Ariel and—

"You're acting like a fool, Don."

Her voice was edged. Whatever possessed her was angry.

Spencer turned, entered the bedroom, and hurriedly began to dress. Paula watched him from the doorway, unsmiling, silent.

He walked quickly past her, out to the waiting space craft.

"Paula . . . goodbye."

"Not goodbye, Don. There'll never be a goodbye for us."

Spencer mounted the ladder, opened the airlock, put one foot inside the rocket. Then, on impulse, he turned.

The trees seemed much closer.

"They are," Paula said, reading his thought. "You only have a few seconds, Don. Eat from the tree, or—"

"Or what?" he demanded.

"Or be destroyed with the rocket."

"Go to hell!" said Spencer as he closed the airlock.

Outside, the trees were all around the silver ship; the clearing had completely vanished.

Sweating and impatient, Spencer turned to the controls —then paused. He slowly raised his head. Something . . . someone was calling him with an urgency he could not resist. Something wanted him . . .

The trees. The trees wanted him.

Moving with a calm deliberation, Spencer opened the lock. They waited for him, offering their shining blue branches in the bright moonlight, offering immortality.

He climbed down the ladder, putting out a hand toward Paula, toward the fruit of the tree.

Hungrily, he ate of the fruit.

Paula welcomed him into her arms. "Now, my darling, we're together again. Forever."

Spencer smiled at her, then looked at the trees. He wondered why he had been unwilling to accept his destiny; men were so weak and foolish . . . so hopelessly *mortal*.

And, on Asteroid K-157 of the Luani Cluster, Donald and Paula Spencer lived happily ever after.

NORTH WIND

Chad Oliver

In the days of our first vast wilderness trek to the West we shamelessly exploited the Indian, slaughtering his buffalo, driving him from his land, breaking our treaties as often as we made them. Will we similarly exploit the aliens of the future?

Chad Oliver, a superb storyteller as well as one of our country's top anthropologists, tackles this delicate question in "North Wind," a neatly fashioned novelet designed to probe the collective political conscience of those who will be working with the "savages" in another kind of wilderness.

THE HEAVY GLASS DOORS whispered apart before him and Norman Mavor walked out of the hearing room. His formal blue suit was still crisply pressed, his straight gray hair neatly combed. He moved down the spotless corridor with a firm step.

Except for his eyes, he might have passed himself off as a man without a care in the world.

His eyes were green—not the shallow green of grass or leaves, but the deep, translucent green of the sea. The eyes were embedded in a lined, craggy face that had seen better days, and at the moment they were more than a little bloodshot.

He looked neither to right nor left, and people kept out of his way. If he heard the barbed comments that followed him down the corridor he gave no outward sign.

He took the private elevator to the roof and climbed into a copter with NORMAN MAVOR discreetly lettered on the sides of the cabin.

Then he waited.

He didn't smoke. He didn't fidget. His eyes were open, looking straight ahead, but it was impossible to tell what they were seeing, if anything.

He just waited.

Ten minutes later, a balding, red-faced dynamo of a man came panting up the little-used stairway, waved excitedly, and piled his somewhat globular form into the copter next to Mavor.

"We tied 'em in circles, Norm," Karl Hauser chuckled, his multiple chins dancing. "Old Fishface and the Development boys never knew what hit 'em!"

"You bet," Norman Mavor said icily. "We won those guys a quarter of their own planet without firing a shot. Ain't we grand?"

Karl Hauser beamed, undaunted. "Save it for the Old Ladies League," he advised. "You need a drink."

"With that I am in complete agreement. Sky Grotto suit you?"

"They sell alcohol, don't they?"

Mavor essayed a smile, not too successfully, and lifted the copter up into the sunlight that washed New York in yellow gold.

Two hours afterward, fortified by a predominantly liquid lunch topped by a drowning hamburger, Norman Mavor checked in at his private office near Lake Success. His grooming was still faultless; only the fact that the lines in his face were less strikingly obvious than before betrayed the lessening of the tension within him.

His office was chiefly notable for its utter lack of curios, gewgaws, knick-knacks, and assorted junk-gadgets. It was clean in its simplicity, and if its stained pine walls and hardwood floors lacked something in warmth, they could at least not be accused of pretense in any form.

There was one photograph on Mavor's desk. It was set in a neat silver frame, and it was a picture of a smug chimpanzee sitting cross-legged on a box.

The chimp's name was Basil, and there was a name-plate on the frame to that effect. Basil was one of the few remaining anthropoid apes; the orang and the gorilla were long extinct, and only a scattering of chimps and gibbons were left to hold the fort.

There was nothing special about Basil, save that Mavor liked the expression on his face. It was hard to take yourself too seriously with a chimpanzee on your desk.

Mavor sat down, and waited.

In precisely four minutes there was a knock on his door, which meant that someone had succeeded in getting past the small army of his assistants to talk to him personally. Mavor loathed the tri-di phone, and seldom answered it.

"Come in," he said.

The door opened and a young, very earnest man hurried in with a folder under his arm.

Enter Prometheus, bearing fire, Mavor thought. He recognized the man: Bill Shackelford, one of the field data analysts. Aloud, Mavor said, "Hello, Bill. How long before the end of the world?"

Shackelford blinked, but made a fast recovery. "I figure a billion years, give or take a few hundred million. Why?"

Mavor shrugged. "When people barge in here," he said, "it's generally a matter of life or death. The lot of the Integrator of Interstellar Affairs is not a happy one, as you may discover if you ever get kicked upstairs into my job."

"I do have something I think you ought to see, Mr. Mavor, or I wouldn't have bothered you."

Mavor nodded sagely. "Let me guess. You have been checking a field report from one of our rover boys, right?"

"Well, yes. That's my job."

"And you have discovered something extraordinary, right?"

Shackelford sat down, as though he had lost some of the wind from his sails. "I didn't exactly discover it, Mr. Mavor—it's in the field report."

"Ah. Let's see now." Mavor tilted his old-fashioned swivel chair back and gazed at the ceiling. "One of the field men has stumbled across a rare item on—ummmm —Capella IV should be about due, yes?"

"No," Shackelford said with some relish. "It's from Arcturus III."

"Arcturus, then. It couldn't have been a plain old primitive culture, because that's too common to bring to my attention. It couldn't be an advanced civilization, in the usual sense, or I'd have heard of it long ago. So what does that leave us, Bill? Either a culture past the Neolithic and into an early urban situation, which might cover the planet without attracting our attention with radio waves or spaceships, or else—what?"

"You tell me, Mr. Mavor."

"Okay." Mavor tilted his chair forward again and put his elbows on the desk. "I'll tell you. The anthropologist on Arcturus has stumbled across something that looks primitive, but isn't. How's that?"

"How did you know?" Shakelford asked, visibly disappointed.

"Basil told me," Mavor said, nodding toward the photograph. "He's a very widely read ape."

Shackelford sat quite still, caught in that maddening impasse of the recently adult male: too old to walk out in a huff, too young to turn the tables with any masterstroke of daily diplomacy. "Well," he said finally, "I'm sorry I bothered you, since you have such a remarkable source of information already at hand."

Mavor squinted his green eyes, damning himself inwardly for his absolute inability to play the buddy-buddy to everyone. He rather liked Shackelford, he knew that the younger man would now go home and tell his wife about what a monster the boss was, and he knew that he had made an enemy. He already had an ample supply of the latter, but he couldn't function any other way.

The silence got tighter.

"I kind of thought you might be interested," Shackelford said finally, fidgeting on his chair.

"Go ahead and smoke, Bill," Mavor said, recognizing the symptoms. "I won't throw a tantrum."

Shackelford produced a cigar, ignited it with a puff, and carefully blew a cloud of smoke into a neutral corner. Mavor, who had been expecting the inevitable pipe, was pleasantly surprised—mentally, if not in an olfactory sense.

"Spill it," Mavor said. "What hath the Noble Savage come up with this time around?"

Shackelford flushed and started pawing through his official folder.

"Skip the technical jargon. Whatever you've got on Arcturus III, plain English will bore through to my addled wits."

The younger man chewed on his cigar instead of counting to ten. "According to Simpson—he's the anthropologist out there—they've got a culture that's still in a hunting and gathering situation as far as technology goes—no cultivated crops or anything—but at the same time they've got a terrifically complex *political* set-up."

"How complex is 'terrifically' complex?"

"They've got big ceremonial centers with resident political and religious officials; they run the show, according to Simpson."

"I take it that most of the people don't live in these centers?"

"No, most of them are scattered along the rivers. They just get together on sacred days and whatnot."

"Sort of like the old Maya?"

"The Maya were agricultural."

"Thank you." Mavor smiled faintly. "How many people are involved in this deal? One tribe?"

Shackelford frowned. "It's hard to tell. I get an impression that it's a bigger affair than just one tribe."

"You *get an impression,* hey? If you don't know, say so."

"Okay. I don't know."

"What else?"

"Simpson says he's on the track of something big, really big."

"Elephant? Hippo? Dinosaur?"

Shackelford retreated behind a cloud of cigar smoke. "He says they've got a lot of dope they shouldn't have."

"Ah, the Wisdom of the Ancients rears its ugly head. Are they splitting atoms with their stone axes?"

"Simpson isn't sure; he's just beginning his research."

"Ummmm. And what does he suggest we do about it?"

"More or less the Standard Procedure for cases like this. He wants us to declare Arcturus III off-limits for a one-hundred-year waiting period, until we're certain what it is we're butting into. The law says—"

"Basil keeps me posted on the law. What do you think of all this?"

"May I speak frankly, Mr. Mavor?"

"I would recommend it highly."

"Okay, then. I think this thing on Arcturus III is one of the most remarkable things I've ever heard of. These people aren't just a bunch of savages, Mr. Mavor—they're unique, they've done something nobody ever managed before." Shackelford leaned forward, his eyes bright. "They've earned their chance. Legally, you're their protector on Earth. It's your *duty* to keep our people off of Arcturus III. That's what I think."

Mavor didn't change expression. "At least you're not ambiguous," he said. "You can go now."

Shackelford hesitated, then got up. His face was very white. He put the folder under his arm and started out.

"Leave the folder here if you will, please."

He tossed it on the desk and left, clearly flirting with an attack of high blood pressure and budding ulcers.

Norman Mavor punched the NO VISITORS button and opened the folder on his desk. He sat straight-backed in his chair, the crease in his trousers still razor-sharp.

His deep green eyes went to work—patiently, and yet not without a kind of steady ruthlessness.

He made occasional neat notes on white cards ready for indexing.

The hours passed, and Mavor hardly moved. He felt a cold knot tying itself in icy loops in the pit of his stomach.

Night came to the city.

On the other side of his office wall, a dark autumn wind whispered down from out of the north.

Mavor had strongly suspected that he was in trouble within minutes after Bill Shackelford had walked into his office. It hadn't been any sixth sense that had warned him, unless its name was Experience.

A preliminary reading of Simpson's report hadn't made him feel any better.

After three days of study, he was certain.

It wasn't the easiest trick in creation for any United Nations brass to disappear for a week in the country. It was still less simple for one of the bigwigs to walk out for a month, for business was always pressing, and generally critical.

No one set off on a junket of 33 lightyears unless it was pretty damned important.

Mavor thought Arcturus III was that important.

Since he was his own boss, with a twenty-year tenure that nothing less than outright impeachment could shake, he got away with it by keeping his mouth shut until the last minute, and then leaving red-faced Karl Hauser, his chief legal expert, to do his explaining for him.

He lined up a UN spaceliner over which he had jurisdiction, and did some backstage red-tape cutting to clear it for use. While the ship's navigation officers were computing a faster-than-light course to Arcturus III, he found out what he could about Edward Simpson, the anthropologist already in the field.

Simpson's official photograph showed a lean, strong face, somewhat lantern-jawed, with dark hair and eyes. It was a rather ordinary face in the sense that it approached the cultural ideal of what a face should be; it would have suited any one of a host of moderately well-known tri-di actors, but it was not striking enough to stick in your mind.

How can you sum up a face in words?"

Mavor tagged it as determined and a trifle cynical, and turned to more revealing sources of information.

Simpson had majored in paleontology as an undergraduate at Harvard, and then switched to anthropology for his Ph.D. at the University of Michigan. His academic record tended to be spotty—he had done extremely well in courses that interested him, and just enough to pass in required work that hadn't caught his fancy. He'd done a fairly interesting dissertation on the prehistoric relationships between the southeastern United States and the Valley of Mexico, and published a solid ethnographic account of an agricultural group on Capella II.

Capable, then, if no ball of fire.

He'd grown up in Maine, where his father was a guide in the game preserves along the Canadian border. He'd married a local girl in Patten, and they had one son.

He was thirty-two years old.

Anything odd?

Anything revealing?

Well, he'd once gotten into warmish water by stating publicly that the UN was run by a collection of windbags, but that was the extent of his subversion, if such it could be termed.

Edward Simpson was either an extremely ordinary young man, or he had a talent for keeping his eccentricities to himself. In any event, he was not likely to have gone off half-cocked.

He knew what he was doing.

Mavor spent a day at home saying goodbye to his wife, Sue, who by this time was resigned to the periodic vanishings of her husband. Sue was even-tempered and not overly imaginative; Mavor had often doubted whether any other woman would have put up with him.

The spaceliner lifted on schedule.

Mavor looked into the viewscreen, and out across the star-blazed midnight that was the sea between the worlds. He saw splendor and loneliness, and the challenge of a universe in which man was but one tiny mystery in a darkness that had no ending.

The ship faded into the gray of hyperspace.

It was September 1, 2044.

The third planet of Arcturus was a green world, warmed by a reddish sun.

After contacting Simpson by radio from the liner, Mavor boarded a landing launch. The gray sphere drifted down out of the great night into a blue sky dotted with white clouds. It came to rest as lightly as a soap bubble on the target area. Mavor got out and the sphere floated up toward the sun, and was gone.

He was alone.

He stood by a small crystal-clear spring that chuckled out from under clean brown rocks. Around him a field of nodding grasses murmured in a fresh, cool breeze. To the east he could see blue mountains wrapped in shadows, and from the south he caught the hint of salt from the sea.

The air was a trifle richer in oxygen than that of Earth, but otherwise identical except for a few trace elements. It had a tang and a sparkle to it. You never really knew fresh air, Mavor thought, until you breathed on a planet that had never known heavy industries, where the internal combustion engine was fifty thousand years away, and smoke only a sweet tendril over a campfire. . . .

He stood still, waiting.

He showed no outward sign of nervousness. He didn't smoke, fidget, or pace.

He waited.

And yet he *was* nervous, and was candid enough with himself to admit it. Partly, it was just the excitement of a new world, a new sky, a new frontier. He had seen many new planets, but he had never gotten used to them.

Every world was a miracle, if your eyes were good enough.

And Arcturus III was more than that. It was a mystery and a challenge and a threat.

It was trouble.

Here was a culture that lived by hunting wild animals

and gathering roots and berries in the forest—the simplest of all economies. And yet, here was a culture ruled by priest-kings, who had a power of life and death over their people.

Remarkable?

The word was impossible.

You don't get dense populations and permanent settlements when you get your food by hunting for it, except under the most atypical conditions. If the population of New York had to eat by hunting deer and rabbits, most of the people would starve in nothing flat. If you hunt, you can't park in one place and wait for the game to jump into your pot—you have to go after it.

Most hunting peoples lived in small bands of perhaps one hundred men, women, and children. There were no sharply defined social classes, and certainly no kings. You've got to have surplus food to support nonproducing specialists, and famine is a constant threat when you hunt for life. At the most, you might find a shaman or two, and a vaguely defined headman without any formal authority.

No chiefs, generally.

Kings?

Priests?

Vast ceremonial centers?

About as likely as a snake running a digital computer.

The cool breeze sighed through the tall grasses. Mavor waited.

The world of Arcturus III didn't play by the rules, and that meant danger. Simpson had stumbled across something that looked very much like a big fat monkey wrench in the gears. It wasn't the first time it had happened, of course—people had a nasty habit of being unpredictable occasionally.

But this time—

"Mavor! Are you there?" The call came from the south, still faint with distance.

"At the spring, Simpson!" Mavor yelled.

A small cloud blotted out the sun, and the wind had a cold edge to it.

Mavor stood quietly, and waited.

Edward Simpson parted the tall grass and stepped forward.

Superficially, he looked like his picture; his features were regular, dominated by a stubborn jaw. He was thinner than Mavor expected, and more nervous. His dark eyes seemed only half-open, but he didn't appear sleepy by any means.

Wary.

The word popped into Mavor's mind, and stayed there. The two men shook hands.

"I didn't expect a visit from the big boss himself," Simpson said rapidly. "Lucky I keep my radio on my wrist or I might have missed your call. What brings you to Arcturus III?"

"A spaceship, generally," Mavor said.

"I meant—"

"Never mind, Ed. Just a speech defect of mine. Looks like you hit the jackpot around here, and I kind of thought I'd wander out and help you count the quarters. Where are they?"

"How much time have you got?"

"Enough."

"Well, the Lkklah—that's what they call themselves—live south of here, most of them. Lkklah means 'people,' of course—"

"Toward the sea?"

"Generally, yes." Simpson offered Mavor a cigarette; when Mavor shook his head Simpson took one himself and returned the pack to his pocket.

"How many of them are there?"

"At least thirty thousand, if my census is accurate. That doesn't count the other tribes around here."

"There are some people who don't have this hotshot culture on the hunting base, then?"

"That's right. It isn't planetwide; I don't know the full extent of it yet."

"Fair enough. Let's take a gander at 'em."

"They move around a lot, Mr. Mavor—"

"You mean those huge ceremonial centers have got wheels on them?" Mavor surveyed the anthropologist with bland green eyes.

Simpson laughed. "I don't think so. But most of the people are scattered in hunting groups, and they're a little shy of strangers."

"I see. Your report mentioned resident officials in the big centers, I believe. Are they out to lunch?"

Simpson threw one cigarette into the spring and lit another. "They go on pilgrimages; I haven't got the exact cycle worked out yet. They'll be in one center or another, but I'd hate to take you on a long wild goose chase."

"That *would* raise certain problems," Mavor admitted.

Simpson stared at him, trying to find some sort of an expression to read. He couldn't find one. He started to say something, then contented himself with a shrug.

"Let's go," Mavor said.

Simpson turned and led the way through the grass.

He set a fast pace, heading south.

Norman Mavor smiled, just a little, and followed him toward the distant sea.

Evening flowed down the salt-wind from the ocean, and delicate rose-tinted clouds hung on the western horizon. Then the sun was gone, and the night turned the world into a shadow.

There was no moon, but the starlight was a silver radiance in the sky.

It was cold, and Mavor jammed his hands into his pockets to keep them warm.

Neither man spoke.

The croaking of frogs and the persistent, irritating whine of some invisible animal blended in with the shuffle of their footsteps.

There was no other sound.

The terrain beneath their feet became rocky and a thorny vegetation pushed out the grass. Then the ground softened and they heard the sibilant glide of water. They came to a good-sized river, black with silver flecks under the stars, and followed a path that wound along its banks.

It was almost morning when they saw it.

In spite of himself, Mavor stopped short and caught his breath.

There, framed by the dark fence of the vegetation and frozen in the pale light of dawn, was magic. No man with an ounce of poetry in his soul could have seen it merely as a "ceremonial center."

Here was a hall where the gods might dance, and spirits sigh down the wind.

You thought at once of pyramids, but that was force of habit. The structures—there were four of them—were square and massive, like blocks of basalt ripped from the depths of a world. They were terraced, with rock stairways cut into their sides.

How big were they?

Mavor reined in his imagination and estimated: sixty feet high, at least, and perhaps eighty feet on a side. And there were smaller structures on top of them—temples of some kind, beyond a doubt.

There were courtyards, altars, market squares.

The place was deserted, but the silence that hung over it was not the silence of centuries.

The place was *used*.

"Well?" asked Simpson, not without an edge of malice. His voice was as startling as a rifle shot in the stillness.

"It's magnificent," Mavor said quietly. Then: "Anyone home?"

"I don't think so. We'll look—these places aren't boobytrapped."

They walked through the courtyards, and peered into the buildings. They were pitch black inside, but a match showed the extent of the rooms. They were amazingly small considering the size of the exteriors; the construction was impressive, but not overly efficient.

They saw no one, and heard nothing.

"Gone to the World Series," Mavor commented.

"They're elusive, sometimes. They may be back here today, or not for months."

"I'll leave my card. I still want to see the people who built this place, Ed."

"How about some sack-time first?" Simpson asked, yawning. "It's comfortable inside the squares, if you don't mind rock mattresses."

"I don't mind," Mavor said.

They ducked inside one of the entrances and stretched out on the floor. Mavor was asleep in seconds, but whenever Simpson stirred Mavor's green eyes opened, and waited.

They slept six hours. Mavor would have preferred to breakfast on synthetics, but Simpson insisted on shooting a deerlike animal in the brush and broiling up some steaks.

The food was worth the extra wait.

It was afternoon before they left the ceremonial center and struck out along the river path, heading south. They did not see a single human being. Mavor did notice that the river was full of fish; they looked like salmon or trout leaping in the rapids. He filed that fact away for future reference.

There was a glazing sunset, and then a growing chill as evening faded into night.

There were still no people.

Mavor didn't complain. He walked along behind Simpson, who had run out of cigarettes and was getting more nervous by the minute. Mavor was tired, but he was ready to walk around the whole damned planet if necessary.

At the Earthly equivalent of three o'clock in the morning, Simpson stopped.

Mavor waited.

"I'll try a signal," Simpson said.

It's about time, Mavor thought, trying to ignore his swollen feet.

Simpson let out a long, moderately blood-curdling yell, and followed it with three short yips.

In seconds, there was an answer.

One long cry, three shorter ones.

About half a mile away, Mavor judged.

"Let's go," Simpson said.

They went.

It took them almost an hour, scrambling over rocks and getting their clothes ripped by thorns.

The camp lay before them, ghost-like in the foggy gray of early morning. It was little more than a low fire and a circle of crude lean-tos—a sleeping place that a month's winds and rains would erase from the face of the planet.

There were three dogs, all yelping.

Mavor counted seventeen people, most of them near-naked, but with skin cloaks against the cold. No tailored clothing, then. He saw some spears and dart-throwers, but no bows.

It looked like an extended family group, and it probably was.

Simpson spoke to one old man in a native language; Mavor couldn't get a word of it, of course, but he listened attentively. Learning native languages was no picnic in the best of circumstances, and out of the question for an official who had to keep tabs on many cultures, on many worlds.

The old man was delighted to see them. He laughed and clapped his hands together. He pulled them over to the fire and insisted that they eat some meat—which wasn't bad—and a kind of cold wild vegetable paste, which would have made the proverbial Duncan Hines beat a hasty retreat with all guns blazing.

The four women kept to themselves, although the younger girls were friendly enough. The men and boys swarmed around them, all chattering a mile a minute, and it was difficult to concentrate on anything.

Mavor kept his eyes open, however, and he took notes.

The day passed rapidly. Both Mavor and Simpson were on the weary side by evening, but the natives were hell-bent on hospitality. The men had snared an animal the size of a buffalo during the afternoon, and that was a fine excuse for a feast.

Mavor and Simpson pitched in and helped with the fire, much to the amusement of the women.

It developed that half-raw kidneys were considered the

real delights here, and the visitors choked them down with a somewhat pale smile.

There was singing—a monotonous chanting of the same syllables over and over again, to the tick-tick-tick of bones tapped gently against two flat rocks. It wasn't pretty, but it was hypnotic.

And, somehow, it was sad.

Late that night, when the orange fires were low and the shadows were soft and close, Simpson leaned over to Mavor. The natives were off on a story-telling binge, most of which was too rough linguistically even for Simpson.

Simpson's usually sleepy eyes were open wide now, and alert in the firelight.

"These people have a saying," he whispered.

Mavor waited.

"They say that in the spring the winds blow from the south, and the trees and flowers and people will live forever. But when autumn comes the north wind blows; the leaves turn brown and fall, and the people know that they too must die. Listen!"

A night wind sighed through the brush and twisted the flickering flames.

Even here, so close to the sea, the wind came out of the north, and it was cold.

"Goodnight," Simpson said, and stretched out on the ground and closed his eyes.

Mavor sat silently, listening to the voices and the wind.

It was late when he slept.

In the morning, after a stomach-searing breakfast, Mavor turned to Simpson.

"I've got news for you," he said.

"Well?"

"I may not be an anthropologist, Ed, but I wasn't born yesterday, either. These people are not the Lkklah you were telling me about. They are just what they seem to be—a band of semi-nomadic hunters. I don't know who they are, and I don't care. They didn't build those ceremonial centers any more than I did."

Simpson eyed him narrowly, but said nothing.

"I don't mind games, son," Mavor said. "If you want to walk me for a hundred years, that's your business. But I'm going to see these Lkklah of yours before I leave this planet. Why don't you stop being so damned clever and get it over with?"

Simpson hesitated, shrugged, and said something to the native headman. Then, without a word, he walked away into the brush, heading back toward the river.

Mavor tagged along after him, and did not look back.

They reached the sparkling river and continued south along the path. Simpson set a killing pace, but Mavor didn't complain. He just watched the river, and noted the fish leaping in the shallows.

Within four hours they hit a stand of sweet-smelling trees that looked like cedars. The smell of salt was strong in the heavy air, and Mavor thought he could hear the sea.

The path through the trees climbed steeply, and then they rounded a turn and the land dropped off sharply before them. The view was excellent, and Mavor saw all he needed to see.

He stopped.

Below them was the sea, almost black beneath a cold gray sky. Between the sea and the rocky cliff they stood on was a stretch of timber perhaps a quarter of a mile wide.

The village was in the trees.

This time it was no simple hunting camp. There were solid plank houses, and lots of them. There were hundreds of people visible, all of them well-dressed in tailored clothing. There were large, graceful sea-going canoes drawn up along the beach.

The houses extended along the shore as far as the eye could see. Thousands of people could have been taken care of without any strain at all.

There were no cultivated fields that Mavor could spot.

But there were rivers.

He counted ten of them from where he stood, winding through the cliffs and emptying into the sea.

He turned to Simpson.

"These are the Lkklah?"

"Some of them. Yes."

"These are the people who built the ceremonial centers back yonder?"

"Yes."

Mavor studied the younger man with his cool green eyes. "Maybe you'd like to sit down," he said.

"You're not going into the village, after coming all this way?"

"No need for that, Ed."

A vein began throbbing insistently in Simpson's forehead.

"Say what you've got to say, Mavor."

"Maybe you'd rather tell me."

"Tell you what?"

"Oh hell, man." Mavor almost seemed irritated, but recovered himself. He sat down on a boulder, his unhandsome face lined and tired.

"I don't know what you're talking about."

"Okay, Ed." Mavor clasped his hands and rested his chin on his thumbs. "We'll put it in teensy-weensy little words so there'll be no mistake. *Don't you know it's a serious crime to fake your data?*"

The scent of the trees was fresh and clean around them, and the beat of the sea was the pulse of unhurried centuries.

But now ugliness was between them on the cliff.

The silence stretched taut.

For a long minute, Mavor thought that Simpson was going to try to brazen it out, even now. But the younger man suddenly slumped and turned his back.

The battle was over.

"How'd you know?" Simpson asked, his voice muffled.

"It's my job to know, Ed. You were too vague with the crucial details in your report. Any time a miracle crosses my desk, pal, I want photographs, statistics, and an analysis somewhat above the sophomoric level."

Simpson turned, his eyes narrowed. "I wasn't that

crude. I said there were complex ceremonial centers, and there were. I said these people had no agriculture, and they don't."

"Bunk," Mavor said bluntly. "You know as well as I do that it isn't the simple technological level that's important —it's the total ecological situation. If you've got plenty of food, and it's reliable, it doesn't make a damn bit of difference where you got it from. If you've got the food, you get the population. If you get the population, a complex social structure is possible—though not inevitable. If your social organization is complex enough, you get specialists freed from food production—and you can build your temples, carve your totem poles, and generally raise hell."

"Thanks for the lecture."

"You're welcome. Look, son, the old Indians on the Northwest Coast of North America had exactly the same deal you've got here. No agriculture, but streams chockfull of salmon—and just about the most complex prehistoric culture north of Mexico. Lots of the Plains Indians had no agriculture, but they had horses, and they had the bison."

"Yeah, yeah. I know all that."

"Good. That means you knew what you were doing. You didn't just make a mistake—you lied in your teeth."

Simpson clenched his fists, but didn't move.

"You were sent to Arcturus III to survey the culture here. It's my job to allocate land for Earth colonies on other planets like this one. I depend on the reports you guys send in. So what do you do? You stumble over this interesting deal where there's a pretty elaborate culture based on a river network that's choked with fish. They go and build some impressive squares out in the brush. It's great stuff, but there's nothing mysterious about it, and you know it. Just the same, you concoct this cock-and-bull story about the Wisdom of the Ancients and advise us to keep hands-off for a hundred years. You admit all this?"

Simpson shrugged.

"Okay, Ed. Now, I'm curious as hell. What in the devil

did you think you were doing—and *why* did you do it?"

Simpson took a deep breath. "You wouldn't understand —not unless you knew the Lkklah. If you'd come with me down into the village—"

"I don't *want* to know the Lkklah—and I don't want to wind up in a stewpot, either."

The look in Simpson's eyes now was neither regret nor fear.

It was hate.

"I thought I was getting a hundred years of peace for some people I liked," he said evenly. "I did it to do them a favor, and if you don't like it I don't give a damn."

Mavor got up, his green eyes narrowed with anger. "You did it to do them a *favor*," he repeated. "You simple-minded jackass."

Simpson started for him.

Mavor stood up straight, a trace of a smile on his lips. He looked Simpson right in the eye and waited.

Simpson stopped.

"It's too late now," Simpson said wearily. "You'll get your lousy planet no matter what I do."

"Exactly," Mavor said.

Mavor punched the stud on his wrist radio which threw a beam to the satellite transmitter and then to the waiting space liner. The landing sphere would pick him up where it had set him down.

"What happens now?" Simpson said. "Do I go back in the brig on bread and water?"

"You do your job," Mavor said shortly. "I'll make it back to the spring."

Simpson frowned. "You don't mean—"

"Don't tell me what I mean and what I don't mean. You're an anthropologist and you were hauled out here at considerable expense to do a job: establish the land-use patterns of the highest culture on Arcturus III. Do your job, and this time do it right. I'll decide what to do about you when I see what your fieldwork looks like— and this time let's have some facts."

"I'm not sure I care to do your dirty work for you," Simpson said. "These people are my friends—"

"Do it or go to jail," Mavor said.

The older man turned and started back along the trail, the north wind in his face. It was a long way back to the pickup point, and he wasted no time on backward glances.

Edward Simpson stood for almost an hour where he was, facing the sea.

There were tears in his eyes.

"The bastard," he said, over and over again. "The dirty, blind, self-righteous bastard."

Then, very slowly, he started down toward the plank houses and the laughter of the people who had been his friends.

The trip from Arcturus III to Earth was uneventful.

On November 21, 2044, Norman Mavor was back in his office. His formal blue suit was neatly pressed, his straight gray hair faultlessly combed. His green eyes were calm and patient.

He looked a little older; that was the only change.

"Well, Basil," he said to the cross-legged chimpanzee, "here we go again."

He flipped a switch.

"Send in Bill Shackelford," he said, and smiled a little. He waited.

Shackelford got there in ten minutes flat. He was smoking a cigar when he came in, and he had evidently fortified himself with a shot of bottled courage.

"I guess this is where I get the old heave-ho," Shackelford said. He looked like he hadn't been sleeping any too well.

"I considered it," Mavor said.

Shackelford carefully took the cigar out of his mouth. "Can me then, Mr. Mavor. I made a mistake, I admit that. But I'm not doing any crawling."

Mavor raised his eyebrows. "You've already heard about Arcturus III, I take it?"

"Word gets around."

Mavor nodded. "Unfortunate business, Bill. But Simpson just made an honest mistake; it could have happened to anyone. I don't fire people for making mistakes, Bill."

"You said—"

"I said I had considered firing you. I didn't say what for."

"Are you asking me a riddle?"

"Hardly." Mavor tilted his chair back. "I want you to take charge of working up the new data from Arcturus III; we've got about two years before the hearing. I want you to make absolutely certain those natives don't get one inch more territory than they're entitled to under the law. Will you do it?"

Shackelford sat down. He looked blankly at his cigar, then slipped it into the disposer.

"It's a dirty job," he said finally.

"I'm glad you think so."

"You mean I'm not fired?"

"Not yet." Mavor reached into a desk drawer and pulled out the morning's New York *Times,* folded to the editorial page. "Did you see where I got my name in the paper again?"

"I saw," Shackelford said, cautiously.

"The usual rave notice," Mavor observed. He cleared his throat. *"Norman Mavor, Integrator of Interstellar Affairs, returned yesterday from another junket, this time to Arcturus III. He announced with evident pride that he had managed to obtain legal rights to yet another planet for colonization. This man, whose job it is to protect the rights of extraterrestrial natives, has shown a consistent disregard for the very natives he is sworn to support. It seems safe to say that no man on this planet has done more to rob native peoples of their homelands than Norman Mavor. . . ."*

"I read it," Shackelford said.

"And agreed, no doubt." Mavor put the paper away. "I think I should start a scrapbook."

"You *don't* like natives, do you?" Shackelford said, almost in spite of himself.

"Not particularly," Mavor admitted.

"And you want me to go over Arcturus III with a fine-toothed comb, to grab all we can get."

"Exactly."

"You know most of the planet will be occupied by simple hunting peoples. That means they won't have private ownership of land—only vague band territories, and a few water holes. Even the Lkklah, from what I've heard, won't have much beyond a coastal strip and a few acres of bush."

"That's right. Legally, the people of Arcturus III don't own their world at all—they just own a few square miles of it. We *do* give them their hunting territories, and marginal safety zones as well. We keep out trespassers. Don't you think that's pretty generous?"

Shackelford began to get very red in the face. "I think it shows a colossal gall!" he said, his voice louder than he had intended. "What's the matter with you? What do you use instead of a heart—a cake of ice?"

Mavor actually smiled. "Loyalty from one's subordinates is always touching," he said.

Shackelford got up and began waving his arms. "You don't have to fire me, Mavor. I quit!"

"Never mind," Mavor said. "Sit down."

Shackelford looked into the green eyes, hesitated, and sat down.

Mavor sized his man up, and wondered.

Was Bill ready?

Or did he need more time, like Simpson?

He looked down at his desk, almost embarrassed. He found it hard to go on.

But he was no longer young, and he was tired.

"Bill," he said softly, "do you know why I almost fired you?"

Shackelford, uncertain what role he was playing, just shook his head numbly.

Mavor hunched forward, for once forgetting the neat press on his clothes. "You came busting in here a few months back with what you thought was a real ding-dong lulu, like the artists of Centaurus VI. You thought we really had something, and do you know what you said to me?"

Shackelford shook his head again.

"These people aren't just a bunch of savages, Mr. Mavor—they're unique, they've done something nobody ever managed before."

Shackelford flushed. "I didn't mean—"

"Yes, you did. You meant that those people were exceptional, and entitled to special treatment. Not just a bunch of savages, as you so charmingly phrased it."

"Well—"

"Well, they *weren't* anything special. Most people aren't. They were just plain old dirty people. No telepaths, no human spaceships, no child supermen with wet diapers. Isn't that a crashing shame?"

"Look, you said you didn't even *like* natives. You've squeezed 'em out of every last square foot—"

"Oh, drop dead." Mavor rumpled his gray hair with his gnarled fingers. "I said I didn't like natives *particularly.* I don't. I'm just old-fashioned enough, just unsophisticated enough, so that I kind of admire human beings in general. I don't give a damn whether they're primitives or live in New York—or both. The odd notion that a man has to be some kind of freak before he's worth anything gives me a royal pain in the sacrum."

"But—"

"Listen, Junior," Mavor said. "This is the old inhuman monster talking, and he may gobble you alive if you don't pay attention. It's only been a few stinking hundred years since primitive peoples were thought of as animals, and hunted down with dogs. This whiz-bang technological culture of ours is still expanding—and if you think one starry-eyed gent can stop it with his mighty idealistic soul you've got rocks in your head. We've got laws now that give them *some* protection at least. Sure, I think they should be let alone to live as they please. We should keep out. Maybe we should have kept out of America, too, but we didn't. It may be news to you, Bill, but I am not the United Nations. I'm just a civil servant with a nasty job."

"You could get out—"

Mavor laughed. It was a strange sound. "Would it help those people out there if *you* had my job?" *Or Simpson,* he thought. *That trick of his would have been uncovered within five years—and then what would have become of the Lkklah?* "Suppose all the people here were positive you were cheating a little in *favor* of the aliens. That's the way they think of them, you know—as aliens. Believe me, it's better this way."

Shackelford stood up, visibly shaken. "But why don't you tell people? Why do you let them—"

Mavor jerked his thumb toward the door. "Run along," he said.

Shackelford left.

Norman Mavor was very tired.

He shook a finger at the picture of the chimpanzee on his desk. "Basil," he said, "you're a fraud. Beneath that hairy exterior there beats a heart of purest gold."

He hated the lectures; they were the toughest part.

"Hooray for me," he whispered, and wondered.

Two years later, in December, they held the hearings concerning Arcturus III.

The copter with NORMAN MAVOR discreetly lettered on the cabin sides floated down through a flurry of snow and landed on the roof of the Adjudication Building. Mavor and Karl Hauser, his balding legal expert, climbed out.

The wind was cold behind the driven snow.

"When autumn comes the north wind blows," Mavor said. "The leaves turn brown and fall, and the people know that they too must die. . . ."

"What the hell is that, old man?"

"Some poetry I heard once. Nothing important. Let's go."

They rode the private elevator down, and then walked along the spotless corridor. Mavor's green suit was crisply pressed, and not a hair on his head was out of place. He walked erect, and his deep green eyes looked neither to the right nor to the left.

"I figure we can argue Old Fishface out of a quarter

of the planet," Karl said jubilantly. "Not bad."

"Oh, we're hot stuff," Mavor said.

Some people recognized him, and there were the usual whispered cat-calls.

Mavor gave no sign that he had heard.

The heavy glass doors of the hearing room hissed open. The Colonial Development Committee was waiting.

Together, their briefcases under their arms, Mavor and Karl Hauser walked into the chamber.

"Give 'em hell," Karl Hauser whispered.

"I'll do my best," said Mavor.

DEATH OF A SPACEMAN

Walter M. Miller, Jr.

This anthology fittingly closes with the work of the same writer who opened it, Walter Miller, Jr.

In "The Lineman," Miller allowed us to share the rugged, active lives of the hard-muscled men who worked the craters of Luna. Now he allows us to share the death of just such a veteran, a tough old spacer dying where he began, on Earth, with the fires of a rocket-strewn universe bright in his memory.

You won't forget Old Donegal.

OLD DONEGAL was dying. They had all known it was coming, and they watched it come—his haggard wife, his daughter, and now his grandson, home on emergency leave from the pre-astronautics academy. Old Donegal knew it too, and had known it from the beginning, when he had begun to lose control of his legs and was forced to walk with a cane. But most of the time, he pretended to let them keep the secret they shared with the doctors—that the operations had all been failures, and that the cancer that fed at his spine would gnaw its way brainward until the paralysis engulfed vital organs, and then Old Donegal would cease to be. It would be cruel to let them know that he knew. Once, weeks ago, he had joked about the approaching shadows.

"Buy the plot back where people won't walk over it, Martha," he said. "Get it way back under the cedars—next to the fence. There aren't many graves back there yet. I want to be alone."

"Don't *talk* that way, Donny!" his wife had choked. "You're not dying."

His eyes twinkled maliciously. "Listen, Martha, I want to be buried face-down, I want to be buried with my back to space, understand? Don't let them lay me out like a lily."

"Donny, *please!*"

"They oughta face a man the way he's headed," Donegal grunted. "I been up—*way* up. Now I'm going straight down."

Martha had fled from the room in tears. He had never done it again, except to the interns and nurses, who, while they insisted that he was going to get well, didn't mind joking with him about it.

Martha can bear my death, he thought, can bear preknowledge of it. But she couldn't bear thinking that he might take it calmly. If he accepted death gracefully, it would be like deliberately leaving her, and Old Donegal had decided to help her believe whatever would be comforting to her in such a troublesome moment.

"When'll they let me out of this bed again?" he complained.

"Be patient, Donny," she sighed. "It won't be long. You'll be up and around before you know it."

"Back on the moon-run, maybe?" he offered. "Listen, Martha, I been planet-bound too long. I'm not too old for the moon-run, am I? Sixty-three's not so old."

That had been carrying things too far. She knew he was hoaxing, and dabbed at her eyes again. The dead must humor the mourners, he thought, and the sick must comfort the visitors. It was always so.

But it was harder, now that the end was near. His eyes were hazy, and his thoughts unclear. He could move his arms a little, clumsily, but feeling was gone from them. The rest of his body was lost to him. Sometimes he seemed to feel his stomach and his hips, but the sensation was mostly an illusion offered by higher nervous centers, like the "ghost-arm" that an amputee continues to feel. The wires were down, and he was cut off from himself.

He lay wheezing on the hospital bed, in his own room, in his own rented flat. Gaunt and unshaven, gray as winter twilight, he lay staring at the white net curtains that billowed gently in the breeze from the open window. There was no sound in the room but the sound of breathing and the loud ticking of an alarm clock. Occasionally he heard a chair scraping on the stone terrace next door, and the low mutter of voices, sometimes laughter, as the servants of the Keith mansion arranged the terrace for late afternoon guests.

With considerable effort, he rolled his head toward Martha who sat beside the bed, pinch-faced and weary.

"You ought to get some sleep," he said.

"I slept yesterday. Don't talk, Donny. It tires you."

"You ought to get more sleep. You never sleep enough. Are you afraid I'll get up and run away if you go to sleep for a while?"

She managed a brittle smile. "There'll be plenty of time for sleep when . . . when you're well again." The brittle smile fled and she swallowed hard, like swallowing a fishbone. He glanced down, and noticed that she was squeezing his hand spasmodically.

There wasn't much left of the hand, he thought. Bones and ugly tight-stretched hide spotted with brown. Bulging knuckles with yellow cigarette stains. My hand. He tried to tighten it, tried to squeeze Martha's thin one in return. He watched it open and contract a little, but it was like operating a remote-control mechanism. Goodbye, hand, you're leaving me the way my legs did, he told it. I'll see you again in hell. How hammy can you get, Old Donegal? You maudlin ass.

"Requiescat," he muttered over the hand, and let it lie in peace.

Perhaps she heard him. "Donny," she whispered, leaning closer, "won't you let me call the priest now? Please."

He rattled a sigh and rolled his head toward the window again. "Are the Keiths having a party today?" he asked. "Sounds like they're moving chairs out on the terrace."

"Please, Donny, the priest?"

He let his head roll aside and closed his eyes, as if asleep. The bed shook slightly as she quickly caught at his wrist to feel for a pulse.

"If I'm not dying, I don't need a priest," he said sleepily.

"That's not right," she scolded softly. "You know that's not right, Donny. You know better."

Maybe I'm being too rough on her? he wondered. He hadn't minded getting baptized her way, and married her way, and occasionally priest-handled the way she wanted him to when he was home from a space-run, but when it came to dying, Old Donegal wanted to do it his own way.

He opened his eyes at the sound of a bench being dragged across the stone terrace. "Martha, what kind of a party are the Keiths having today?"

"I wouldn't know," she said stiffly. "You'd think they'd have a little more respect. You'd think they'd put it off a few days."

"Until—?"

"Until you feel better."

"I feel fine, Martha. I like parties. I'm glad they're having one. Pour me a drink, will you? I can't reach the bottle anymore."

"It's empty."

"No it isn't, Martha, it's still a quarter full. I know. I've been watching it."

"You shouldn't have it, Donny. Please don't."

"But this is a party, Martha. Besides, the doctor says I can have whatever I want. Whatever I want, you hear? That means I'm getting well, doesn't it?"

"Sure, Donny, sure. Getting well."

"The whiskey, Martha. Just a finger in a tumbler, no more. I want to feel like it's a party."

Her throat was rigid as she poured it. She helped him get the tumbler to his mouth. The liquor seared his throat, and he gagged a little as the fumes clogged his nose. Good whiskey, the best—but he couldn't take it any more. He eyed the green stamp on the neck of the bottle on the bedtable and grinned. He hadn't had whiskey like that since his space-days. Couldn't afford it now, not on a blastman's pension.

He remembered how he and Caid used to smuggle a couple of fifths aboard for the moon-run. If they caught you, it meant suspension, but there was no harm in it, not for the blastroom men who had nothing much to do from the time the ship acquired enough velocity for the long, long coaster ride until they started the rockets again for Lunar landing. You could drink a fifth, jettison the bottle through the trash lock, and sober up before you were needed again. It was the only way to pass the time in the cramped cubicle, unless you ruined your eyes trying to read by the glow-lamps. Old Donegal chuckled. If he and Caid had stayed on the run, Earth would have a ring by now, like Saturn—a ring of Old Granddad bottles.

"You said it, Donny-boy," said the misty man by the billowing curtains. "Who else knows the Gegenschein is broken glass?"

Donegal laughed. Then he wondered what the man was doing there. The man was lounging against the window, and his unzipped space rig draped about him in an old familiar way. Loose plug-in connections and hose-ends dangled about his lean body. He was freckled and grinning.

"Caid," Old Donegal breathed softly.

"What did you say, Donny?" Martha answered.

Old Donegal blinked hard and shook his head. Something let go with a soggy snap, and the misty man was gone. I'd better take it easy on the whiskey, he thought. You got to wait, Donegal, old lush, until Nora and Ken get here. You can't get drunk until they're gone, or you might get them mixed up with memories like Caid's.

Car doors slammed in the street below. Martha glanced toward the window.

"Think it's them? I wish they'd get here. I wish they'd hurry."

Martha arose and tiptoed to the window. She peered down toward the sidewalk, put on a sharp frown. He heard a distant mutter of voices and occasional laughter, with group-footsteps milling about on the sidewalk. Martha murmured her disapproval and closed the window.

"Leave it open," he said.

"But the Keiths' guests are starting to come. There'll be such a racket." She looked at him hopefully, the way she did when she prompted his manners before company came.

Maybe it wasn't decent to listen in on a party when you were dying, he thought. But that wasn't the reason. Donegal, your chamber-pressure's dropping off. Your brains are in your butt-end, where a spacer's brains belong, but your butt-end died last month. She wants the window closed for her own sake, not yours.

"Leave it closed," he grunted. "But open it again before the moon-run blasts off. I want to listen."

She smiled and nodded, glancing at the clock. "It'll be an hour and a half yet. I'll watch the time."

"I hate that clock. I wish you'd throw it out. It's loud."

"It's your medicine-clock, Donny." She came back to sit down at his bedside again. She sat in silence. The clock filled the room with its clicking pulse.

"What time are they coming?" he asked.

"Nora and Ken? They'll be here soon. Don't fret."

"Why should I fret?" He chuckled. "That boy—he'll be a good spacer, won't he, Martha?"

Martha said nothing, fanned at a fly that crawled across his pillow. The fly buzzed up in an angry spiral and alighted on the ceiling. Donegal watched it for a time. The fly had natural-born space-legs. I know your tricks, he told it with a smile, and I learned to walk on the bottomside of things before you were a maggot. You stand there with your magnasoles hanging to the hull, and the rest of you's in free fall. You jerk a sole loose, and your knee flies up to your belly, and reaction spins you half-around and near throws your other hip out of joint if you don't jam the foot down fast and jerk up the other. It's worse'n trying to run through knee-deep mud with snow-shoes, and a man'll go nuts trying to keep his arms and legs from taking off in odd directions. I know your tricks, fly. But the fly was born with his magnasoles, and he trotted across the ceiling like Donegal never could.

"That boy Ken—he ought to make a damn good space-engineer," wheezed the old man.

Her silence was long, and he rolled his head toward her again. Her lips tight, she stared down at the palm of his hand, unfolded his bony fingers, felt the cracked calluses that still welted the shrunken skin, calluses worn there by the linings of space gauntlets and the handles of fuel valves, and the rungs of get-about ladders during free fall.

"I don't know if I should tell you," she said.

"Tell me what, Martha?"

She looked up slowly, scrutinizing his face. "Ken's changed his mind, Nora says. Ken doesn't like the acad-emy. She says he wants to go to medical school."

Old Donegal thought it over, nodded absently. "That's fine. Space medics get good pay." He watched her carefully.

She lowered her eyes, rubbed at his calluses again. She shook her head slowly. "He doesn't want to go to space."

The clock clicked loudly in the closed room.

"I thought I ought to tell you, so you won't say any-thing to him about it," she added.

Old Donegal looked grayer than before. After a long silence, he rolled his head away and looked toward the limp curtains.

"Open the window, Martha," he said.

Her tongue clucked faintly as she started to protest, but she said nothing. After frozen seconds, she sighed and went to open it. The curtains billowed, and a babble of conversation blew in from the terrace of the Keith man-sion. With the sound came the occasional brassy discord of a musician tuning his instrument. She clutched the window-sash as if she wished to slam it closed again.

"Well! Music!" grunted Old Donegal. "That's good. This is some shebang. Good whiskey and good music and you." He chuckled, but it choked off into a fit of coughing.

"Donny, about Ken——"

"No matter, Martha," he said hastily. "Space-medic's pay is good."

"But Donny——" She turned from the window, stared at him briefly, then said, "Sure, Donny, sure," and came back to sit down by his bed.

He smiled at her affectionately. She was a man's woman, was Martha—always had been, still was. He had married her the year he had gone to space—a lissome, wistful, old-fashioned lass, with big violet eyes and gentle hands and gentle thoughts—and she had never complained about the long and lonely weeks between blast-off and glide-down, when most spacer's wives listened to the psychiatrists and soap-operas and soon developed the symptoms that were expected of them, either because the symptoms were *chic*, or because they felt they should do something to earn the pity that was extended to them. "It's not so bad," Martha had assured him. "The house keeps me busy till Nora's home from school, and then there's a flock of kids around till dinner. Nights are a little empty, but if there's a moon, I can always go out on the porch and look at it and know where you are. And Nora gets out the telescope you built her, and we make a game of it. 'Seeing if Daddy's still at the office' she calls it."

"Those were the days," he muttered.

"What, Donny?"

"Do you remember that Steve Farran song?"

She paused, frowning thoughtfully. There were a lot of Steve Farran songs, but after a moment she picked the right one, and sang it softly . . .

"O moon whereo'er the clouds fly,
Beyond the willow tree,

There is a ramblin' space guy
I wish you'd save for me.

"Mare Tranquilitatis,
O dark and tranquil sea,
Until he drops from heaven,
Rest him there with thee . . ."

Her voice cracked, and she laughed. Old Donegal chuckled weakly.

"Fried mush," he said. "That one made the cats wilt their ears and wail at the moon.

"I feel real crazy," he added. "Hand me the king kong, fluff-muff."

"Keep cool, Daddy-O, you've had enough." Martha reddened and patted his arm, looking pleased. Neither of them had talked that way, even in the old days, but the out-dated slang brought back memories—school parties, dances at the Rocketport Club, the early years of the war when Donegal had jockeyed an R-43 fighter in the close-space assaults against the Soviet satellite project. The memories were good.

A brassy blare of modern "slide" arose suddenly from the Keith terrace as the small orchestra launched into its first number. Martha caught an angry breath and started toward the window.

"Leave it," he said. "It's a party. Whiskey, Martha. Please—just a small one."

She gave him a hurtful glance.

"Whiskey. Then you can call the priest."

"Donny, it's not right. You know it's not right—to bargain for such as that."

"All right. Whiskey. Forget the priest."

She poured it for him, and helped him get it down, and then went out to make the phone-call. Old Donegal lay shuddering over the whiskey taste and savoring the burn in his throat. Jesus, but it was good.

You old bastard, he thought, you got no right to enjoy life when nine-tenths of you is dead already, and the rest is foggy as a thermal dust-rise on the lunar maria at hell-dawn. But it wasn't a bad way to die. It ate your consciousness away from the feet up; it gnawed away the Present, but it let you keep the Past, until everything faded and blended. Maybe that's what Eternity was, he thought——one man's subjective Past, all wrapped up and packaged for shipment, a single space-time entity, a one-man microcosm of memories, when nothing else remains.

"If I've got a soul, I made it myself," he told the gray nun at the foot of his bed.

The nun held out a pie pan, rattled a few coins in it. "Contribute to the Radiation Victims' Relief?" the nun purred softly.

"I know you," he said. "You're my conscience. You hang around the officers' mess, and when we get back from a sortie, you make us pay for the damage we did. But that was forty years ago."

The nun smiled, and her luminous eyes were on him softly. "Mother of God!" he breathed, and reached for the whiskey. His arm obeyed. The last drink had done him good. He had to watch his hand to see where it was going, and squeezed the neck until his fingers whitened so that he knew that he had it, but he got it off the table and onto his chest, and he got the cork out with his teeth. He had a long pull at the bottle, and it made his eyes water and his hands grow weak. But he got it back to the table without spilling a bit, and he was proud of himself.

The room was spinning like the cabin of a gyro-gravved ship. By the time he wrestled it to a standstill, the nun was gone. The blare of music from the Keith terrace was louder, and laughing voices blended with it. Chairs scraping and glasses rattling. A fine party, Keith, I'm glad you picked today. This shebang would be the younger Keith's affair. Ronald Tonwyler Keith, III, scion of Orbital Engineering and Construction Company——builders of the moon-shuttle ships that made the run from the satellite station to Luna and back.

It's good to have such important neighbors, he thought. He wished he had been able to meet them while he was still up and about. But the Keiths' place was walled-in, and when a Keith came out, he charged out in a limousine with a chauffeur at the wheel, and the iron gate closed again. The Keiths built the wall when the surrounding neighborhood began to grow shabby with age. It had once been the best of neighborhoods, but that was before Old Donegal lived in it. Now it consisted of sooty old houses and rented flats, and the Keith place was really not a part of it anymore. Nevertheless, it was really something when a pensioned blastman could say, "I live out close to the Keiths—you know, the *Ronald* Keiths." At least, that's what Martha always told him.

The music was so loud that he never heard the doorbell ring, but when a lull came, he heard Nora's voice downstairs, and listened hopefully for Ken's. But when they came up, the boy was not with them.

"Hello, skinny-britches," he greeted his daughter.

Nora grinned and came over to kiss him. Her hair dangled about his face, and he noticed that it was blacker than usual, with the gray streaks gone from it again.

"You smell good," he said.

"You don't, Pops. You smell like a sot. Naughty!"

"Where's Ken?"

She moistened her lips nervously and looked away. "He couldn't come. He had to take a driver's lesson. He really couldn't help it. If he didn't go, he'd lose his turn, and then he wouldn't finish before he goes back to the academy." She looked at him apologetically.

"It's all right, Nora."

"If he missed it, he wouldn't get his copter license until summer."

"It's okay. Copters! Hell, the boy should be in jets by now!"

Several breaths passed in silence. She gazed absently toward the window and shook her head. "No jets, Pop. Not for Ken."

He glowered at her. "Listen! How'll he get into space? He's got to get his jet licenses first. Can't get in rockets without 'em."

Nora shot a quick glance at her mother. Martha rolled her eyes as if sighing patiently. Nora went to the window to stare down toward the Keith terrace. She tucked a cigarette between scarlet lips, lit it, blew nervous smoke against the pane.

"Mom, can't you call them and have that racket stopped?"

"Donny says he likes it."

Nora's eyes flitted over the scene below. "Female butterflies and puppy-dogs in sport jackets. And the cadets." She snorted. "Cadets! Imagine Ron Keith the Third ever going to space. The old man buys his way into the academy, and they throw a brawl as if Ronny passed the Compets."

"Maybe he did," growled Old Donegal.

"Hah!"

"They live in a different world, I guess," Martha sighed. "If it weren't for men like Pops, they'd never've made their fortune."

"I like the music, I tell you," grumbled the old man.

"I'm half-a-mind to go over there and tell them off," Nora murmured.

"Let them alone. Just so they'll stop the racket for blast-away."

"Look at them!—polite little pattern-cuts, all alike. They take pre-space, because it's the thing to do. Then they quit before the pay-off comes."

"How do you know they'll quit?"

"That party—I bet it cost six months' pay, spacer's pay," she went on, ignoring him. "And what do real spacers get? Oley gets killed, and Pop's pension wouldn't feed the Keiths' cat."

"You don't understand, girl."

"I lost Oley. I understand enough."

He watched her silently for a moment, then closed his eyes. It was no good trying to explain, no good trying to tell her the dough didn't mean a damn thing. She'd been a spacer's wife, and that was bad enough, but now she was a spacer's widow. And Oley? Oley's tomb revolved around the sun in an eccentric orbit that spun-in close to Mercury, then reached out into the asteroid belt, once every 725 days. When it came within rocket radius of

Earth, it whizzed past at close to fifteen miles a second.

You don't rescue a ship like that, skinny-britches, my darling daughter. Nor do you salvage it after the crew stops screaming for help. If you use enough fuel to catch it, you won't get back. You just leave such a ship there forever, like an asteroid, and it's a damn shame about the men trapped aboard. Heroes all, no doubt—but the smallness of the widow's monthly check failed to confirm the heroism, and Nora was bitter about the price of Oley's memory, perhaps.

Ouch! Old Donegal, you know she's not like that. It's just that she can't understand about space. You ought to make her understand.

But did he really understand himself? You ride hot in a roaring blast-room, hands tense on the mixer controls and the pumps, eyes glued to instruments, body sucked down in a four-gravity thrust, and wait for the command to choke it off. Then you float free and weightless in a long nightmare as the beast coasts moonward, a flung javelin.

The "romance" of space—drivel written in the old days. When you're not blasting, you float in a cramped hotbox, crawl through dirty mazes of greasy pipe and cable to tighten a lug, scratch your arms and bark your shins, get sick and choked up because no gravity helps your gullet get the food down. Liquid is worse, but you gag your whiskey down because you have to.

Stars?—you see stars by squinting through a viewing lens, and it's like a photo-transparency, and if you aren't careful, you'll get an eyeful of Old Blinder and back off with a punch-drunk retina.

Adventure?—unless the skipper calls for course-correction, you float around in the blast-cubicle with damn little to do between blast-away and moon-down, except sweat out the omniscient accident statistics. If the beast blows up or gets gutted in space, a statistic had your name on it, that's all, and there's no fighting back. You stay outwardly sane because you're a hog for punishment; if you weren't, you'd never get past the psychologists.

"Did you like horror movies when you were a kid?"

asked the psych. And you'd damn well better answer "yes," if you want to go to space.

Tell her, old man, you're her pop. Tell her why it's worth it, if you know. You jail yourself in a coffin-size cubicle, and a crazy beast thunders berserk for uncontrollable seconds, and then you soar in ominous silence for the long long hours. Grow sweaty, filthy, sick, miserable, idle—somewhere out in Big Empty where Man's got no business except the trouble he always makes for himself wherever he goes. Tell her why it's worth it, for pay less than a good bricklayer's. Tell her why Oley would do it again.

"It's a sucker's run, Nora," he said. "You go looking for kicks, but the only kicks you get to keep is what Oley got. God knows why—but it's worth it."

Nora said nothing. He opened his eyes slowly. Nora was gone. Had she been there at all?

He blinked around at the fuzzy room, and dissolved the shifting shadows that sometimes emerged as old friendly faces, grinning at him. He found Martha.

"You went to sleep," said Martha. "She had to go. Kennie called. He'll be over later, if you're not too tired."

"I'm not tired. I'm all head. There's nothing much to get tired."

"I love you, Old Donegal."

"Hold my hand again."

"I'm holding it, old man."

"Then hold me where I can feel it."

She slid a thin arm under his neck, and bent over his face to kiss him. She was crying a little, and he was glad she could do it now without fleeing the room.

"Can I talk about dying now?" he wondered aloud.

She pinched her lips together and shook her head.

"I lie to myself, Martha. You know how much I lie to myself?"

She nodded slowly and stroked his gray temples.

"I lie to myself about Ken, and about dying. If Ken turned spacer, I wouldn't die—that's what I told myself. You know?"

She shook her head. "Don't talk, Donny, please."

"A man makes his own soul, Martha."

"That's not true. You shouldn't say things like that."

"A man makes his own soul, but it dies with him, unless he can pour it into his kids and his grandchildren before he goes. I lied to myself. Ken's a yellow-belly. Nora
made him one, and the boots won't fit."

"Don't, Donny. You'll excite yourself again."

"I was going to give him the boots—the over-boots with
magnasoles. But they won't fit him. They won't ever fit
him. He's a lily-livered lap-dog, and he whines. Bring me
my boots, woman."

"Donny!"

"The boots, they're in my locker in the attic. I want
them."

"What on earth!"

"Bring me my goddam space boots and put them on my
feet. I'm going to wear them."

"You can't; the priest's coming."

"Well, get them anyway. What time is it? You didn't
let me sleep through the moon-run blast, did you?"

She shook her head. "It's half an hour yet . . . I'll get
the boots if you promise not to make me put them on
you."

"I want them on."

"You can't, until Father Paul's finished."

"Do I have to get my feet buttered?"

She sighed. "I wish you wouldn't say things like that. I
wish you wouldn't, Donny. It's sacrilege, you know it is."

"All right—'annointed,' " he corrected wearily.

"Yes, you do."

"The boots, woman, the boots."

She went to get them. While she was gone, the doorbell rang, and he heard her quick footsteps on the stairs,
and then Father Paul's voice asking about the patient.
Old Donegal groaned inwardly. After the priest, the doctor would come, at the usual time, to see if he were dead
yet. The doctor had let him come home from the hospital
to die, and the doctor was getting impatient. Why don't
they let me alone? he growled. Why don't they let me

handle it in my own way, and stop making a fuss over it? I can die and do a good job of it without a lot of outside interference, and I wish they'd quit picking at me with syringes and sacraments and enemas. All he wanted was a chance to listen to the orchestra on the Keith terrace, to drink the rest of his whiskey, and to hear the beast blast-away for the satellite on the first lap of the run to Luna.

It's going to be my last day, he thought. My eyes are going fuzzy, and I can't breathe right, and the throbbing's hurting my head. Whether he lived through the night wouldn't matter, because delirium was coming over him, and then there would be the coma, and the symbolic fight to keep him pumping and panting. I'd rather die tonight and get it over with, he thought, but they probably won't let me go.

He heard their voices coming up the stairs . . .

"Nora tried to get them to stop it, Father, but she couldn't get in to see anybody but the butler. He told her he'd tell Mrs. Keith, but nothing happened. It's just as loud as before."

"Well, as long as Donny doesn't mind——"

"He just says that. You know how he is."

"What're they celebrating, Martha?"

"Young Ronald's leaving—for pre-space training. It's a going-away affair." They paused in the doorway. The small priest smiled in at Donegal and nodded. He set his black bag on the floor inside, winked solemnly at the patient.

"I'll leave you two alone," said Martha. She closed the door and her footsteps wandered off down the hall.

Donegal and the young priest eyed each other warily.

"You look like hell, Donegal," the padre offered jovially. "Feeling nasty?"

"Skip the small talk. Let's get this routine over with."

The priest humphed thoughtfully, sauntered across to the bed, gazed down at the old man disinterestedly. "What's the matter? Don't want the 'routine'? Rather play it tough?"

"What's the difference?" he growled. "Hurry up and get out. I want to hear the beast blast off."

"You won't be able to," said the priest, glancing at the window, now closed again. "That's quite a racket next door."

"They'd better stop for it. They'd better quiet down for it. They'll have to turn it off for five minutes or so."

"Maybe they won't."

It was a new idea, and it frightened him. He liked the music, and the party's gaiety, the nearness of youth and good times—but it hadn't occurred to him that it wouldn't stop so he could hear the beast.

"Don't get upset, Donegal. You know what a blast-off sounds like."

"But it's the last one. The last time. I want to hear."

"How do you know it's the last time?"

"Hell, don't I know when I'm kicking off?"

"Maybe, maybe not. It's hardly your decision."

"It's not, eh?" Old Donegal fumed. "Well, bigawd you'd think it wasn't. You'd think it was Martha's and yours and that damfool medic's. You'd think I got no say-so. Who's doing it, anyway?"

"I would guess," Father Paul grunted sourly, "that Providence might appreciate His fair share of the credit."

Old Donegal made a surly noise and hunched his head back into the pillow to glower.

"You want me?" the priest asked. "Or is this just a case of wifely conscience?"

"What's the difference? Give me the business and scram."

"No soap. Do you want the sacrmaent, or are you just being kind to your wife? If it's for Martha, I'll go *now*."

Old Donegal glared at him for a time, then wilted. The priest brought his bag to the bedside.

"Bless me, father, for I have sinned."

"Bless you, son."

"I accuse myself . . ."

Tension, anger, helplessness—they had piled up on him, and now he was feeling the after-effects. Vertigo, nausea, and the black confetti—a bad spell. The whiskey—if he could only reach the whiskey. Then he remembered he was receiving a Sacrament, and struggled to get on with it. Tell him, old man, tell him of your various rotten-nesses and vile transgressions, if you can remember some. A sin is whatever you're sorry for, maybe. But Old Donegal, you're sorry for the wrong things, and this young jesuitical gadget wouldn't like listening to it. I'm sorry I didn't get it instead of Oley, and I'm sorry I fought in the war, and I'm sorry I can't get out of this bed and take a belt to my daughter's backside for making a puny whelp out of Ken, and I'm sorry I gave Martha such a rough time all these years—and wound up dying in a cheap flat, instead of giving her things like the Keiths had. I wish I had been a sharpster, contractor, or thief . . . instead of a common laboring spacer, whose species lost its glamour after the war.

Listen, old man, you made your soul yourself, and it's yours. This young dispenser of oils, Substances, and mysteries wishes only to help you scrape off the rough edges and gouge out the bad spots. He will not steal it, nor distort it with his supernatural chisels, nor make fun of it. He can take nothing away, but only cauterize and neutralize, he says, so why not let him try? Tell him the rotten messes.

"Are you finished, my son?"

Old Donegal nodded wearily, and said what he was asked to say, and heard the soft mutter of Latin that washed him inside and behind his ghostly ears . . . *ego te absolvo in Nomine Patris* . . . and he accepted the rest of it lying quietly in the candlelight and the red glow of the sunset through the window, while the priest anointed him and gave him Bread, and read the words of the soul in greeting its Spouse: "I was asleep, but my heart waked; it is the voice of my beloved calling: come to me my love, my dove, my undefiled . . ." and from beyond the closed window came the sarcastic wail of a clarinet painting hot slides against a rhythmic background.

It wasn't so bad, Old Donegal thought when the priest

was done. He felt like a schoolboy in a starched shirt on Sunday morning, and it wasn't a bad feeling, though it left him weak.

The priest opened the window for him again, and re-packed his bag. "Ten minutes till blast-off," he said. "I'll see what I can do about the racket next door."

When he was gone, Martha came back in, and he looked at her face and was glad. She was smiling when she kissed him, and she looked less tired.

"Is it all right for me to die now?" he grunted.

"Donny, don't start that again."

"Where's the boots? You promised to bring them."

"They're in the hall. Donny, you don't want them."

"I want them, and I want a drink of whiskey, and I want to hear them fire the beast." He said it slow and hard, and he left no room for argument.

When she had got the huge boots over his shrunken feet, the magnasoles clanged against the iron bed-frame and clung there, and she rolled him up so that he could look at them, and Old Donegal chuckled inside. He felt warm and clean and pleasantly dizzy.

"The whiskey, Martha, and for God's sake, make them stop the noise till after the firing. Please!"

She went to the window and looked out for a long time. Then she came back and poured him an insignificant drink.

"Well?"

"I don't know," she said. "I saw Father Paul on the terrace, talking to somebody."

"Is it time?"

She glanced at the clock, looked at him doubtfully, and nodded. "Nearly time."

The orchestra finished a number, but the babble of laughing voices continued. Old Donegal sagged. "They won't do it. They're the Keiths, Martha. Why should I ruin their party?"

She turned to stare at him, slowly shook her head. He heard someone shouting, but then a trumpet started softly, introducing a new number. Martha sucked in a hurt breath, pressed her hands together, and hurried from the room.

"It's too late," he said after her.

Her footsteps stopped on the stairs. The trumpet was alone. Donegal listened; and there was no babble of voices, and the rest of the orchestra was silent. Only the trumpet sang—and it puzzled him, hearing the same slow bugle-notes of the call played at the lowering of the colors.

The trumpet stopped suddenly. Then he knew it had been for him.

A brief hush—then thunder came from the blast-station two miles to the west. First the low reverberation, rattling the windows, then the rising growl as the sleek beast knifed skyward on a column of bluewhite hell. It grew and grew until it drowned the distant traffic sounds and dominated the silence outside.

Quit crying, you old fool, you maudlin ass . . .

"My boots," he whispered, "my boots . . . please . . ."

"You've got them on, Donny."

He sank quietly then. He closed his eyes and let his heart go up with the beast, and he sank into the gravity padding of the blast-room, and Caid was with him, and Oley. And when Ronald Keith, III, instructed the orchestra to play Blastroom Man, after the beast's rumble had waned, Old Donegal was on his last moon-run, and he was grinning. He'd had a good day.

Martha went to the window to stare out at the thin black trail that curled starward above the blast station through the twilight sky. Guests on the terrace were watching it too.

The doorbell rang. That would be Ken, too late. She closed the window against the chill breeze, and went back to the bed. The boots, the heavy, clumsy boots—they clung to the bedframe, with his feet half out of them. She took them off gently and set them out of company's sight. Then she went to answer the door.

EDITOR'S POSTSCRIPT

THIS is my fifth science fiction anthology. I began, in 1965, with *The Pseudo-People,* for Sherbourne Press, followed by *Man Against Tomorrow* for Avon that same year. Next came an edited collection of novellas for Avon, *Three to the Highest Power,* in 1968. Finally, in 1969, my two "linked" anthologies: *A Sea of Space,* from Bantam, and *A Wilderness of Stars,* from Sherbourne.

I owe a great debt of thanks to the authors who provided me with the 53 stories used in my five anthologies, and I am also indebted to the publishers who supported these projects. The present volume will probably be my last edited science fiction anthology, since it completes the five-book cycle I planned back in early 1965. I had hoped to share with the reader my favorite science fiction gathered over some two decades of extensive reading in the field. Nearly all of the stories I selected were new to book form; a few were written directly at my request.

As editor, I have done what I set out to do five years ago. Now, as novelist and short story writer, I must move forward to my own work. Editing these five books has brought me pleasure and satisfaction. I hope the science fiction readers who buy them will enjoy reading the stories as much as I enjoyed putting them between covers.

WILLIAM F. NOLAN
Los Angeles, California

HOW MANY OF THESE NEW SCIENCE FICTION STORIES HAVE YOU READ?

DAUGHTERS OF EARTH 75c
by Judith Merril

EMPHYRIO 75c
by Jack Vance

MORE THAN SUPERHUMAN 75c
by A. E. Vogt

NOVA I 75c
by Harry Harrison

OPUS 100 95c
by Isaac Asimov

THE POLLINATORS OF EDEN 75c
by John Boyd

SHOCKWAVES 75c
by Richard Matheson

THIRTEEN O'CLOCK 75c
by Cecil Corwin

THREE FOR TOMORROW 75c
by Robert Silverberg, Roger
Zelazney & James Blish

TO LIVE AGAIN 75c
by Robert Silverberg

UBIK 95c
by Philip K. Dick

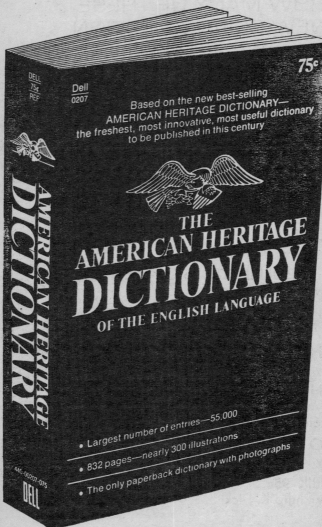